The 86th Degree is a love story written with so much emotion that you are infused with empathy. Denied love and the desire to be loved are parallel with abuse and abusers. Barb weaves passion, romance, and mystery into her novel set in the education field that she knows so well. **Jeanne Anderson**

When I read, I want to escape. When I read *The 86th Degree*, I escaped into a story of love both uplifting and forceful. **Barb Ross**

The 86th Degree brims with complex human relationships. The reader will love Amber Helm immediately and yearn for her to win as she fights for her man, her profession, and the gift of loving herself. **Jo Sundet**

The 86th Degree is a story of healing as much as one of love. I was enthralled following Amber as she fills the holes on her way to becoming a complete woman. **Linda Williams**

Sometimes it takes the fight to rescue someone else before you can save yourself. In this relevant novel, the lives of a spirited and dedicated teacher, a past love, and a troubled student collide. The reader will follow and support Amber Helm through her trials and realization to a satisfying denouement. **Karen Anderson**.

Think the latest buzz in the teachers' lounge is about grades? If you do, Barb Harken's sassy first novel—a tale about a young teacher's lost love, her feelings, desires and ultimate betrayal—will change your mind. With only so much time to read, don't wait. Discover if family ties are lethal. **Vi Steine**

The 86th Degree

by
Barbara Harken

Robert D. Reed Publishers • Bandon, OR

Robert D. Reed Publishers
P.O. Box 1992
Bandon, OR 97411
Phone: 541-347-9882 • Fax: -9883
E-mail: 4bobreed@msn.com
web site: www.rdrpublishers.com

Cover Designer: **Cleone Lyvonne**
Typesetter: **Barbara Kruger**

ISBN 978-1-931741-94-1

Library of Congress Control Number 2007908765

Manufactured, typeset and printed in the United States of America

Dedication

To Mike who has the best of Dad,
and to MaryLou, sister-in-law extraordinaire

Acknowledgments

Thank you to Marcia Klinefelter for all her patience and support.
Thank you to the other Barb for cheerleading.
What a couple of pals.
And thank you to the Cedar Valley Writers' Gals
for suggestions, truth, and love.

Prologue

"Two stars and a sticker. Even smelly Aimee Marten didn't get two stars."

The little girl sat in the back seat of the Mercedes, her school papers pressed tight into the curve of her chest. She was seven years old, a skinny thing tall for her age, mostly knees and elbows, her coloring genetically coordinated—coppery red hair, pale skin and lashes, and a stamping of freckles from head to ankle. Her mother had hoped for a princess. She'd given birth to a gangly elf with red curls.

Of course, the little girl didn't know that. How could she? She dwelled in that private world of children where all little girls are priceless and every day a new adventure, her dreams spun from imagination, a web glistening with happy endings. Every day on the ride home from her private school—The Oak Ridge Academy—she'd crane her neck to watch the northern suburbs of Chicago pass by while the family chauffeur whisked her home, inventing stories about the huge brick houses crammed onto postage size lots, homes to children with no way out. Evil wizards lived inside some. In others, skeletal trees emerged from the basement, their leafy tentacles searching for children in need of rescue. The stories never ran out of monsters. And always a brave princess with red hair would come to their rescue.

And today. Today was special even for a princess bent on saving Northbrook. Today was her day alone. Edens Expressway went by in a blur. A breeze from the lake had kept the spring air chilly, and the clouds to the east were edged with gray. But inside, all warmth. She had two stars and a sticker.

Her mother would be proud.

When the car pulled through the gate and headed up the curved drive of the Helm estate, the child placed the papers in her lap and carefully smoothed them, especially the edges. A report of such status had to be ready for display. When the vehicle stopped, she didn't even wait for Harrington to open the door for her before she barreled toward the double doors of the Lake Forest home. Papers wadded in her excitement, she was thrust forward by an energy owned by her special news, her feet scattering pea gravel onto the paving stones of the driveway and her momentum nearly knocking down a huge urn that dared bar her straight path. Frizzled hair, caught in two pony tails, fought to escape the beaded bands that held them tight, and today's grit, smeared across the front of her dress, would surely call for an eventual upbraiding. But no matter. The happy face sticker and gold star at the top of the school papers clutched in her hand were proof positive of her position as stellar student.

"Mommy! Mommy! Nobody else got a star and a sticker. Just me!" She opened the door and bounded into the foyer, the slight tap of her shoes against the marble her special announcement. The house waited for her, she was sure, couldn't wait to invite her in to celebrate; she had known this as surely as she knew the daily route home. Sitting there in that back seat, she had let today's story ride her, pictures of the golden girl tap-dancing across the floor, each flap and glide sending the music of her success upward until the whole world knew that she was the only one with both coveted signs of success. Oh yes, that hall would ring.

"Oh, for heaven's sake, child, this is not an amusement park."

The criticism wafted from the front sitting room, a sigh as much as an admonition. The little girl, so caught up in her fancy, halted, dropped her arms to her sides and automatically straightened her posture before she walked slowly into the room. She knew that sigh, icy reproof laced with the firm belief that children were showpieces of parental excellence—and heaven help the child who forgot. The little girl should have known that that sigh, too, a sign of low blood sugar attacking the mother, a side affect of too much insulin that morning.

But as is the nature of children, a seven-year-old caught up in imminent celebration sometimes forgot. She only heard the reproach, and her joy was set aside like a forbidden dessert, calling in sweet want but momentarily untouchable.

She went slowly, squeezed by a whiff of indecision, the woman's tone hanging over her, the sheer pluck of childish faith nudging her along. "I have a sticker and a star. Wanna see?" She thrust the papers forward in hope. Surely her mother would pull her onto her lap, wrap her arms around her while they both read the wondrous story—all four sentences a tale of an ogre tracking through fantasy swamps. Washed with pride, her mother would kiss the top of her head, the woebegotten state of the child's hair ignored considering the importance of the moment. She stepped forward, the papers still held out, their edges clutched by childish hands. "Mommie, I wrote it just for you. Look." The sheer bliss of imminent success had overcome a short lifetime of recognizing the warning signs of a diabetic's war on her own body and the repercussions of children not perfectly attuned to the needs of the mother.

Hope may spring eternal somewhere, but in this house it faltered and fell. The mother sat in her chair in front of floor-to-ceiling windows, an ill woman breathing deeply, a sheen of moisture on her upper lip, both face and eyes pale. "Papers? What . . . papers?" She closed her eyes, blinked them open, stared off to the right. Her hands shooed away the child who stood there like a supplicant offering the spring sacrifices in a bid for favor, but not quite sure whether or not the goddess would be pleased.

"Not now, child. Mommie isn't feeling well."

The child leaped toward her mother. She was close enough to smell the tang of acidosis but too bent on her mission to recognize the threat. When the papers rested on the mother's lap and the little girl flung her arms toward her mother's waist, the woman pushed her away, sending the papers flying and the child reeling back onto the floor.

"Dammit, child, just go upstairs. We'll look at your papers after dinner."

Head down, the child reached for her story and stood up. Without raising her head, she turned and made her way slowly toward her room, climbed the curved stairway to the second floor, each step a plod, her arms at her side, her hands still clutching her prize. Mommy had said the "D" word. Not even Harold, the gardener, said naughty words when Mommy was near. Her body flushed with censure as she made her way up those stairs. After supper would have to do. She walked into her room, plopped onto the bed and sat there, arms wrapped around her small torso, hands tightened onto her elbows in a defensive position. She had made her mother angry. She only wanted to show her the proof of a perfect day. If she could be perfect, Mommy would smile and call her a darling. Didn't Mommy always say, "That's what little girls do, precious child; they make their mommies happy."

Instead, she had done something wrong and her mother had made her disappear like a bad thought. So, the child waited upstairs on her bed, staring at crumpled papers, her fingers tracing the outlines of a star and a happy face, waited until she would be called back into a state of grace.

Downstairs, the mother, too, sat in wait. As minutes passed, her peevishness began to morph into confusion, her body growing more and more clammy as it slid closer to insulin shock.

"Help me," she moaned to an empty room. Her lips started to foam with spittle.

The little girl's father, harried from a last minute crisis at the bank, entered the room with an apology on his lips. Now his fear dried on his tongue and his feet felt the hard edges of the wooden floor as he raced toward his wife, one word on his lips. "Lillian!'

Upstairs, the child waited. Waited until the crunch of gravel and shadows of red and blue drew her to the window. Her mother wasn't downstairs waiting for her. Her mother lay on a strange bed with wheels, covered with a blanket except for her head. Strange men loaded her into a big white truck. As they closed the door, the little girl gasped over and over. Something had happened to Mommy. Something bad. As her eyes widened, a voice somewhere in her head shamed her. Daddy said to never, never bother Mommie when she was sick. She needed her rest or she would go the hospital and maybe never come back. Papers forgotten, she watched in horror as the red and blue lights whirled their message.

Your fault. Your fault.

Chapter 1

Friday.

10:02. The mechanical click of the wall clock broke Amber Helm's concentration. Nice going. First day back at school and already late, too caught up in bulletin boards to notice the time. Ten o'clock meetings start at ten.

The shine was off the apple now. In fact, the apple was about to turn to sheer worm food if she didn't get her behind going. Stepping over piles of books and bulletin board supplies, Amber made her way to her desk, grabbed a folder packed with paper with one hand, a pen with the other while she slipped on her sandals, then turned toward the door, snapped back to the business of school inservice time. She was almost through the threshold when a "Whoops" escaped her mouth and she turned back to grab her coffee cup, a chunky white mug with *Carpe Diem* stamped in bold black letters. Seize the day all right. Seize your butt down that hallway, girl, and into the study hall before everyone knows you're late.

This was her third year of teaching, the one promised to all new teachers, that pivotal time when rookies turn professional, when the first-year panic and the second year of reassessment both gel, and the real teacher emerges. The thought hung sweet within Amber Helm. For the entire morning, she had been veteran teacher, armpit deep in unpacking her teacher gear, little beads of pleasure buzzing up and down her neural pathways as she watched the bare room begin to take shape, the morning coffee she usually found so indispensable growing cold because she had so much to do. The mug had remained two-thirds full for the last hour, discarded like Amber's sense of time.

She was Amber Helm, tardy and about to be conspicuous. Scooting in third gear toward the meeting room, she balanced papers, purse, and mug with a growing sense of panic. The coffee in her cup sloshed and ran over, leaving wet brown globs on the floor. She slowed to a trot, gritting her teeth. "Why am I always the last one at these meetings?" she muttered to no one in particular even though she very well knew the answer. Plotting out creativity prompts beat out meetings hands down. Playing in bulletin board paper and stencils was far more fun than watching the clock. Amber wagged an internal finger at herself. You stayed up on that ladder too long, little girl. Good going. You dedicate your life to the perfect school year, and right off, you have to give yourself a detention.

She hardly had time to laugh at herself before the twinge—that internal voice snagging her attention, shaping its way around the teasing, turning it from humor to burden.

You're not the least bit humorous, young lady. The world operates on standard time and proper procedures, not on Lady Amber's by-your-leave. Maybe you don't notice responsibility, but others do.

Damn. She slowed her pace and listened. She had no choice, really. Spawned from some deep place within her, little bits of conscience would edge their way into her life without warning or invitation, like the words of an old hymn, never really forgotten, and so ingrained, their presence could be felt without the slightest conscious effort. Some women had guardian angels. Amber had guardian baggage.

She always swore to herself that the voice belonged to the earthbound ghost of Miss Pfiffner, the tutor Lillian Helm had hired to instill social graces in her hapless daughter, a spirit still searching for the swan lodged in the hapless duckling, forever censorious, dragging around chains of nit-picking. Amber straightened up. *Right. Blame it on a poor dead woman. The dead can't fight back.* A little piece of spunk defended her against the critic.

Neither can the living, sometimes.

That bit of rumbling faded as she neared the study hall and the din of the high school faculty members. For a meeting that was supposed to start at 10:00, all was typical friendly chaos. Good. No tardy for Amber, at least not today. She breathed a sigh of relief and slipped into the room, settling just inside the heavy doors, allowing herself to take in the sounds and sights. A few watchers like herself lined the perimeter, their coffee cups symbols of fellows-in-arms.

Sara McGovern saluted her with her cup, and Amber waved back. Still thanking the tardy gods for a reprieve, she slid over to the back table and the large aluminum urn that held the requisite first cups of coffee for the entire faculty. Amber stayed close to the table, fresh coffee in hand, surveying this strange mixture of balding heads and thick mops, coaching shorts and cargo pants, the old and the new all gathered to herald in another school year.

Swallows came back to Capistrano. Chicago was sure that this year the Cubs would break the jinx. Yup, some things never changed, one of them the opening rites of the school year.

Nearby conversation ranged from the trials and tribulations of the golf course and the impossibility of maintaining knees and backs after the age of forty to predictions of how many days would have them sweltering before the first frost.

Some of the faculty were more goal oriented. Guidance counselor Marti Butler sat two rows behind them, poring over last minute schedule shifts that threatened to snow her under every year. She was aided and abetted by Language Arts Curriculum Director, Joann Roling, who at that very moment worked her way toward Marti, a quickly snatched Styrofoam cup of coffee in each hand. They had been entangled in the problem since seven-thirty, and things weren't looking very bright for them. White and generic Styrofoam, a sure sign that neither had even made it to her office yet.

The rest of the staff just mingled and shared strategies, a few new jokes that had hit the e-mail circuit over the summer, the usual apologies for not keeping in touch. Shoulders jabbed in good fun and promises made that once again would be broken, but never in malice. Another school year in full swing.

"Amber, how's it going? We're counting once again on your leadership this year." English Department Chair Duane Murphy broke her concentration with a slap on the back that half-choked her before he maneuvered past to greet the next teacher. Perhaps greeted wasn't the right word. Duane worked a room like a cheap politician, all eyes and gums and that jarring slap he mistook for networking. As hot liquid slid through all sorts of wrong passages, Amber's instinct told her to dump the rest on his head before he moved too far away, but she squelched the thought quickly. Let him be Duane. She eyed the room again once again. Time to move forward from the treats area and take her seat.

Moments later she sneaked up behind her favorite coworker, and often partner-in-crime, Maggie Witkowski. The lanky Maggie had evidently decided to take her usual spot near the back of the room. Struggling to fold her six-foot two-inch frame into place, she mumbled all the while about idiot desk designers who think high schoolers are four-foot midgets. The teacher could hardly have noticed Amber. She was too busy grabbing the rim of the molded desk and trying to heave her right leg across the seat and through the opening without tipping the whole thing over. Amber easily slipped into the desk right behind her, grateful for a thirty-inch inseam, and set down her folder and coffee cup. Maggie shifted her weight and exhaled, a sigh of obviously frustrated relief that she had conquered the monster. Amber waited for Maggie to lean back, then whispered, "Maybe you shouldn't have taken so much growth hormone when you were a kid, Witkowski."

Maggie almost came out of her seat. "Sweet Mary, Martha, and Joseph!" She turned around and bared her teeth. Then her hands mimed a sound choking, the sort of drama that made Queen Maggie famous. "I don't know what makes me madder, that you scared the living daylights out of me or that you slide into one of these like it's nothing. Just because you took ballet while I sat on my butt and tortured Barbies doesn't mean you should get all the grace."

Amber just shook her head and laughed, then put her hand on Maggie's shoulder. "Mags, I really have missed you. How was Maine?"

Before Maggie had time to respond, Duane's voice broke through. His normal spouts sounded even more grating as the sound system warmed up on its own schedule. "I guess it's time to start." The mike squeaked a burst of annoyance. Even technology had little time for the man. He mopped his ever perspiring upper lip and flicked on the overhead's light, cluelessly sure that his color-coded transparencies had some bearing on the lives of the teachers before him.

"I think—um—we've dispensed with all the welcomes and can get right down to business." He tapped the mike. "You've no doubt picked up your syllabi from the office . . . "

Not far away, a low moaning from at least half of those assembled melded with the rustling of paper as the rites of in-service began and the abstractions of standards, benchmarks, and performance goals replaced the earlier clamor. Maggie stayed turned toward Amber. "Surely, whole forests have sacrificed their lives to get American education up and running this school year. Where's ecology when you need it?"

Her tanned hand, marked by long nails painted brick red, ran through the short black thatch she called hair, and she scratched her head in mock wonder. "Just think, yesterday I was lying in slothful splendor reading trashy romance and listening to Harry Konnick, Jr. Now I'm listening to Duane Bullshit, Sr. What kind of officious power monger elected him department chair anyway? All he does is bore us to tears and sweat."

"Be nice." Amber pretended to carefully study page 1 of the syllabus outlined for all on the overhead screen. "You know he tries." She raised her eyes toward the front of the room. "Turn around, Witkowski, before we're both in trouble."

Maggie ignored the order and grinned, then, ever the conspirator, leaned in to whisper. "No problem. But before he starts his drone, tell me, poor little rich girl. Have a good summer with Mom and Daddy Warbucks and the country club crew?" Amber pursed her lips and pointed toward Duane, the scowl she usually reserved for the truly rowdy pointed at her unruly friend, but Maggie, knowing full-well that Amber was at least half teasing, talked right past the hint. Who could listen to Duane when summer gossip beckoned?

"Any polo playin' stud muffins make your panties wet enough to want to leave us workin' folk? Give me all the good, juicy gossip. How do those rich boys look on their gold-plated saddles?" Amber's parents, Charles and Lillian Helm, were often the brunt of Maggie's teasing. According to Maggie, a "trying-to-be-devout" graduate of the Catholic education system, the Helms were "richer than God and almost as rich as the pope."

Wealth wasn't the problem. Rather, Maggie regularly mocked their disdain for their daughter's choice of profession. Not only had Amber seen fit to work rather than marry and devote her time to pursuits worthy of her station in life, she insisted on a working in an environment the Helms regarded as "inner city" in spite of the fact that the student population of Clausson High School was predominantly middle class. They tskked on a regular basis when Amber spent money on supplies for "those ragamuffins" and insisted on buying her a brownstone near Lincoln Park so that she wouldn't be "raped and mutilated by some serial gangster malcontent upset by a well-earned failing grade." Their daughter found it much easier to placate them with regular visits and laughing promises to be careful than fight them for total independence. And truth be told, she enjoyed the house and the black Miata convertible they had given her for her birthday, luxuries she never could afford on a teacher's salary—even if she had to occasionally swallow some crow. She might be mistress of her realm at Clausson High School, but to Charles and Lillian, Amber was still the child who ate too fast and never pulled up her socks. Maybe that was why Maggie's gibes hit deeper than her friend knew.

Oh, yes, Amber wanted to laugh and flip off a fantasy about a multimillion-dollar prince riding in on his white Porsch, but she settled for, "*Hush!* We're as bad as the kids." Maggie scowled, more for effect than displeasure, and both teachers duly settled down and garnered their attention on business at hand, boring though the business might be. During the presentation, a few hands went up for clarification, but mostly the discussion resembled the steady drizzle of rain that marked the days before students came back when the temperature climbed to at least ninety. Finally a "Thank you, and let's make it so" signaled the end of the meeting and both Amber and Maggie stood up to make their escape.

"Yup," Maggie snorted behind her hand. "He's been hanging out at trekkie conventions again, hoping to get lucky with an android." Before Amber could do much more than turn her head in reply, Duane's voice sounded into the Mike, "Amber and Maggie, may I see you a minute."

Maggie rolled her eyes in mock horror. "Oh oh, Murph's got our number. Get ready to rumble." Maggie broadly smiled and winked, then turned to lead them up to the chairman who still held onto his microphone like a trophy—or perhaps a phallic symbol—

as he waited, pulling his few pitiful strands of dark blonde hair across his balding head.

She stopped halfway and bent her head to Amber. "I'm serious, Toots. The old boy's got his polyester pants in a tizzy over us and our wanton ways. We just ain't got no respect for the old master's transparencies no more. And after all the time he spent dusting off those piegraphs."

Caught in the middle of a slew of teachers headed in four different directions, and, truth told, in no hurry to meet with the ever-clammy Duane, Amber slapped Maggie with a swing of her hip and allowed herself one naked grin. Then they both edged their way forward through the line of fellow teachers making a beeline for their rooms before they, too, might be called.

Finally, the study hall was just a huge room housing only the three of them. "So, Duane, how was your summer?" both girls chimed almost as one in the universal greeting of all teachers who had lost contact over summer break.

He approached them like a mother hen ready to wing in her brood. "Just fine, ladies, but no time to talk about that now." His head bent toward them in a conspiratorial nod. "We're not supposed to announce this until the department meeting this after noon, but I *had* to tell you. After all, the Melnick Grant last year could never have worked without your leadership."

Maggie looked away and bit her lip to avoid the temptation to deliver a well-placed retort or perhaps a snigger, and Amber managed a "Thank you, Duane."

"Exactly. That's why I just had to get you two aside." He raised his head and spoke to the air, as if the gods of pedagogy themselves were listening. "You know how I've been on a veritable quest for hands-on opportunities for our children. Why, the *hours* I've spent . . . I just can't begin to tell you." His hands slid back and forth, palms slipping with sweat and making little burping noises, then stopped abruptly. Maggie and Amber continued to put on their best teacher faces even while they both fought the laughter. Thankfully, Duane was entirely too caught up in his own self-important monologue to notice. "Liz and I have spent endless time in Central Administration working on that Artist-in-House grant, and guess what!" He slapped his hands together in child-like glee. Before either teacher could mouth the obvious answer, he pointed his index fingers at them. "We got it!" He paused as if to let the sheer wonder of it all sink in. "On Monday, Ethan Michaels, a Writer-in-Residence from the Iowa Writers' project, will be with us as our first official publishing author! He'll work directly with the department on Monday and Tuesday to help facilitate our *Start the Year Out Write* project and then actually team with us in the classrooms to help make it work. Five weeks with a real writer!"

She only felt the start in the back of her eyes. That meant it was a small shock, didn't it? Her brain had simply tripped its alarm button.

He's in Wyoming writing the almost great American novel. He swore by Wyoming. Yeah. He's in Wyoming.

She pushed the next exhale a little harder. Her heels started tapping against the floor, and her teeth bit down on the edge of her tongue.

Imagine. Two writers named Ethan Michaels. For a few seconds there, she had felt a stab of panic. The very presence of the possibility was absurd. Ethan, her Ethan—or her Ethan once upon a time in a whole different universe—was no doubt off living his dreams out West on some mountain top, wearing cowboy boots and pearling wisdom to the locals. Some other Ethan Michaels was coming to Chicago. Surely, she was safe. Dear lord. Let her be safe.

Back to Duane, girl. Her voice turned serious. "So, Duane, how did you find the time to do all that writing?" Normally the man could be counted on to prattle about himself.

"Amber, his bio mentions some summer school classes at Freston College. Isn't that where your Uncle James teaches?"

Duane, let me count on you. You're a narcissistic boor. Make it about you the all-knowing. She felt that stab again, this time in her left temple. She wasn't quite sure what to do with her hands.

When all else fails, try again. "I remember how I felt last year when we were writing our grant. Foundations fatten themselves on paperwork, I swear."

Evidently, Duane was unmoved. "I remember you talking about how much you learned about finding your voice in Iowa. I'm sure that was where your uncle teaches."

Damn the man. The room had a buzzing sound, something she hadn't noticed until now. Must be a short in the wiring somewhere. Amber put on her best smile and nodded. "Why yes it is, Duane. And come to think of it, I bet I had our Ethan Michaels in that class I took while I lived with Uncle James." Her temple was throbbing by now. She reached up and massaged it.

Hopefully the simple movement would give her some relief and enough time to stifle her feet and figure out what to say. The man standing across from her was unrelenting and the truth was pretty much out of the question.

Once upon a time, three summers ago, she had met Ethan Michaels. She had more than met him, for crying out loud; she had rolled him into her life like a metaphorical piece of sour candy, a bitter shock followed by a comfortable tang and then a yearning for more. Then she had closed herself to him. His was a taste she had put aside like so much of her life, all those dangerous flavors that would bring nothing but trouble. Amber had learned from an early age never to make trouble.

Oh yes, the truth pretty much wouldn't cut it.

Ethan Michaels was coming here. Ethan Michaels would be here, back in her life after three years.

Duane was right in the middle of ". . . so of course I knew I was right when I read the name of that college" when Amber muttered, "Excuse me, I've got to go somewhere about something," then pushed past the two forms—one, a rotund man staring in wonder, the other, a tall woman surveying the situation, her eyes charged with curiosity.

Amber shoved the door open and took her body out of that room and into the hall. She felt the tingle of her neck hair rising, heard the slap of her sandals as she walked down the same hall that used to be so comforting. An endless row of high school pictures lined each side—the football teams, graduates, some hero from 1935 who had sent the basketball team to state competition, all the ghosts of children turning to adults under the watch of George T. Clausson professionals, this story of the high school. She had looked at them every day for three years. They represented the heart of the school's history, and she never tired of searching the faces for their secrets. Now she stopped and peered at them as if they were strangers intruding on her thoughts.

"Where were the pictures from three years ago," she wondered, "from the year when her world had turned upside down that summer?" Anyone watching her might comment, "Now that's a teacher deep in thought over lesson plans" as long as the hall's shadows hid her face and eyes. When she reached the end of the hall, she turned the corner and fled. Finally, there was her room, a haven for the moment, a place where she could sit and wonder just what the hell she was feeling. She keep twisting her hands, rubbing her fingers tightly as if to force feeling back into her body. She'd read about people who twisted their hands in moments of high emotion; she laughed at the triteness of the action. She'd never succumb to the banal. Yet here she was giving Lady Macbeth a run for her money.

A sense of dread kept filling her and she'd beat it down, but it would slide back in and fill her, tell her to face facts and get ready, and she'd beat it down again. There was nothing wrong here. Well, maybe a little wrong. It's not every day that your past pops up to bite you in the butt. But this panic rising like gorge. It was ridiculous, nothing to make her head pound and her stomach clutch and those damn heels of hers beat on the floor.

She moved quickly down the rows of desks toward the back of the room. If she made it to the chair, the floor wouldn't crack and open up, a huge maw of concrete disappearing down a sink hole and pulling her with it. Her eyes darted to the right and she grimaced at the image of her tumbling into chaos like Alice thrown into the rabbit hole. Where had that come from? And where was her coffee cup?

Collect yourself, girl. Stop that stupid hand wringing and get hold of yourself. You're an adult, not a gangling ninth grader flipped out over this week's crush. Summer romances are for summer. That's the rule. They never carry over. It's unnatural.

Tell that to the panic that's eating at you right now.

She slid into a chair positioned in the back corner, an orphaned recliner recycled for reading day, and armed with enough graffiti and duct tape to be declared a natural disaster. It was supposed to allow students to curl up and lose themselves in the wonder of reading. Now it was a haven for the onslaught of emotions that started in on the teacher who had dragged it in, thinking that once again, she was the good teacher, the one who went the extra mile for the kids. Some good teacher.

Just wait until the artist-in-residence shows up and . . . . Good lord, what would he do when he saw her and knew, after all this time, they'd be stuck together for five weeks?

When Maggie came in twenty minutes later, Amber was still curled up in the chair, waiflike, staring out the window at nothing in particular.

"What's up, girl? You looked like Murph wanted you to share his transparencies and . . ." By the time she had made her way into the room far enough to see Amber's face, Maggie stopped in mid-gibe and took Amber's hand, tried in infuse some life into its white limpness, her warm fingers massaging out of friendship, and even more, questioning.

"Amber, talk to me. I know anybody Duane dreams up will be iffy, but how bad can this Michaels guy be? Who knows, maybe he even grades papers."

The attempt at humor fell flat, but at least Amber turned to look at her. The color was back, but Amber eye's still held a faraway glaze. She withdrew her hand. Physical contact at this instant was more than she could handle. Conversation, yes.

Touch, definitely a no.

"Mags, remember when we were toasting St. Pat's Day at Kelly's and I started to cry over those silly Irish songs?"

"Yeah," she laughed. "I thought you were going to water down your green beer before we had given the old sod enough respect. So?"

"Remember how I kept looking at the guy at the end of the bar, the tall one with the dark hair and darker attitude?"

Maggie sent her eyes skyward trying to retrieve an image and then laughed. "Hon, that evening's memories are pretty much drowned in green." When the quip only met silence, she turned serious, searching her friend's face for clues to this whole enigma, her eyes fixed on Amber's.

Silence reigned for a just a moment. Then Amber spoke in a hushed monotone. "In so many ways, just looking at some stranger

I'd never see again, he . . . was . . . Ethan." That pronouncement brought on a roll of explanation tumbling in disarray. "Not Ethan exactly, of course, but all that darkness, that brooding, carnal, look through your soul. . ." She stopped and looked at her knuckles. Little pieces of memory snapped around in her head but made no sense at all.

Maggie looked at her. "Ethan?"

Amber looked at her friend, stunned that she had so quickly forgotten. *Well, what do you expect? To Maggie he's just a name she's heard for the first time. He's not a danger to her.*

"Ethan Michaels. Duane's coup for the English department."

Amber stared at a friend who, for once in her life, was truly, truly speechless. Maggie's open mouth moved twice, like a freshly docked fish gulping for air, then her eyes rolled as things clicked. "The writer in college, the dark Ralph Lauren kind of hottie . . ." She laughed in disbelief and rose to her feet. "You've got to be kidding. Holy Mother Lucretia. Amber, this is awesome. Ethan Michaels. Our Ethan Michaels coming to us this very Monday as Mr. Important. Ethan Michaels is your long lost love. *Mr. I Bolted from Him, Wasn't I Stupid himself!*"

Amber looked at Maggie as if her friend had just qualified for Bedlam. "I'm sorry if I don't quite catch the humor in all of this," iciness lacing her words. The ice turned to anguish.

"Maggie, what am I going to do?"

"Thank the gods for another chance, I'd say." Amber's face remained locked, still edged with panic. Maggie switched to humor. After all, a little humor trumped shocked and catatonic any day.

But just in case, she backed toward the door a little before she cocked her head and suggested, "Buy red panties?" Amber just cradled her arms and moaned. Maggie extended her hands as if the next offering were obvious. "Just think . . . now you won't have to ask Santa for a new silver Jingle Bells vibrator for Christmas."

"Margaret Mary Witkowski . . ." She only resorted to full names when she was in front-load panic. "I am about to have the absolutely worst debacle of my life. This is no time for sex-toy jokes."

Maggie stood in the doorway, hands in her pockets, legs slightly rocking, watching Amber. She and her friend could exchange endless stories filled with all the girl things that had made up their friendship, rituals of shoe shopping at Marshall Field's, champagne and giggles after a disastrous dating experience, life's rituals that bonded women and gave them their own secret code. But this was beyond her. "For the two years I've known you, we've had enough men weave in and out of our lives to make . . . well at least a great Conga line." Her face turned serious. "But I've never seen you this flipped out." She paused, whether to find the words or let what she about to say sink in.

"Girlfriend, the one thing you had better do, and I *mean* better do, and do it fast, I might add, is figure out why a visit from an old love is putting you into apoplexy."

At that point, Maggie let her friend struggle alone with her ghosts.

Amber stayed quiet, letting Maggie's question wrap around her like fog, silent and damp and concealing. *The cool wetness of August nights. The taste of the man who had held her. The coil of dread turning to panic as he held her and whispered a promise to face the threat of Lake Forest and its sway. He had laughed at her, said no dragon's breath could touch the two of them, that all parents eventually understood.*

Summer romance? Not likely. Maggie's question was the elephant in the room. Tilting the chair back, she reached toward the book shelf for a book to hold, any book to hold onto as a symbol of security. *Odd Girl Out* the title read. Amber shook her head. "Ain't that the truth."

Chapter 2

The three beers with Maggie on Friday night helped. Saturday was a no brainer. Nothing like the challenge of clean sheets and underwear to keep a girl focused, that and the pouring into chores, the sweet smell of Windex, the scrubbing and polishing. Color coding the underwear drawer might have been overkill, but a girl just never knew when the placement of undies might be important. Amber had been busy with the unspoken exorcism against imminent danger—give order and shine to her immediate world, and she could ignore the impending threat of Monday.

Then came Sunday. Duties over but no calming rest for Amber. She stumbled through the day. When she went for a walk, the late summer humidity frizzled her hair. When she thought about tomorrow, the idea frizzled her mind.

Her world had been so beautifully constructed. Good teacher. Good daughter. Competent. In control. Balancing the world of career woman and reverent daughter with never a merging of the two. Now the beautiful walls that kept her world solid might crumble. Ethan knew her. Knew her secrets. She had run from him, but he was back.

Her world was one of cards, and anything nudging the order could bring it all tumbling down.

By Sunday evening, every one of Amber's coping mechanisms lay in tatters. Time to pull out all stops.

Chocolate.

She started with the obvious choice, chocolate kisses stuck in the back of the pantry, a half-bag left over from last Easter. After that, time for decision. Tapping her nails on the metal rim, she stood at the sink, tiny beads of foil littering the counter on both sides, wondering what to eat next. Chunks of baking chocolate? The six-pack of pudding in her refrigerator? How about Kahlua poured over ice cream? She immediately dismissed the thought of any liquor. The last thing she needed tomorrow was a fat head. And she might need the baking chocolate in the near future. No point in being unprepared.

That left the pudding. Definitely, the pudding. Six brown friends waiting for her. She grabbed a spoon from the silverware drawer next to the sink, inhaling the promise of her next move, and went toward the refrigerator. The ensuing frenzy was more than delicious, it was pure heaven. Finally sated—just as she dug out the last dollop of chocolate pudding in the last of the handi-pak containers of a six-pack with her fingernails—she allowed herself a moment of idle musing. Nails were such handy things. They could get inside those nasty plastic edges where the last of the pudding held out. Such a thought demanded celebration.

"Gotcha." She licked the glob with carnal pleasure. When she had slid the first of the pudding down her throat, she had felt an immediate rapture of addictive experience. Now her mouth caressed the tip of her tongue as she scanned the kitchen, eyes wily in pursuit of one more possible cache. If the need for her own personal scarlet A reared its head, at least she would wear it satisfied.

Late Friday, Duane Murphy, her immediate boss and royal pain in the backside, had stopped into her classroom after she had abandoned him that morning, his ego no doubt quite askew, to make sure that her sudden departure that morning had been some kind of female thing. He had made it perfectly clear that she was to use all her professional and worldly charm to ensure that Ethan Michaels had a most "auspicious time" during his stint at George T. Clausson High School. He would need, *they all* would need, the warm and wondrous hand of Amber Helm. "Your name isn't *Helm* for nothing, my dear, for that is indeed where you belong. At our helm." After rattling off a few inane tasks "he was sure that Amber could handle with aplomb," he had floated toward the door smiling at his wit, gums applauding his play on words. Then he left the room, never noticing that Amber hadn't replied.

How could she? What would she say? Right now, armed with thirty-six hours of denial and enough sugar to hallucinate, her mind played an imaginary tape.

Of course, Duane, I'd love to escort Ethan around. We have so much more in common than you could possibly know.

I didn't mention? Oh silly me. Ah yes, our visiting dignitary thoroughly enjoyed more than just my helm one fine summer. Why, the last time I saw him, after a particularly salacious encounter under an August moon, he labored under the impression that we were in love, and when he woke up, I would be beside him still warm and rosy.

At least until I walked out on him.

How very Bronte of me. Do you think our grant budget could stand a bit of lavender and maybe some heather? We could spread it in the multipurpose room and play Catherine and Heathcliff on the moors. And you could provide the wind.

Her sarcasm evaporated, only grief remaining. Amber stood there, silent, elbow on the counter, arm supporting her head, fingertips splayed on her forehead. The conversation with Duane had stripped any sense of composure she had been able to muster after the original announcement. With every upward tone in Duane's voice, she had felt more guilty, more terrified about meeting a ghost from the past, one that had done its own bit of haunting in the three years since she had last seen him.

Her brain sent her another signal. *Find sugar.* She lifted her head and looked around. At this point, she might even settle for a petrified gummy bear.

The phone rang just as she rummaged through a drawer on the outside chance that at least a couple of peanut butter cups had somehow miraculously been left over from last spring's Perk Points—even though no respectable female in her state of mind stood a chance of having extra chocolate in the house. It was never there when you needed it most.

The phone kept on with its insistence, two rings now. The damn thing was only at the end of the counter—maybe five feet away.

She stood with her back to it. Answering meant abandoning her chocolate quest. For just the briefest moment, she continued to ignore it, but then, good girl that she was, habit overcame temptation, and she turned.

Lord, why didn't she have an answering machine that beeped after four rings?

"Okay. I give." She eyed the damn thing while counting the rings, now at six, before she picked it up. How could things get any worse?

Before she could even begin a hello, her mother's voice begged, "Darling, what have you been doing? Whole wars have been fought and won in the time it took for you to answer."

Things were worse.

Amber closed her eyes and sighed softly enough—she hoped—not to be caught acting, then put on her best daughter voice. "Mother. I was just hauling down some books when I heard the phone ring. Sorry, dear." Sorry? You can't begin to know how sorry.

"Well, it was quite a wait, but that's all right, pet, I have you now. And don't worry. I'm sure you'll get organized one of these days."

Amber felt the pressure build above her right eye. It tightened to a knot and threatened to pound. Nothing new. She held the phone at arm's length as if it were poxed.

I've made my bed, Mother. Done my laundry, folded it with perfect corners and put it away in freshly cleaned closets. A dull blackness started to mass in the back of Amber's mind.

And I've lined up the wooden stakes and holy water, have a cudgel or two just in case . . . .

Watch it, young lady, that's your mother you're talking about.
Don't you know any better?

She stiffened in reply. No, sarcasm was definitely not appropriate, even now. Amber pressed the phone to her ear.

Her mother's voice hadn't missed a beat. "And what an amazing coincidence. Kikki and I spent hours yesterday wrestling with your bedroom problem. There's a perfectly divine Poiret bench for under the window. You can toss out that wicker thing you picked up at that place on Halstead."

The sheer weight of Lillian's mothering pressed on Amber, raised the ache that had settled behind her eyes to all-out throbbing. Kikki was Lillian's decorator whose service had been this year's birthday present to Amber, just a reminder that even though the society matron's daughter had chosen to help the unfortunate Plebeian class by teaching, and had deserted hearth and home, she should never forget her roots. The gold plated ones. Amber had hoped for a gift certificate at Barnes and Noble to buy books for her kids. So much for hope.

She chewed on her lower lip, her discomfort rising. Dealing with her mother was a full-time job even under normal circumstances. Nothing about her life right now suggested normalcy. She had to get her mother off that phone and off her back. Now.

"Mother, you know I appreciate all you and Daddy have done for me. I never could have afforded this place without you. But I'm a big girl now, and I like wicker, even if it makes you think of church basement auctions. Besides, Maggie and I made every effort to check for fleas and rat pellets before we took the chair." Her right eye ticked. Sarcasm did not play well with Lillian Helm.

"Now don't get testy with me, darling, just because I do my best to help you. Those little stores you insist on frequenting are perfectly fine for your teacher friends"—she pronounced friends like a benevolent despot might have pronounced *the people*, then her voice turned soft, its insistent edge replaced with maternal cajoling—"but you know very well that Kikki could add such ambiance to your bedroom and hide those . . . seconds you have up there. The space under the window sets the whole tone for the bedroom, and you have nothing more than. . . stuff. Kikki has such a flare you know. Doris Templedorn swears by Kikki's magic."

Of course. Anything less than the wave of Kikki's wand was unacceptable.

Amber pictured her mother's lips thinning with every attempt to confirm her silken control. A homicidal resentment rolled through her. She gripped the phone and thought of necks. Her mother hated Amber's stuff, Amber's treasures, the ones picked from the one-of-a-kind shops she and Maggie loved. Her mother had always hated those places, the unmatched castoffs, the clutter, the retro clerks, all the things that made Amber cherish them. Every time Amber showed her a purchase, Lillian held her breath in fear, her mind probably caught in some horrific vision of her precious daughter running off on a Lillith Faire, driven by the gypsy muses of flea marketing.

Amber tried to slow her breathing and return the phone to her ear just as her right eye started to quiver. She needed to end this conversation before she cracked up and dragged herself around the kitchen, an ancient Quasimodo, hunched over and looking for release, but tied to her mother by that damn phone and the ever-present Kikki.

Please, oh please, dear God, make my mother go away, and I'll even let the omnipotent Kikki sleep overnight and paint the walls puce. Urged on by demons and a dip in blood sugar, Amber hunted through one more drawer for one piece of candy, hoping she wouldn't drop the phone she had cradled with her right shoulder and escalate the moment. Multitasker to the end.

The sheer weight of Lillian's mothering pressed on.

"I've never heard you so—so very hurtful, dear." There was the pregnant pause, then, "Is something wrong? Your daddy and I fret so much about you living alone there . . ."

Here it came—the guilt clobber. Amber took in extra air and, without thinking, clenched her teeth against her mother's voice ". . . in the midst of that element." Lillian's tone tightened. "At the very least, you could give us the satisfaction of knowing that your surroundings are appropriate."

"Mother, I'll visit Kikki's gallery next week.

"No, I don't need Harrington to pick me up."

The knockout shift in power seemed to come from nowhere with one of Lillian's famous sighs and a "Well, just make sure that you do. I will just be so stressed until this is taken care of, and Amber . . . you know what stress does to me in my condition."

The official Lillian Helm knockout guilt blow. Amber didn't even realize she was nodding her head, so automatic was the response. The daughter hadn't a prayer. Too many years had stitched a crazy quilt that still rested deep within. Ethan was a crisis. Lillian was a way of life.

"Are you having your reactions again? Have you talked to Doctor Betts? What about the new insulin?" Twinges of fear worked their way through Amber's body, fear so involuntary she welcomed them like an aunt come to stay without an invitation. The emotion inched its way from her duty-filled brain through her muscles as she felt herself growing smaller and smaller.

"Amber? Are you listening, dear?"

"What? I'm sorry." Amber pressed the panic where it couldn't hurt her, down and inward where it always seemed to lie in wait. "I was just distracted by some noise in the hall. You were saying?"

"I was saying how, new insulin or no, Doctor Betts has made it clear that at my age, stress is absolutely forbidden. I'd think that you would set aside your fancies and think of me, at least occasionally."

"Oh, Mother, I'm sorry. I just . . . "

"I never want to worry you, love, but my health is so precarious and any little thing . . . . Well, enough of that. I have to dash off now and meet with the girls about the Fall Festival at the club. Never a moment's rest. And never a bit of appreciation."

Rush off? What about stress? Amber could only roll her eyes and grimace. She got me again. She wields guilt like a club, and I just stand there waiting for the next blow. She offered herself a sympathetic smile. "Well, Mother, you know I appreciate you. Be careful and don't work too hard. And try an amble instead of a dash. Love you." She placed the phone into its cradle and wandered into her living room, one hand rubbing her forehead. A sense of irony hit her. She dealt with belligerent teenagers everyday. Water rolling off her back. But a wisp of a woman bullied her with charm and guile, and all she could do was stew in her futile attempts to free herself from the fear that the slightest veering from perfect child might harm her mother. Some adult.

She was a wimp all right.

By the time Amber had walked the twenty feet from the kitchen to her living room, those twinges had attacked her neck again. Lillian's unsolicited intrusion stayed housed in her body long after every conversation between mother and daughter, pricking at her like a thistle spine, tiny but stuck beneath the skin. She settled into her favorite chair, an overstuffed Pottery Barn warren of comfort set parallel to the window overlooking the park, and she rubbed at the back of her neck. A cold spasm shot through her, shook her jaw and hit her arms all at once, then settled into her entire body. The rain that this morning had laid a wet blanket over Chicago had lessened its hold, and the evening air was damp and cool. No doubt that was the reason for the chill that gripped Amber. Surely it was the weather.

Wrapping herself in a cashmere throw, she tried to sink into the depths of the chair. The chill lessened to a vague impatience as she sat there, cocooned, the softness of the cashmere playing against her skin, rubbing across it like a kiss. The noise of Chicago was right outside her door, but it sounded so far away, an echo bouncing beneath the water. Lulled into that sense of semi-awareness halfway between the now and sleep, she floated into a memory.

Ethan's face peered at her, hazy yet compelling. That very first day they had met, that long ago time, she had instantly resented his face. The arrogance in its stark lines. The darkness of his eyes and hair. She had resented everything about him, in fact, the first day she had seen him striding into the summer class and owning it. Seconds passed, minutes perhaps, while she sat there in her apartment and let the images wash over her. Then she turned her head, searching for something she could not name. She gazed out the window at couples strolling in the park across from her building, some arm in arm, others holding hands, all caught in the embrace of what she had felt that summer long ago. The mist and the dusk stealing the light turned them to shadows, but Amber knew them. Once, she had known what they knew as miraculous.

She and Ethan had been such a couple, young kids swept up the euphoria of hormones and endless talk. She had gone on with her life—or so she thought—that bittersweet memory of young love something to hold onto during a melancholy excursion to the past. She had moved on. They both had moved on. He hadn't ever tried to contact her, after all.

You certainly wanted him to. Let him prove his love, carry you away.

She tried to flick away that thought. Tears began to well, and she could no longer keep herself from drinking in the aching. Tonight, the sadness rode her, something about her mother's petulance and those damn lovers out there in the park was too much.

Enough with the traipse through self pity. Forget the doom act and think.

She took courage in from deep within her gut and rubbed the moisture from her right eye. She was in the present, not the past.

The past had been . . . well, no use even trying to define it. The present held the adult Amber, the one in charge of her own destiny.

The present meant maintaining safety. Safety meant image.

She'd wear that really great gold bangled bracelet Daddy had given her for her birthday, so subtly golden, it would drape on her wrist, look elegant with her freshly done nails. If she started now she could even work in a pedicure and spiff up her tan with a little bottle glow. By tomorrow she would be a goddess, a goddess in charge of the moment. She would ooze aplomb, reach out her hand for his, take it with just enough pressure to suggest awareness but never invitation of any kind. Her "Hello, Ethan, how wonderful to see you again" would welcome but never woo. He, of course, would be speechless.

Yeah. Right, the small voice snickered. *Ethan? Speechless?*

She knew better. Ethan Michaels, writer guru and purveyor of wisdom, would never be speechless. He's probably worn down half the mountains in Wyoming with his analysis. Then reconstructed new ones out of manuscript drafts.

She tightened the throw around her and smiled. Decision made. She'd master the present. Let him just try to invade her world and unseat her with his scrutiny. Project Goddess would set him in his place. She wondered, for a moment, if he still smiled first out of the left side of his mouth before his right caught up. And if his eyes still darkened to coals when he was aroused by something. What a minute, Amber. Don't even go there, girl. You're in control, not in lust. And you only have until tomorrow to get yourself ready.

The urge for chocolate reasserted itself, little Mars Bars and Snickers dancing in her mind. Some sort of ritual had to launch this night. It might as well be chocolate. She jumped out of the chair and strode to her hall closet, then yanked it open, a veritable goddess of victory. *Ah, no one ever said that chocolate was only for losers.*

Two minutes later, trenchcoat thrown over her sweats and a Cubs baseball cap hiding all but a few greasy tangles of hair that escaped at the back, she made her way to the convenience store at the corner. She knew no one would care she looked like hell right now, but those feet hurried themselves along just in case. No surprises for her. Ten minutes later, she was headed back, a family pack of Snickers in tow.

So busy had she been plunking down the money she always stuffed in her coat pockets, she had stormed out the door, oblivious to anyone around her.

There hadn't been much to see. Just the clerk and one customer who'd stopped to pick up some razor blades and a six-pack, standing there midway in aisle one. The lone customer watched her as she walked away, stood there still, in fact, his eyes straight on her, steel-like and focusing, like a hunter honing in on his prey.

His form never changed, except for a twitch of jaw muscle that pulled against his lips. He walked toward the counter just as the clerk hollered to an empty space, "Hey, Ma'am, you forgot your change!" The poor clerk looked so helpless, standing there with a five-dollar bill in his hand. The customer walked up and took the money. "Don't worry. I know her. I'll be sure that she gets it." The clerk looked at him, face wary and fingers pinching the bill in protection. Ethan held up his hand. "Sorry. This is Chicago, not Iowa. I forgot for a moment." He paid for his purchases and left.

Chapter 3

Ethan Michaels pulled into the parking lot at 8:00 and parked his gray Corsica between a red Honda and a purple Kawasaki. He opened the door of the car. A creak reminded him that the door needed WD40, squalling its displeasure again when he shut it.

The building before him looked pretty much like any other high school in the Midwest, dark brick, aged in this case, probably as much by Chicago pollution as weather and time, rows of windows the shaded eyes of sentinels that guarded the school's wards from intruders like him. He squared his shoulders once he was out of the car.

Another August. Another new school. Another chance to sell writing as a learning tool, and maybe help make his way toward a university job while he was at it.

He headed across the gravel of the parking lot toward a freshly patched sidewalk. The grass on both sides had been edged as well as mowed. Good sign.

A couple of oaks held their own, separating the city street from the campus, its perimeter marked on one side by a chain link fence. As he walked toward them, his mind latched onto a scene from *The Wizard of Oz*—nasty trees grabbing at Dorothy and her crew, and he laughed at himself. C'mon. They edge when they mow. The trees were fine. It was just him. He always felt a flicker of uneasiness when he came to a new place, probably why he ritually surveyed the landscape, as if to find the character of each school he visited.

So far, this one said, "Watch your step."

Turning onto the front sidewalk, he nodded toward the closest tree, smiling at his own state of foolishness, and marched forward, finally climbing the entrance steps, vast slabs of concrete capable of supporting a horde of marauding barbarians.

Not really a friendly place at first glance, but looks could be deceiving. Or maybe it was just him. This was his fourth job as guest guru. He should be used to it. Move in. Sell the truth. Move on. He liked what he did, after all, and he understood about paying dues. But, in spite of the extra pay and the resume building opportunities, more and more, he dreaded those first few days, that initial time of community building when everyone was a stranger. Working with teachers was great. Working with kids even better. But oh, those first few days . . . . Maybe he just ached for connectedness.

Knock it off, Michaels. At twenty-six, you're a rookie; you can't dictate the terms of your career, even if you want to. And the job will be over before you even start if you stay out here bellyaching all day. When you get back, talk to Dr. Maxwell. Right now, grab your briefcase and head on out. Something nagged at him. He felt like he was trying to retrieve a word lost somewhere in memory or a name that toyed with his brain. An itch on his mind, nothing more. But he hated that he couldn't put a finger on the underlying cause of his annoyance. Some leader he'd be.

The morning's haste to start out in Chicago had erased last night's glimpse at a ghost, the tug of recognition gone already, or at least set aside in the rush to begin a new venture.

His appointment with the department head was for 8:30, but, out of habit, he came his usual thirty minutes early. He always wanted to get a feel of a new school, walk down the hall, take a peek at the classrooms when no one watched. *Michaels, you're the peeping Tom of bulletin boards.*

That's how he survived.

A car zoomed into the parking lot, the imminent death throes of its muffler competing with the blasting of its radio. Ethan turned to see the driver's head jam to the music's roar while his passenger tossed out a half-smoked cigarette through the window and joined in the car dance. Then they tore out, the flow of Jay-Z's kingdom and blueprint crashing for several blocks. Great start. Kids who head-banged and cruised. Would there be more of the same waiting for him?

C'mon, Michaels, get in there and hit the ground running. Wow 'em with your charm and Weird Al Yankovich. The important thing is a great start, and you're not doing much out here whining in the parking lot.

A laminated sign had been fixed to one of the metal doors of the entryway. Visitors welcome. Please sign in. Immediately inside those doors, more steps led to more doors and a hallway perpendicular to the steps. A huge swath of bright blue cut across the upper wall; pumpkin orange stars and black lettering had been painted over the background blue to firmly establish that this was Comet Land Ablaze in Glory, an obvious art class endeavor above the oak trophy cases attesting to the legend of the Clausson Comets. The hall itself was deserted now. While Comets might blaze, summer still owed its students two days of vacation.

Ethan took all this in with a writer's dispatch for detail while he climbed the inside stairs and then stood in the hall to get his bearings, professional demeanor fully on alert, wondering if this school would be any different from the others he had served, and if intelligence blazed as vividly as school pride. He felt around in his pocket for the visitor's pass, and after pulling it out, set the briefcase down while he attached the pass to his requisite navy blazer before he headed down the hallway to find the office. His instructions had said to take a right at the entrance and then another sharp right. Briefcase in hand, he set out.

He found the office sign almost right away, made a mental note for when he was done with his preliminary survey. The language arts wing was supposed to be up the stairs and to the right. Before he could make his way, the office door swung open and a teacher almost collided with him. The man had been walking out, head turned toward the secretary for some passing comment. Ethan backed up two steps to avoid a crash, hollered a quick "Hey" that brought the assailant to a halt just as the office door banged shut. Two washed out blue eyes widened and thin lips formed a sudden "Oh" of shock. The poor man brought his hands up instinctively, sending a pen skidding across the hallway. For some reason, Ethan thought of the three little pigs, in particular the second pig, smart enough to use sticks but not quite bright enough to fend off the wolf. There was something annoying about this guy—beyond the fact that he had plowed into him—something not real, something artificial. His head was covered with a few strands of blonde hair futilely trying to cover a pink head, nondescript face, pudgy and far too white for this time of year, nostrils flaring below eyes so pale they almost seemed noncolored. Right now those eyes bulged in shock, a reaction heightened by the lack of brow and eyelash color. He had the look of a man who had just been discovered dipping into the till and wanted to run, but instead, stood frozen in his tracks, wondering how to maneuver his way out of trouble.

Ethan made the first move. He set his briefcase down and brought both hands up in mock surrender. "I really think it's too early in the day to dance." He did his best to look apologetic, nonthreatening so maybe the guy wouldn't back up and try it again.

The dancing partner in question collected himself, telltale perspiration beading on his lip from the past few seconds. He brought his hands together in a silent clap, his eyes trying to catch the name on the visitor's pass in front of him. "I'm so sorry, Mr. . . ."

Ethan cut in. "Michaels." On that, the sweat on the man's lip almost doubled, and he brought his hand to his chest almost as if to ward off a heart attack. A faint splash of red spotted his cheeks. "Oh, my, my, my. You're Ethan Michaels." He laughed as if he had just shared some great bit of news, his gaze sweeping up to Ethan's face. "Isn't this just a bit of serendipity." His attention stayed on Ethan's face while he grasped Ethan's free hand with both of his and shook it. "I'm Duane Murphy, department chair. Welcome to Clausson High." His hands kept their grasp while he rambled on, and Ethan felt an uncomfortable sense he was about to be asked to go steady. "I can't *tell you* how thrilled we are that you're here." The hand clasp went full throttle forward, almost pulsating in its short, jerky movements. "I was just telling Mrs. Pruitt, our secretary, that we could start looking for you anytime, and what do you know, here you are."

Duane abruptly quieted, removed his hands from the continuing handpump and flung one upward. "Oh my, that was terribly inane, wasn't it?" He brought the hand to his mouth, and looked skyward as if he were some martyred sage. "But better inane than insane, especially in teaching, wouldn't you say. . ." his right hand flipped upward again in obvious punctuation "although those little rapscallions often drive us in that direction, don't they? But then, we do love them, don't we?"

Ethan said nothing. How could he? He was standing in an empty hallway, in a strange school, while a total stranger blathered on and on just like he was someone's long lost relative. *And serendipity?* If this clown's initial greeting was any indication, this would be quite the stint. What's next? Tweedle-Dee and Tweedle-Dum? Ethan tried to push his energy level up and garner a friendly smile, at the same time chastising himself for his rude appraisal. He was a professional, on company time.

First impressions were essential, and while this certainly was not the best of all possible beginnings, things couldn't help but improve in this place of learning that prided itself on Comet glory.

He calmly took back possession of his hand. *Be friendly, Michaels, not too familiar, but friendly.* "Actually, I wanted to explore a little before I checked in, get a feeling of the school I'll call home for the next few weeks." He gave his best "Aw shucks" look, the left side of his mouth creeping up in a half-smile, his shoulders lowering a little in friendly relaxation. "I have to admit," he said with a chuckle, "this is by far the most hands-on welcome I've had in a long while." Walking over to retrieve Duane's fallen pen, Ethan felt the surge of energy in his back, let it spread to his shoulders and settle in his arms. He would get the feel of the place, the smell and the vibes and the essence of what made each school unique. The kids were the priority, the kids and what he could bring to their lives. Often, he made a difference. And once in a while, someone he touched made a difference to him.

His newfound best friend, Duane, was still chattering about grants and bureaucracy and the lack of time for those who truly loved the muses. Time to turn the focus toward something productive. He was on the clock, and he was ready, even if his partner of the moment was something out of *Rocky Horror Picture Show.* No problem. Let's do the Time Warp again.

"Tell you what," Ethan said once he had stood up and moved toward the gushing teacher. "I'll trade you a pen for a cup of coffee and a doughnut. If there's one thing I know about in-service days, it's that where there's a meeting, there's a doughnut. How about it?"

Duane took the pen from Ethan's outstretched hands and widened his smile. "Let's get to the lounge," he gushed as if they were best buddies, "and I'll make sure that you even have sprinkles." He eyed the brown leather by Ethan's feet. "And don't forget your briefcase. We'd hate to lose your expertise before we even begin, wouldn't we." He took off, two steps in front of Ethan, never noticing the rolled eyes and measured sigh strategically softened and charged with frayed patience from the newcomer bent over to retrieve his briefcase and then follow a man who slightly reeked of pixie dust.

The dance had begun all right.

Just as they reached the door of the teacher's lounge, an all-call sounded from the office.

"Duane Murphy, you have a call on line one."

"Whoops," the guide almost giggled, "Business calls. Busy, busy, busy. Just help yourself. We have plenty of cups, coffee, and all the doughnuts a teacher could love. I'll be back in a jiff." Duane turned and scurried down the hall back to the office, leaving Ethan alone with his hand on the door knob.

Oh, well. 'Busy, busy busy.' Better get in there and fixate on caffeine. This could be one long morning.

He opened the door and stepped in. Only one teacher was in the lounge at that moment, a woman, a very attractive woman at least from the back. A red head with shoulder length curly hair and a very nicely rounded ass.

He stepped back.

The ghost he had refused to acknowledge in the parking lot. The one that had shocked him last night.

He knew that ass even from the back, even from the space of three years. He waited for the shock of the moment to fade. So, it hadn't been a time warp thing. At least this time, the anger didn't rise in him as it had done last night. He was ready to acknowledge proof positive of chaos theory. The great passion of his life, or at least one summer, was part of the faculty package.

She was facing the wall directly across from the door, pouring herself a cup of coffee into a chunky mug. From his angle, he could make out that the *Carpe Diem* boldly stamped on its side. Carpe Diem. Seize the day. He scoffed for just a second, wound tight with the thought of what he wanted to seize and the sweet panic of vacillating control. Just then, she turned around. All thoughts of mastered restraint went awry. He looked her in the eye, had to focus on that, had to keep leverage even as the world seemed to slap him in the face. *Go ahead and recognize her, Michaels, acknowledge you know her, but don't you dare react. React, and you're a dead man.* He curbed an urge to swear and walk out of the room. But the same muscle that had pulled at his jaw last night while he watched a woman in a trenchcoat and Cubs hat leave a convenience store, that muscle pulled at him now.

They both looked at each other, for the first few seconds two strangers guarding territory, all the *if's* keeping them on opposite sides of the room. Amber's face was still, except for her eyes that moved over him, the action sustained and puzzling. Ethan made sure his eyes stayed steady. *I'll watch her, yes. There's plenty to watch. But this time I won't get hurt.* An awkward silence hung for several seconds, and then Amber walked over to him, reached out her hand. Without thinking, Ethan drew back. Once, he had touched her shoulder, let her know that she was safe with him. Now he stood with his arms at his side, sizing up the moment. *Move ahead, Michaels, take the initiative.*

He took her hand. Right then a jolt shot through him, sort of free-floated its way up his arm and into his throat. Five fingers on five fingers in a teacher's lounge in the northeast fringes of the city of Chicago, their only witness an aluminum coffee urn offering up its perking burp.

He went first. "So how's your Uncle James?" He watched her eyes widen almost imperceptibly and her mouth try to give up a smile. He knew the question would send her back.

"Oh he's fine, the same old professor trying to sell C.S. Lewis and John Gardner." Her body relaxed as she spoke about him. "Last week he called me in horror. Some freshman wanted to write a paper on *The Crucible*, that it was a rallying cry to all Christians to beware of witchcraft. He told me he didn't know whether to walk away or suggest a lobotomy." She laughed, just a light laugh to match the nervous banter.

"Don't worry, he didn't do either. He made an appointment. You know how he never gives up."

Not like some of his family. The thought hung in the air between them.

"Grace Remington died year-before-last." Ethan heard the softening in her voice. He understood.

"Sorry to hear about that. She was a good woman. I know she meant a lot to both of us."

More words hanging between them. Dr. Remington. The class. He'd better be careful or those word might weave a web and he'd be caught. Again. Change gears.

Ethan had never been much for surprises. Surprises meant loss of control. So what he had to say, that one small question, had nothing to do with revenge. It was just a bit of defense.

"So how were the Snickers?"

It left her silent while he stood there and smiled.

Chapter 4

The morning had disappeared, the minutes falling one onto another. Amber sat at her desk, idly watching out the window, her finger playing with her hair, twirling a clump round and round into a tight knot while it lightly played on her scalp. She wondered if the mayonnaise in the tuna salad in her refrigerator would keep another day. That, at least, seemed like a perfectly good thing to wonder about on a late August morning. When the Miracle Whip starts tasting like cheesy socks, who knows what could happen. Freud could have a heyday, laugh from his grave at that one—a woman, finger in her hair, eyes fastened on an overcast sky, who really thought she was concerned about the state of her sandwich spread.

She let go of her hair and sat forward, letting the phantom conversation she had practiced this morning replay itself.

Hand on chest in pure amazement. "Oh, you didn't go to Wyoming?"

Benevolent smile post-compliment. "Oh, yes, Ethan, you look wonderful, too."

Slight laugh and shake of the head. "Funny how all those plans we make take a sudden turn when reality steps in."

What ever possessed her to think up that fantasy, much less believe it? All that calm poise. What a crock. For a solid year after she ran, every time she spied a tall, dark, craggy man out of the corner of her eye, somehow he morphed into Ethan, made her catch the start in her throat, her chest tingle with . . . what? Fear? Regret? Abject stupidity? What ever, the last thing she could have hoped for was a graceful upper hand.

The good news? He'd work only with junior and senior classes. That meant they wouldn't be working side-by-side in the classroom—her classroom for pity's sake. The bad news? He was here! She'd see him every day. Share a doughnut and a cup of coffee, reminisce about good old Grace Remington and her looping techniques. Her voice might hold steady but she'd remember in her skin the feel of his arms, the depth of his voice, the texture of his tongue.

She replayed the meeting today.

The whole of their six weeks together that summer had come down to staring at each other twenty feet apart, sharing nothing more than idle chitchat. That and a swift kick in the face from fate.

"Say, Sweetcakes. Ready for the Days of Our Past Lives?" Maggie peeked around the corner. Maggie's eyes held the nervous query of a shopper scanning National Enquirer headlines at the supermarket checkout, concerned, intrigued, and a bit guilty at being caught even looking. Amber came up sharply. "Witkowski, don't you ever knock?" She forced a smile to let Maggie know the abruptness of her tone was in jest. A lie right now was so much safer.

Maggie laughed. "Sorry, I didn't know you had gone clear to China. What's the matter? Getting nervous over Tall, Dark, and About to Drive you Crazy?"

Amber just closed her eyes and shook her head. Instead of sitting down with her best friend and hashing out all the guilt and shame and longing that rumbled around inside her, the absolute need to deal with the panic and ache that kept taking turns controlling her, Amber quieted the chaos and kept it light. Light humor trumped despair.

"You wouldn't believe it. We've already met."

"No!" Maggie dashed across the room, grabbed the computer chair right next to Amber's desk and sat down, all ears and eyes and focus. "Tell me all about it and don't you dare even leave out a comma." She leaned forward and thumped her index finger on the wooden slab. "And hurry, because I've got to unload textbooks and hang two theater mobiles before we get out of here for lunch."

Amber just shrugged. "All I did was get a cup of coffee in the lounge, just a stupid cup of coffee." She looked off for a second, waiting for some cosmic bit of wisdom to come tumbling through the window and land on her lap, something to keep it light and dull the roiling inside her. No such luck. She pressed on.

"I'd been rolling the great confrontation in my head all morning."

Maggie circled her hand and nodded. "And?"

"He wanted to know if I liked my Snickers."

That answer brought Maggie to a halt, and she sat there, a look of wonder stretched across her face like Amber had just said *Let's go herd some cats* or announced that Edith Whitehead, the dowager media specialist made porno films in the back room of the library. She glanced at the clock once, perhaps to get her bearing, and turned back to her friend, her mouth in a twist. "So what's with the Snickers?"

"Last night I fought my own Chocolate War. I was trying to get ready for this whole stupid, stupid day, and I figured *without chocolate there is no hope*. I wanted . . . no, make that needed, really, really needed a chocolate fix , so I had been scrounging for at least one lick and . . ."

"You're blathering. You always blather when you're stressed. Breathe deep, Amber. Focus. Chocolate."

"Okay. Chocolate war. I lost. Ran down to K&C."

The call for focus had lasted for about two seconds and Amber veered off again. This time, though, Maggie just sat there silent while Amber reeled.

"I was going to be a goddess, right? Bowl him over." She stood up. "Look at me. My hair is done. My nails are done. I've got on a $200.00 linen skirt on a work day, for God's sake. I am ready for the man."

Maggie repeated the question, slowly, the kind of dumb repetition people do when no one understands them and they think they just need to speak more slowly. "So. What. Does. This. Have. To. Do. With. Ethan?"

Amber returned in kind. "Maggie, he had to have seen me last night. That or he has a crystal ball. I looked like hell! I had that grubby Cubs hat Fred gave me when I told him I was a Yankees fan even though I lived in Chicago. My hair was a grease ball, all stringy, sticking out all over. I had on absolutely no make-up and you know what that looks like." She stopped just long enough to grab a breath and maybe regroup, tightening her lips like she always did when she was stumped. "He had to be in the K&C picking up toothpaste or something."

Maggie couldn't help it. She almost doubled up in laughter. "You, my dear, must have been very, very naughty in a previous life." She wiggled her eyebrows. "Or maybe in a recent one, say about three years ago?"

Amber pressed her lips together in a sarcastic smile and pushed her hands against her thighs. "You are so hysterical. Thanks for the support. I have images of the next weeks playing roller coaster in me, and you crack jokes."

Maggie put her hands on top of Amber's. "If you don't laugh, babe, you'll cry." She paused and grinned. "Then you'll have water retention."

Amber was not amused. "Remind me to nominate you for friend-of-the-month. You can celebrate by rubbing my nose in humble pie."

Amber took Maggie's hands off hers and bent down, her arms locked over her head. She heard her friend's gentle breathing. It acknowledged her right to pause and regroup. When she raised her head, she smiled.

"News from the front, then. Pleasantries from Ethan this morning were wrapped in a silken scarf of resentment. While I stood there with quaking knees and concrete-filled shoulders, he acted like a dorm buddy at a class reunion."

The metaphor was too close. While the outer Amber spoke of the morning, her mind spoke to her in an image—Ethan waking up on another morning and finding nothing but a hasty goodbye. Her face turned neutral, her voice dropped off. "He's here." Amber stared ahead, her eyes focused on the blank chalkboard. "And I bet he hates my guts."

Maggie's reply came at her like a fog, rolling in low and almost unnoticed, a whispery thing. Maybe Maggie had begun to understand Amber's state. Then again, it could have been Amber's mind-rambling that made the sound so distant.

"It's been three years, close to forty months since you've seen this guy, love affair or no." Maggie paused while the numbers lay between them. "Marriages don't last that long. Time wounds all heels and all that jazz?" Maggie leaned forward, put her hands back on Amber's knees. "Amber, I asked you before, when you first told me Ethan was coming, to think about why you're flipped out. What is driving you so that an old boyfriend, lover, whatever he was. . . what is it about this guy that is making you crazy?"

Amber closed her eyes. Her jaw and neck strained with tension. "You really want to know, Mags?"

Maggie's hands tightened their grip. "Yes," she said.

"I've been thinking about running."

"Running? As in a race?" The words came out quickly, teasing. Maggie paused and spoke more quietly. "Maybe, as in running away?" When Amber's face tightened, Maggie's voice took on a lighter tone. "That would be an awful waste of a perfectly good $200 skirt."

The phone intercom broke in. "Miss Helm, call on line 2. Can you take it?"

Amber walked toward the file cabinet that acted as storage and phone caddy. "Sure." Turning to face Maggie to let her know their conversation wasn't over, she lifted up the phone, said "Amber Helm" in her best teacher voice but then softened as she said, "Mother."

Maggie left her seat, mouthing "I'll talk to you later" and gestured toward her room down the hall, her body language making it a command more than an invitation.

"Amber, I just called to make sure that we were still on for dinner Tuesday night. I know how sometimes you get all caught up in your job and forget your family." Lillian's voice was like butter laced with the slightest tinge of criticism.

Amber didn't even flinch. "Now, Mother. Of course I'll be there for dinner. Besides, how could I resist Carelton's cooking when I know I'll be facing hot lunch for nine months. I'll see you at seven. Of course I remember how important it is that you eat on time." She'd lived the timing for too many years to forget. "Seven. Exactly." After a bit of mindless mother-daughter chitchat, she ended with a "Love you, too."

Some things were stable. AT&T stock, papers to grade every weekend, and crown roast with her parents every Tuesday night. Perhaps it was a godsend. Lord only knew she needed some stability right now. Stability certainly beat the panic that circled her now.

She would put herself back in control. Control was the answer, had been the answer her whole life. Forget last night. Put away this morning. Turn proactive. Master the chaos that would drop her to her knees and ruin her.

The whole thing centered on timing.

Ethan would settle in, get used to the idea of working with her. Her whole brouhaha a moment ago was nothing more than wobbly nerves. Most of his reaction earlier was due to shock. Give the shock time to wear down, and they would both adjust. Timing. That was the key.

If she had any luck at all, which so far had definitely not been the case, she could probably avoid seeing Ethan until late this afternoon. Duane would keep him in meetings for the rest of the morning, and the administration would spring for lunch, to which the lowly teachers, no doubt would not be invited. He'd have to meet the other seven language arts people, so if she were statistically in the middle, that would put her past 2:00. And, she laughed to herself, statistically she was ahead, because no way in hell would Maggie wait to meet the man of Amber's dreams—or nightmares—depending on the perspective. Maggie would wend her way, somehow to be one of the first in line. She had at least until 2:00.

Chapter 5

Amber started studying the clock at 1:00 after its familiar click, lifting just one eye toward its face—slowly, blink by blink, so that it would not betray her and slow down. One hour. Perfect occasion to slog through some literature refiling, maybe get lost in them, busy herself in the world of metal file cabinets and plastic tabs. Stephen Crane deserved special treatment. And Hemingway. If she didn't straighten her files on old Ernie once in a while, he'd get ornery and use even fewer words. File away, she told herself.

She stared at the clock once again, more an act of defiance than curiosity. What the heck, she could pass the time until Duane, bless his officious little heart, bid her come to his office to meet his golden boy. Who knows what could happen. She might even be putting the finishing touches on those nasty folders, and the two would just pop in to see her in teacher-of-the-year-mode.

Yup. They would be impressed all right. And besides, school would start on Wednesday and she needed to get organized, man from the past or no. Lunch with Maggie was over. Duty called. Besides, how long could one hour last when she had so much to do? A little voice running loose somewhere in her frazzled brain made some crack about work as sublimation, but she quashed it and let herself believe that cleaning files full of worksheets and old tests, and organizing transparencies separated her world from chaos. Ethan Michaels was not the only priority in her life right now. Last year's tests needed tending, just in case some assessment Gestapo lined up a raid to check her sense of organization. A girl needed her priorities.

By 1:45, Amber had rearranged A through J in the file. The tabs of each hanging file angled exactly one tab over from the previous file. Literature units were filed both by author and title, color coded with green and orange sticker circles. Writing activities connected to literature units were coded blue. General George Patton, himself, could not be more proud of her progress.

By 1:50 her eye was wandering toward the clock again. Same at 1:51. Time for a new strategy. Competency. She had to send them both a message of competency. She could start on some hands-on activities for writing strategies. Ethan was so very keen on writing strategies. Her hands fidgeted at the computer keys but nothing even remotely usable, much less competent, appeared.

Just a memory of a summer class three years ago.

Competency. That's what had started their whole relationship. She was a college girl, living with her professor uncle for the summer, plodding along in her quest to garner enough skill to teach, one little step at a time, a response to literature class here, a writing proficiency class there. Uncle James had raved about Grace Remington's seminar, so there she was, poised and ready and secure in the knowledge that her uncle would be there when her confidence wavered. After all, she wasn't some Toni Morrison or John Gardner trying to outwit the muses. She was just an ordinary college student trying to get ready to teach.

The first time Ethan walked in, Amber watched the way he moved, the look of him, misplaced jock, all lean muscle and black stubble and hubris. Hey Mister, the PE Complex is two blocks away. And *cat* is spelled with a *c* instead of a *k*.

She was smug with self-assurance. She'd be a winner for sure next to this guy.

Two days later, he opened his mouth to give peer commentary and she ate her words. Lucky her to be paired with someone that totally honest and so damned willing to cut to the quick. Not that she didn't deserve it. She'd written about golden vistas and the arms of the universe, mostly because she hadn't any idea what she had really wanted to say. He had laughed at her and demanded she search herself. That or drop the class. She explored the pain of seeing *Amber Helm prays for breasts* on the bathroom stall in eighth grade; he forgot to tilt his chair and told her that maybe there was some hope for her after all, but don't most middle school kids worry about body image. What was really and truly hers? They worked on that, both in and out of class. Days later, when she had finally probed deep enough to face some of the terror within herself, they were in the kitchen of her uncle's house and she was crying, her mascara a black river beneath both eyes.

But as they say, that was then, and this was now. Now Amber sat, her room deathly quiet except for the faint rhythm of her breathing. The woman in the now shook her head as if to ward off an insect—or a shudder. Too many ghosts and too much unease. They sifted down on her like fat, invisible snowflakes. Time to collect herself. The trouble was, the clock's face kept casting a more and more baleful look at her as the seconds slugged by. Amber gave up on the strategy sheets to just sit and watch the clock, her legs up on the swivel office chair, her arms wound around them, her chin stuck on her knees, and her mind lost somewhere between now and a summer that was. Some days life just refused to cooperate, no matter what the behavioral objective.

Damn that clock anyway. It was right above the door, so when Ethan appeared, materialized, in fact, out of the darkness of the hall, Amber jumped, almost losing her balance, arms flying, voice shrilling like cartoon character terrified of a mouse. When she collected herself, she sat there in mute embarrassment, her face flushed.

"I seem to have that affect on women. Leave them screaming all the time." Ethan took a few steps toward her, hands in his pants pockets, tie and sports coat long ago discarded.

So, floor, what do I have to do to make you open up and swallow me? The hole is connected to hell, you say. And what is this I'm in right now?

"Ethan, you startled me."

Clever. Really clever.

Ethan at least looked like he didn't hate her, even smiled when he spoke. "Look. I promise not to bite. The line about the Snickers was probably pretty cheap. You don't like to be caught off guard."

You know that about me. You know more than that. That's what scares me.

He took a few more steps forward. Then he took his right hand out of his pocket and ran it through his hair, the left side of his mouth turned up in the thought of a smile. "It's not enough that we're thrown together like this after . . ." He stopped and cupped his face with his hand, rubbed his mouth. "I guess you could just say 'all this time.' I saw you in a store last night on the way to my old roommate's apartment."

Amber was sitting on knives and didn't dare breathe, much less move, commitment to control stomped into oblivion.

"You remember Dave? The unrepentant slob? He's a loan officer in Lincoln Park, complete with white shirt and burgundy tie. Who would have thought." A little laugh.

What the heck. The room's about to spontaneously combust. Let's keep it light and talk about good old Dave and his perpetually dirty socks. So how is Dave? Did he ever learn the value of laundry detergent?

Ethan looked at her, his face inscrutable. Well, so much about Dave. She found the nerve to stand up and greet him. "Ethan," she laughed, hoping to sound ever so light in spite of the internal mud that bubbled in her gut and numbed her fingers, "I honestly had no idea what to say this morning." Her tone deepened and her words slowed down. "I probably don't even know what to say right now. At least more than welcome to Clausson High School and the wonders of the teenage mind." A part of her wanted to stay rooted to the floor, but she knew she had better move forward and continue. She stuck out her hand just as she had done this morning. Back to light and friendly. "But promise me one thing. No more cracks about chocolate. A girl has to keep her secrets."

Ethan watched her, his eyes hooded. Amber knew that look. Probably not the time for humor.

The smart thing to do would be to end it right there. Act like an adult after all. Where there can be no genuine peace, there could at least be compromise. Just shake his hand, say "Have a nice life," and go on with getting ready for the school year. Ethan was here to help kids learn, had walked into her life after three years to work with her classes for a few weeks, just like he would work with the entire language arts department, so her bruised sense of wrongdoing was more than out of line. It was cheap, if not immoral. Change your state, girl. Light and simple. Professional.

Yeah. Tell that to your heart. It's doing a pretty professional job of thumping in your chest right now. And those sweaty palms aren't from the humidity outside, girl.

He ignored the offer of the hand. Amber's heart did an awkward skid.

"I know about a girl and her secrets." His voice was steady, deep. "At least I thought I did." Were his words edged with regret? He leaned back and looked at her. She saw in his face the Ethan of summer nights for just a moment, but then his eyes became hooded again and she lost that momentary glimpse.

What could she say? She owed him more than that stupid note she had left, the "We had a beautiful time together, and you helped me see myself and grow, but now it's time to move on" drivel that had seemed her only option at the time.

Give him the truth. Stop stalling and tell him. He deserves the truth, grim and petty as it is. But she couldn't move her lips to say the words.

"I should go now." His words cut her guilt. Go?

"Ethan . . ." She bit her upper lip, waiting.

Amber stood there, rocking, her teeth into her lip. Maybe the pain would awaken something, give her enough courage to take a step forward, a token step to renew what had begun that summer in a small Iowa town. But pain has a way of driving itself inward, and Amber could not take that step, coward that she was. She closed her eyes and stood there, silently rocking her life away. When she finally opened her eyes, he was gone.

Chapter 6

4:00 on Monday.

The second day of inservice was over. Finally. Time for the requisite dirty martinis and cosmopolitans. The faculty usually gathered at the favorite hangout—Gilley's Irish Pub—but Amber wasn't up to war tales about years gone by and the latest in administrative injustice. Sure, the weather man had promised a starry night with a welcome bit of coolness, but Amber had been on edge on all day. Maury Adamson's plea for at least one semester without Zwaniker kids had run stale. And she definitely wasn't in the mood for comments about the new-boy-on-the-block. She shelved the last handful of textbooks and used her left hand to work out the knot in her neck. That and the cement that passed for shoulders told her that her best plans for tonight should include a warm bath and a soft pillow.

Moving to the window, Amber kept at the tightened muscles while she looked out at a student parking lot not yet crammed with cars. She swept her scan to a grassy football field not yet full of screaming fans. She was ready to feel the buzz of students as they chattered. Only two more days.

A knock on the door alerted her, and she turned and waited. The afternoon sun was great for throwing light on the writers' wall across the room, would bless the ink and the images of student work, but it darkened the doorway until the clouds of November even things out. Whoever designed this place didn't know much about feng shui. Anyone in the doorway was a total stranger until second quarter.

"I've been standing here wondering whether to come in or just let you fall asleep at that window."

Ethan. The knot in her neck tightened.

He leaned against the frame, not much more than a tall darkness.

There were words somewhere in her head, but for the life of her, she couldn't find any. If Ethan as a shadow in the doorway reduced her to a tongue-tied teenager, how was she going to manage these five weeks?

She watched him as he moved into the room, the shadows fading as he came closer, caught the light playing on him—the shadow of dark that roughened his face. He hated to shave. Black stubble used to creep down the sides of his neck. He'd wear that stubble like he wore his summer tan—casual, indifferent to the opinion of others—even when the opinion of most of the females within Amber's earshot had been laced with craving.

Enough of that. Why would she remember that anyway? She ran her hand across the top of her head and laughed. A volleyball could bounce against her neck and be called a spike, but no way would she let Ethan Michaels know it. "I always feel exhausted by the end of the first inservice day. No resistance after a summer of nothing."

Summer. Good job, Amber. You could talk about anything, but you come up with summer. Her eye twitched but she held the smile.

"All that adrenaline spent before the kids even get here, I want to just pass out on the sofa and stash the end pillows over me." She rubbed her neck again. "By the end of September, I've built up enough endurance to face the kids. I can even face partying with the teachers."

"What are you doing tonight?" His voice was casual, as if he often stopped by with the question. She forgot about the knot. The flipping action in her stomach had her full attention.

He stepped forward and added quickly, hands in the air, "Don't worry. I'm not asking for a date. Think of this as a truce of sorts. We left each other today in a state of . . . I don't even know what to call it." He raised one eyebrow as if searching for an answer or asking for Amber to provide one. Before Amber could even think of a reply, his face returned to normal and he shrugged. "I don't know the best watering holes and I'm already hungry." He grinned, a naughty boy grin. "Besides, you sort of owe me. I almost rescued your five dollars."

"Five dollars?"

"Sure. You were so busy running out of the store Sunday night, you forgot your change."

Amber looked at him with a stoic face, but a swath of red crept up her neck, and she felt hot.

He put his hands together in prayer position. "You can buy half of the first round. We can practice being nice to each other. I promise no interruptions." He unfolded his hands and raised two fingers. "Scout's honor."

All that worry for nothing. Two coworkers going out for a drink. No noise. No replay of faculty complaints already old and worn. The cords of tension started to recede. Her stomach steadied, and the throb went back to mere ache. Amber stepped toward him, arm extended and hand ready for a pact. "You've got a deal. I'll take you to Pour Fools. Best hot spinach dip this side of Lake Michigan. Double Blue Moons until 6:00. Best of all, subtle music and relaxation."

She paused as she went to her desk to grab her purse. Turning, she said, "But Dutch treat."

He smiled. "Wouldn't have it any other way. We're just going as a couple of thirsty teachers looking for spinach dip and pita chips."

Twenty minutes later, they were sitting in the back corner of the Pour Fools Tavern, a yuppie bar with plenty of maple wood and sleek aluminum, their tall glasses a kind of common ground. Second beer of the night. All the body kinks were gone. Happy Friday.

Sure, when they had first sat down she had fidgeted like a teenager on her first date, but the ice had been broken. She and Ethan were two adults ready to let go of the past.

Ethan scanned the bar. "I can see why this is a godsend after a full day with kids." A clattering drowned out his comment as the El train roared by, spiriting home commuters for the evening.

Ethan yanked his head toward the sound, then looked back, his brows furrowed and his mouth puckered. He leaned forward. "How does anyone carry on a conversation in this place? I've read about the infamous El, but hordes of rushing barbarians couldn't make that much racket." His shocked face made Amber laugh.

"Don't worry. Anyone familiar with Lincoln Park knows to just shut up and wait. That or take advantage of the noise and tell a lie. No one would even know."

"Gee, do people in Chicago worry about lying?" His face was an absolute blank, not a stitch of expression registering, eyes still and looking right at her, mouth a straight line.

Amber leaned forward in her chair with a total lack of guile, just a girl talking to an out-of-towner. But she held her fists in her lap, pressing her thumbs tightly.

"Actually, most of us are quite honest. We might get caught up in things we can't control—but overall, we have the courage to tell the truth. Why do you ask?"

"No reason. Just making conversation." His voice was so light that Amber might have believed he meant it, if not for the subtle hint of sarcasm laced in his tone.

He watched her spool the warm cheese onto a pita square and lift it. When she bit down, the cheese ran onto her lips and she ran her tongue over them to catch it, savoring the spill. He grabbed a piece of the pita bread, slammed it into his mouth, and chomped down hard. Then he reined in his focus. Easy, fella. You're supposed to be Mr. Cool here.

"So, Amber, big city woman in the land of Lincoln and roaring trains, let's play catch-up.

"We really didn't get to know that much about each other back then."

You know plenty about her, you jerk. That's why you want to run out and catch the quickest cab back to Dave's. Either that or slam her up against a wall and shake out an explanation. He tuned out the voice. This was just a few hours in a local bar between two adults who happened to share some history best left forgotten. Tread lightly. Stay safe.

"I know your favorite color is orange, favorite author is Tolkien. How about your favorite music? Dave Matthews? Leonard Skynner?"

Colors. Authors. Music. Safe topics.

"Actually, I like Blues and soft jazz. That's why I love to come here. Great music every weekend to soothe the mind ravaged by chaos of teaching."

Good answer, Amber. Nice safe territory. Stay on track.

"Did you know that Chicago was the first city to use the word *jazz*?"

Ethan gave her a full-mouthed grin, the same one she had watched him use to spill trust into any audience.

"Nope. Sorry. I'm just a country Iowa boy at heart with a bit of rock 'n' roll oldies thrown in. Kenny Chesney, old Dion and the Belmonds records. Yeah. And Paul Revere and the Raiders. My idea of a good time is the Great Jones County Fair, with emphasis on *Great*. You get the best of right-now country and golden oldies. Lucky I didn't have to get here any earlier. I never miss the Great Jones County Fair."

"I picked you as a jock, at least the first time I saw you—then a writer/critic, even something of a shrink. But I can't imagine you as a 'Good Old Boy'. Guess you're missing the red truck and the John Deere cap."

He sat upright, cocked his head and raised his brows. "Don't dismiss the jock. I'll have you know I was the town hero on the baseball diamond, pitched like a madman. That and I played back-up quarterback—too slow to start, I guess, but I could hurl a ball. Got it from Grandma Amanda."

"Your grandmother played baseball? Was she one of those woman baseball players who played during World War II? Kind of a Geena Davis throwing for Tom Hanks?"

Ethan widened his eyes in mock horror. "Grandma Amanda would set you straight on that one. She had been born the year Pearl Harbor was bombed. Called herself an early Baby Boomer with a god-sent mean right arm. She pitched on the neighborhood sand lot team until she sprouted breasts and had to retire her glove. Took to dresses and chasing boys since the fifties had no call for girl athletes, even in Iowa. Kept up with her pitching though. Threw rocks at rabbits when they tried to lunch on her garden. Hated the things."

Amber took a sip of her beer. A waitress passed by, and the music segued into some Miles Davis. Amber closed her eyes and swayed for a few beats, then, eyes open and back to reality, smiled, her head still keeping tempo with the music. "So, about Grandma and her rabbits."

Ethan had watched her sway. A memory wisped its way into his brain—Amber with her eyes closed, swaying. He beat it back and swallowed. *Keep it light, buddy*. Rabbits, Michaels.

He didn't miss a beat. "Never killed one though. She'd hurl the rocks like a major leaguer with a fast ball—good enough to land them close enough to scare them away but not close enough to do any damage. Grandma saved a lot of lettuce that way. Not to mention, rabbits."

Amber threw back her head and laughed full out. "You could catch the humor in anything. You've always had a way of making me laugh." She took a swallow of beer while Miles Davis' trumpet made *After Round Midnight* sound like a work of art.

Good thing the room was dark. She couldn't see his eyes glazing. He matched her drinking, gulping the cold beer. Something had to cool him.

"I'd love to see your grandma whipping those stones. When I was little, I never dreamed about Bambi or Thumper. I wanted to be a hunter going on a safari, or a cop chasing the bad guys." She stopped for a moment, turned wistful. "Not a chance, though. My whole life has been nothing but 'Be a lady' and 'Why would you ever want to do that?'"

Ethan leaned back. "I know. You told me."

The laughter died. Amber bit her top lip and played with the orange slice, running it around the edge of her beer glass. Ethan grabbed her hand with his own. "I come from strong stock. I can take a little hurt."

A long tense moment sat there between them.

Amber brushed one hand through her hair, then held it at the back of her neck. When she spoke, her voice was so soft Ethan had to strain to hear her. "What I can't take is that I was the one who did the hurting." Her words sounded choked.

The conversation fell flat. No more tales of childhood. No more friends having that innocent drink. The air between them hung heavy with words unspoken, even the music and the buzz of Pour Fools walled out of range.

Ethan stood up and threw two twenties onto the table. They left, beers unfinished, spinach dip left to turn cold.

Amber drove home. Ethan hailed a cab and rode back to the school to pick up his car.

Rabbits, colors, choice of music—all fine. Backstory pain? No way.

Tuesday morning. Day three of teacher workshop, and they were all back in the study hall again. A few things had changed since Friday. The janitor had hung the school flag in the upper corner of the study hall, right behind the teacher's wooden desk. The coffee and cookies were gone—this was serious business, after all, not a back-to-school social. The chalk board next to the flag had a message written in bold swirls, *Welcome, Mr. Michaels.*

Amber had purposefully sat near a back window, just enough to blend in with a crew of teachers gathered on demand, most of them irritated that more precious time had been stolen from their work day, a few at least willing to listen, others sure that this was nothing more than another politically orchestrated ploy to make the administration look good. She had chosen to stay as far out of harm's way as she could manage without looking odd. The last thing Ethan needed, she told herself, was any kind of distraction at such a pivotal time. The least she could do was provide him the professional courtesy of anonymity while he began his community building.

Besides, she wasn't the one who needed to hear his speech. She knew what he stood for.

A faint riff of jazz played in her mind, pulling her back to last night at the Pour Fool's Bar. Her mind slammed shut against the memory. No time for distractions. Any unfinished business needed to wait until Ethan had established himself with the faculty. Professional courtesy demanded she not make waves or raise questions. Professional courtesy. Of course.

So why was her pen beating on her binder? And why did that music keep coming back, pulsing where it wasn't wanted, like the throb of a freshly finished root canal. Here she was, put in charge of making sure he felt comfortable by the great Duane, himself, and she felt like her nerves were raw and being attacked by thick ropes of lizard skin. Last night, listening to his tale of a rock-throwing grandma had been too damn close to the ease she both feared and longed for. That, and the ride home had been damn lonely.

"Amber."

She blinked, her attention drawn back from somewhere deep inside. Sally Fiene was looking at her, evidently wondering whether to laugh or blush. "Sorry, I didn't mean to startle you."

"Hey, Sally, no problem." She widened her eyes and smiled for effect. "I was off in Paradise lying on a beach while essays graded themselves under sheltering palms."

Sally let loose the understanding smile. "I just wanted to know if you wouldn't mind checking in with me later today or tomorrow. I'm going to use that biosketch idea you presented last year. Your kids did such a fantastic job, I thought I'd try it with *To Kill a Mocking Bird*. Think you've got some time?"

Ethan was in front of the room, sitting on the edge of desk propped up on a wooden platform, his one loafered foot firmly planted on the floor, the heel of the other propped against the thick wooden edge that ran along the desk's wooden skirt. He had shed his tie and opened the top button of his denim shirt.

"I mean . . . if you don't have time. . ."

Amber's fingers went up to her forehead, and she shook her head once, as if to clear her mind. "Sally, I'm sorry. I've been in LaLa Land all day today. I'd love to come in and help. Always ready to spread the wealth, and *Mocking Bird*'s one of my favorites. How about right before lunch?"

"Great. Just pop in. I'll be there. Lord knows there's enough to do to keep us in our rooms for another week. I really appreciate this." She began to turn away, then turned toward Amber. "Why is it that they fill our time with guys like him?" she said. She scowled and rolled her eyes toward the front of the room. "Look at him, Mr. 'I'm here to bring you the mountain.' If he were any more sure of himself, he'd have descended from a cloud."

Amber paused, her stomach doing a flippy thing. "Give him a break, Sal. He can't be any worse than Harry Silverdorf and the seven essentials of bonding. And besides, Duane's got *Write Way* pens for us—but only if we pay attention."

Sally laughed. "Gotcha." With a "And thanks again," Sally walked to her own little group who had chosen their seats closer to the front.

Great help you are, Amber. He's on the hotseat and you recommend him for Duane's trinkets. Just one big ball of help.

Oh, and don't forget the professional courtesy. On that, she feigned interest in an Educational Leadership magazine article Liz Aaron had dropped off, while she let her attention meander back to Ethan. The lead article, the latest in individualized instruction, couldn't compete with the man in front of the room.

The sport coat had never even made it past the desk, and Amber knew from his rumpled, black hair and the way he played with his folded hands, his thumb moving in subtle agitation that Ethan was primed and ready. She had seen that movement often enough in a world light years away, a weird mannerism they both shared. They had laughingly decided it suggested genius.

The drumming of her pen on the magazine caught her attention, and she stopped. When had she started doing that again? She put down the pen, turned toward the front of the room. Outside, the line of trees planted that acted as a buffer soon would wear shades of gold and red—but she registered only trunks, globs of green, tall sticks that another time she would recognize as light poles. Her consciousness still prickled from the competing bits of guilt that fought for supremacy. Inside the long room, a few voices dispelled any hope for a smooth blending of faculty and Ivory Tower expert sent to teach the teachers.

A sound brought her back. A voice deep, challenging. She blinked, focused to catch the words. "Yeah, and what place is there in the curriculum for high school kids to practice writing across the curriculum? Don't we have enough to worry about just covering content?" Fair question. Especially in a system tied to testing as the ultimate weapon against an imaginary onslaught of irresponsibility. The central office loved testing. Life was so simple when it was reduced to multiple choice.

Fair question all right for the bureaucrats. Like multiple choice would cure cancer or inspire poetry.

"I have to say, you sure know how to cut to the chase." Ethan's fingertips pressed against his knuckles the way they did when he was impassioned. "It's no surprise to any of us here that the expectations on teachers have increased tenfold since the days when standards had more to do with marching band flags than

testable outcomes sent from the state capital." That brought a few
nods from the faculty. Ethan slipped off his perch and stuck his
hands in the pockets of his khakis. He looked toward the door for a
moment, perhaps searching his thoughts, maybe even looking for a
bit of divine guidance—although in Amber's experience, Ethan had
never been one to look to outsiders for the answers to much of
anything. He surveyed the room full of teachers, nodding his head
almost imperceptibly, then spoke to the teacher who had posed the
challenge.

"Before I even get officially started, I want to make something
clear. You all—every one of you—are in that trench daily, fighting
to teach, fighting to reach the kids." He looked out at the crowd for
a moment and then zeroed in on Steve again. "I have nothing but
the greatest respect for what you do, and what you have to endure.
That's part of why I'm here."

Once, Amber had heard this tone and mistaken his passion for
arrogance. People often did that with Ethan. She had learned
quickly though, that, right or wrong, the man at the front of the
room, this stranger in the faculty's midst, acted out of his
convictions. Ethan Michaels took no prisoners when it came to
those things he loved. A spasm of quick warmth rippled through her
and she smiled. The moment was fleeting. The man acted just as
much against those things he hated. Amber let out a quick thanks
that she was surrounded by colleagues and thus obscure. The Ethan
in front of the whole faculty was a safe Ethan. It was the close-to-
you-in-your-face Ethan that worried her.

His hands were still now. He had cooled his tone with that "Ah
shucks" smile of his, the one that brought out his dimples, the one
that disarmed the unwary who took self-deprecation as a sign of
deference.

"The research is pretty clear on the connection between what
we can imagine and what we can write. In fact, the stuff coming in
says that narrative discourse, this *story-stuff* that seems to be so
darn ephemeral, is absolutely important for learning of any kind to
take place."

He stopped just a moment for effect, the country preacher on
the verge of a come-to-Jesus moment. He looked out to the front
three rows now, as if they represented the entire room.

"But folks, is that such a surprise? Think about it. When have we ever . . ." He used his index fingers like six-shooters to make the point. "When have we ever not learned through the stories we have to tell? The ones we have from what is the crux of our being." He paused again. "The one that's in our voice."

His gaze widened the search, connecting with even more educators. Now they rested on Amber, not so very hidden near the window in the back of the room.

"We all have the story. We all have the voice to tell it." Amber watched him with an old hope, wondering if that bit of eye contact had meant anything, the deepest part of her knowing exactly that it had. But Ethan's eyes kept working the room.

"Folks, there's a lot of hurting kids out there. And yes, they have to learn to spell. And yes, they have to learn to conquer the comma splice, and infer, and learn that reading means visualizing and connecting and all those other intangibles.

But those kids are our mission. We need to help them learn to find themselves and find the voice to tell us—and them—who they are."

He stopped. His bottom teeth bit into his upper lip while he collected himself. Then he gave one of those good-old-and boy laughs again and scratched the back of his head.

"You'll have to forgive me. My mom always thought I should be a minister, I get so fired up." A few teachers laughed, two or three nodded their heads.

Another quick pause and a smile. "That or a vacuum salesman. I promise to stop preaching. And I promise, *I promise. . .*" He raised his right hand in a boy scout hand vow. "I solemnly swear to give you some great hands-on stuff to make your lives easier. I've been in the trenches, just like you, and I know the tremendous sacrifice you give in time and energy. . . not to mention comparable wage-earning power. The least I can do is offer you something tangible that won't just collect dust on the top of your file cabinets. " That brought on even more nods of agreement.

Maggie had been sitting behind Amber. She leaned forward and whispered, "I don't know about letting him in my classroom, but anybody that hot could give me hands-on anything. If you don't buy red panties, I will."

Amber wished she had a quick retort but too many emotions—
and maybe a few old hopes—were tugging at her, each vying for
her attention like a crowd of students all demanding immediate
gratification. She stayed knotted. Kids she could discipline. The
tussle inside her was something else. Ethan's presence was a well-
packaged bomb with no clear directions for disarming.

The room had cleared of a few teachers, but most of them
stayed. Standing there among her peers, Amber knew one certainty.
She did not want to make small talk about the writing project. She
did not want to hear complaints about changing lesson plans,
accolades for the visionary artist who would lead them out of
mendacity—whatever the hell that meant—or anything in between.
God, but teachers were a disparate group. Love him, kill him, use
him, send him back to Iowa with all the other corn. It all swirled
around her. All she wanted was to get back to the safety of her
room.

No such luck.

"And when will we be working together?" She flinched like a
naughty child caught raiding the cookie jar, beat back the urge to
jump out of her skin and tried collect herself.

His mouth curved at her response, the edges of his lips stretched
in humor. Amber gritted her teeth. He always had liked to catch her
unawares. Even on her own turf. So much for the safety of her
room. It might as well be on the moon.

He looked down at the sheaf of papers in his hand, then up at
her. "I don't have you on my list. Aren't we teaming?" His eyes
swept her as he spoke, and she caught the control in his voice. He
was choosing his words with care. The checked firmness of his
voice let her know that he was as nervous as she was. She also
recognized that stab of control as if no time had passed between
them.

His guard was raised. Up close, even in a room filled with
fellow teachers, he would be guarded. But his eyes stayed on her
after the words were out. The man was challenging her with a
muted sword.

Out in the hall, a janitor rumbled by with a cart no doubt loaded
down with texts needing to be delivered. Voices played against the
rattle of the cart, a subtle din of indistinguishable conversation,

staff members twisting around them like a living fog, oblivious to what might appear to be two associates getting to know each other, if the staff had even bothered to notice.

Ethan glanced toward the noises. "And so goes the end of summer. Time for the greatest of plans, right, Clausson teammate?"

Amber fumbled for what to do next. The hall noise had stirred something in her, muddled the touch and sound of his words.

Why can't you just talk to him?

He is the one man you can talk to. She shuddered. Ethan knew that, too.

Please, God, don't let him read me. Please, God, don't let him touch me. If he touches me, I'll botch it, either grab onto him or run away.

Just like she had taught students during skills sessions, she turned her fears to images, then blacked them out one at a time until she centered on the essentials. That hesitant control in his voice. The touch of what had coursed through her while she stood there listening to him. She felt their history stare at her from the inside. He had been her safe place, had pulled pain from her she hadn't known was there, so deeply was it kept, holding her while she touched emotions and let them fill her. She smiled at the thought, the smile one of gratitude, a smile that stretched from her mouth to her eyes and sought to honor him as thanks for a sense of grace she had never let herself own before his help. "I knew you'd wow 'em. That commitment of yours is just too genuine."

She paused for a second, raising her head a bit and looking straight into those dark eyes. "Not to mention the firm avowal of hands-on activities." Then she turned serious and ever-so-quiet. "Ethan, I want you to know . . . I need to explain."

He hushed her with a look and an equally soft. "No. No explanations. I thought about what you said . . . and what you didn't say last night." His hands were in his pockets and he rocked on his heels. Amber couldn't see the tension in those fingers, but she felt it, felt the anger that Ethan was stilling with all his might at this moment.

Here, in a room filled with people and empty understanding, his next words, just a bit lower in pitch, came out like bullets. "I don't want to know." He scabbed over the anger, cementing his protection, then let out just the hint of a snort as he looked at her. "I read that somewhere. Seems appropriate."

He was right. Events cannot be unmade. Events wear their history, one after another leading the vulnerable toward the cliff.

The intercom sounded its usual static warning before a godlike voice announced, "All those renewing mandatory child abuse training certification should report to the cafeteria in five minutes."

Amber heard the message. She heard both messages quite plainly. Ethan turned his back on her, walked forward to greet someone he didn't know. His stiff back spoke volumes.

The intercom sounded again. "Mandatory child abuse training in three minutes."

Amber closed her eyes and told the air, "I've got to go to the meeting." She turned and hurried out of the room.

Ethan kept his back to her. His voice was a whisper, raw and low. "That's right, Amber. Leave.

"That's what you're good at. Leaving"

Pictures of abused children were bad. Endless images of the worst of abuse magnified into twelve-foot horror scenes was an abuse of its own kind. Not one teacher said anything. No one even squirmed, restless to finish the child abuse training and be gone to other projects. At least, that's what they said. No one could process power-pointed abuse in graphic detail. The room held a hush, its only sound the motor of the LCD player cooling the projector.

Someone cleared his throat. Another shut down the pictures in her own mind. Leonard Drivens spoke, finally, as if voted representative for the faculty members present. "Why report them? We should shoot the bastards." The words had been strong, even for a gruff old shop teacher, but thirty minutes of children bruised, scalded, and tattooed with cigarette butts brought out the crust in anyone. And unsaid in the training room, but known by all, was the knowledge that often the worst bruises were the ones unseen. A bruised soul does not heal, not without time and righteous therapy.

Amber walked out and headed back to her room after the training. The light was dim in the hallway, and the shop teacher's tirade left a din in the background, occasionally punctuated by a loud word or two among the garbled conversation of the teachers still outside the training room.

Her classroom was a haven. Finally she was alone with her thoughts, swirl that they were, a mishmash of images, some of them the scenes from the training, others the cousins of those images, the memories of kids over the years she had suspected may have been abused. As teens, they hadn't the physical damage of younger, more vulnerable children. They wore a look or an attitude, though, some withdrawn and sad, others haunted or angry. But Amber never had anything concrete enough to take to the authorities. School promised them protection, but kids, for whatever reason, kept the secret enough to keep their parents out of jail.

"What would keep a kid in such hell?" The sound of her own words surprised her. She stood there, her words circling her. Some other time she might have waited, might have listened, might have even tried to interpret her mood. But circumspection demanded a peaceful setting. This was not the time.

She walked to her desk and sat down, surprised at the sense of isolation that filled her, the chill that reached at her from the walls.

Minutes later, she shook her head at the thought of that lapse of focus, her lips pursed as she collected herself. You're just on the rebound from the meetings—both of them. Battered children on top of battered ego.

Yes, things had not gone well with Ethan, all right. That was an understatement. But struggle and chaos are the first stages of problem solving. Surely they would move to understanding.

Oh, please, teacher lady, what part of that first scene with him did you miss? Since when does 'I don't want to know' really ask for silence? If you really want to set things right, get back to him and grovel if you have to. You owe him, and don't think for a minute that he doesn't know it.

How had she moved from child abuse to Ethan?

Like there's a difference? Neglect is a form of abuse even if you don't mean it.

The critic cut her no slack.

Kids weren't the only victims of neglect. Or pounding.

Make things right or leave the poor guy alone to get on with his life.

Amber wanted to run back to the knot of teachers grousing about abused kids and join the din. Focus on something outside herself. She needed all the help she could get to deal with the punishing voice in her head. But the more she wanted to run, the faster the voice scolded.

Instead of running away, little girl, try running toward. Do what you have to do, but get on with the doing. Make it right. Make it right, now.

She cursed her conscience, but the resentment cracked and faded away. A wave of righteousness filled her—it stamped a silly smile on her face and made her feel curiously buoyed even while she felt slapped and foolish by her new knowledge.

She headed toward the second floor where Ethan had his temporary office, absorbed in this new-found grit while she walked through her guilt, her terror, all the stumbling and jabbering she could possibly do to make herself feel any more the fool than she already had. By the time she reached his office, she was manic.

She knocked on the door and opened it at the same time. Ethan was sitting at his desk, a pile of manila folders heaped and ready for file drawers in front of him. He was busy searching through one when he looked up. He half-way stood up, hands on the desk supporting him, but didn't say a word.

Amber had plenty to say. "So what about that morning has you most confused? The note? The fact that I ran out? The absolute trashy way I left without any forewarning?" The words tumbled so fast that Amber didn't acknowledge the lack of reaction on Ethan's part. He had finished standing up; his upper torso was leaning forward—surely that was a welcoming gesture—but his face was void of any response to her outburst.

Some of her drive faltered at the sight of him there, but Amber steeled herself and headed into that room, talking nonstop, her head down to avoid eye contact—this was embarrassing, for God's sake—her hands moving, fingers splayed. "I'm not leaving until we have this out. I mean, it wasn't just summer sex, I know that . . . " Her voice had taken on a peculiar tone for a statement; it sounded more like a question. She started to raise her head. Seeing his face might not be so bad after all. "That night before had been so incredible, and I think I was just so scared." On that, just as Amber faced Ethan and caught the raise of his eyebrows and an all-out grin, her ears caught a cough from the blind side of the room. She froze. She couldn't have moved, in fact, if sirens had started ringing and she needed to run or burn. Her hands dropped to her side just as Ethan stated the obvious. "Marti dropped in."

She felt the heat creep upward through her body, fill her chest and edge up the outside of her neck to billow out in her cheeks, a landscape of shame and guilt.

Dropped seemed to be the definitive word. Like as in, Amber wanted to . . . .

"She wanted to talk over a few things I brought up today, you know, the importance of assessing instead of just testing."

The word *testing* had a particular emphasis, a slight punch. It fit so well with all the other damning words that ran through Amber's mind at that very second while her feet came unstuck and she backed out of the room. "Don't mind me, guys. Carry on." She closed the door gently on "Catch you both later," and then she rolled away from the door window and leaned, head and upper back against the wall, knees locked and mind praying not to pass out.

Why hadn't she looked? She shook her head. Look at what?

She fled down the corridor, turned the corner and stopped in the Senior hallway, panting like a deer who just had outrun a hunter. Then she stationed herself against the wall, letting the heat have its way, replaying Ethan's face for a hint of reaction, hearing again Marti's polite cough, watching the ghost of her own embarrassed self slink out.

There in that hall, she pressed the small of her back against the wall, leaning her head until her neck muscles cramped, a crazed woman making plans for tomorrow. Here's the to-do list. Leave a post-it on the mirror as a reminder to kick yourself. Bring out the Stupid Award. What-the-hell—invite Ethan and Marti as guest presenters. You can have your picture taken with your foot so far back in your mouth, the straps'll come out of your nose.

The adrenaline rush started to ebb, sapping her, leaving her feeling like she had taught a whole week of classes in one day. Her legs and shoulders shook, and she slipped toward the floor, sinking against that locker, sliding down it metal hardness while a whole new emotion grabbed her before she hit the floor. She sat there in the hallowed hall of Clausson High School, Miss Professional-I-Can-Get-You-A-Grant Helm, and let go, let herself feel this crazed new emotion, let its bubbles rise and claim her.

She laughed. Laughed at the way Ethan's head had snapped up and then froze. Laughed at Marti's stilted diplomacy, laughed at herself, at the way she had slunk out like a naughty urchin caught pilfering candy. At first it was just a titter, one of those things couldn't get any worse reactions. Then, spurred on by the absolute lunacy of the moment, it grew—huge, starting from her belly and pushing its way upward. Sitting there on the floor, she grabbed herself with both arms and let the laughter flow, rolling in the absolute joy of the moment. So great was the silliness that filled her, she hardly had room to breathe.

Her eyes watered. Her stomach ached. If she had any more fun, she might pee her pants.

By god, if she was going to be a moron, she'd be the best damn moron around. And she'd spare no recourse doing it.

All the air went out of her. She flung her arms over her head. God, she was a moron.

Chapter 7

"A mix of the finest in new continental style juxtaposed with the best of the past . . ."

That's what the tour brochure would have said about the home of Charles and Lillian Helm. Unfortunately, said tour never materialized. Lillian had looked at the committee—after they had proposed her home as a part of a fund-raising effort—and said, "Just because we call this area the public rooms doesn't mean we want the public in them." Lillian Helm certainly could twist a phrase. She had looked like she wanted to twist each neck of the committee members sitting there, the club members who suggested that she open her home to dirty feet and wayward hands. And at Christmas, no less, as if the strain of the holidays didn't push her enough toward the edge.

This was Tuesday evening, however, and months after that bit of gauche behavior on the part of those who would take advantage of Lillian's style. On this Tuesday, in the dying days of late August, Lillian, Charles, and their daughter, Amber, dined together as family as they should—on Cirque Chibois plates from Tiffany's set at an eighteenth-century Piedmontese table in front of walls covered in hand-painted silk wallpaper the beloved Kikki had found in London. On any given day, Amber could have cared less.

Right now her attention was turned toward the room's fireplace. Two Chippendale china dogs bordered a picture on the mantle, a portrait of Amber sitting astride her horse, riding champion cup in hand. The portrait hadn't been moved since Amber had sat for it in fifth grade, all perfect posture and perfect form, the blessing of a daughter ready for taking her place as young lady. Lillian loved to be reminded of her daughter's perfect form whenever possible. All Amber could remember about that scene was the itch of her collar and the smell of horse sweat. But she remembered it with regularity. Like a ritual, every Tuesday night during her scheduled visits, by the time the soup was served, Amber could feel the phantom itching creeping up her neck and down her back clear to her bra line. Looking at the portrait had become sort of an exorcism. If she stared it down, maybe her neck would escape the phantom itch.

"So Amber, darling, how are things at your school?" The words broke her concentration. Lillian's smile was a study in the maternal. "What exciting things will be happening with your children this year?"

Her mother was asking about her job. Lillian Helm was intruding where she usually loathed to travel.

All right, Mother, what's up? Amber hated surprises when they came from her mother. But she answered enthusiastically—just in case.

"We're really excited about a new reading program where reading teachers will mentor content-area instructors to help kids tackle their textbooks. Reading literacy is so much more demanding now than when I was in school—the vocabulary is so much more complex, and . . ."

"That's interesting, Darling. Pass the truffle before you're tempted, Charles; it's bad for your heart and you know you can't resist." Lillian's radar had caught Charles without her conversation breaking stride. She had turned to her husband long enough to chastise and now returned her gaze to Amber. "So, are there any new faculty members this year? So many fascinating people you work with. I love to hear all those stories."

Liar. You tolerate my job because it's the only time I've put my foot down. You either criticize my friends and coworkers or you ignore them in hopes they'll disappear. If I date anyone without the pedigree of country club membership, you shudder in fear of mongrel grandchildren. Lillian, this is scary.

The worst of all truths hit her.

She knows. She knows about Ethan. Don't even ask how. She's read it in the entrails of the prime roast, tonight's blood sacrifice. She's divined it. Doesn't matter. Oh my God in heaven, she knows.

Amber pressed down the panic that grabbed her just as her

father asked, "A little cognac?" She nodded and took the glass he offered with one hand, clutched the linen napkin in her lap with the other. Should she test them, those parents sitting there so doting, smile at them and tell them, did she have the courage? Her throat constricted, her heart, too, her insides knotting and tight.

She smiled. "Well, there is one guest writer from the Iowa Writers Grant who'll be helping with a writing project." She stopped and raised the napkin to her mouth, touched her lips once with its elegant softness before she spoke. "But I don't think I'll be seeing much of him. He'll be more hands-on with the creative writing group."

Lillian smiled back. "Oh really? I'm surprised you won't be seeing him. You've always had such an interest in that sort of thing." Lillian paused and turned to her husband. "No cognac for me, Charles. I don't want to throw off my sugar balance."

Chapter 8

Ethan sat in his car across the street from Amber's house. The night had that kind of pre-fall wetness, a welcoming coolness tinged with enough moisture to demand a swipe or two from car wipers. His watch said 9:30. Time to go. Time for answers.

He pocketed his car keys, opened the door and stepped out. The night's dampness hit him in the small of his back and along his collar line. He ran his hands down the sides of his pants to dry imaginary dew. The sight of this place-- her house, her turf, these brought up other images. Her face today at school, caught tight in shock, her whole body closed in while she retreated from his office. Grimacing, he cleared his mind and focused. Time for closure. No more smiles masking unspoken anger and hurt, no more half-truths and unfinished conversations. Tonight, there would be answers and the finish of whatever had tentatively hinted at beginnings.

Down the street, at the corner, a cat let out a wail. Resisting the startle that grabbed him, he closed the car door and leaned against it, taking in the sense of her home. Well-lit neighborhood, street lights on vintage iron poles every three houses or so. Her lights were on upstairs, the one on the front porch as well. Security all the way. Count on her to have a red door. Matched her temperament.

By the time he stepped over the strip of grass and ducked by a tree that separated the sidewalk from the curb, he had detailed the possibilities. The key here was control. If she stammered, if she cried, if she threw tire irons, it was all the same. He would be in control.

It had been so easy Monday morning. Maybe not easy, just within the realm of containment. Another brick building like all the others. Another gaggle of teachers and kids. Big artist man on the verge of burnout, wanting to run back to Iowa City and refill, do the writing that kept him going. Publish a story or two, get on that great American novel tract. Be professional. Do the gig and leave.

He could have. He'd made it through the first meeting, even the so-called non date. The time after was tough, but he'd held firm, nothing doing with her "I'm sorry." Water over the dam, over the whole damn thing, in fact. But today, her face in his office, the bite of her eyes, green and full of spit and fire, the mouth—those lips full and determined before she melted in embarrassment. Too close to what got him hooked in the first place.

Shaking his head, he beat back the thought of her and stirred his sense of resolve. He needed the edge, needed the answers that would calm this haggling that had roped his bones ever since Amber had left his office. His sense of practiced composure started to unwind. Things had seemed so easy in the car. Time to regroup.

Game on.

He ignored the railing that matched the iron of the street lamps and outlined Amber's tiny lawn. The hand-laid bricks leading to her front steps didn't warrant so much as a glimpse. Same with the pots of perennials. He was back to the rehearsing, letting his words take clearer form, trying to think of a joke maybe. Jokes lightened the moment, let the answers fall more easily.

Then he could go on.

He used the heavy black knocker rather than the bell. It felt firm in his hand. By the second knock, he blew out a firm breath, lips pressed for the exhale in hopes that he wouldn't have to stand there much longer. The knocking turned to pounding, then abated. *Come on, Michaels. Control.* Right. He ran his hands through his hair, blew out one more breath, and knocked again.

The hall light went on and the door opened. Amber stood there for a second with the same shocked look from this morning. Then her whole face snarled at him. He moved forward just as her arm pushed on him. No more Amber armed with apologies.

"If you've come here to gloat, it isn't going to work, my friend."

"Gloat?" Gloat, my ass. Where was the apologetic Amber from last night, the firebrand who had today announced that he was more than a good lay?

He brushed away her arm, and strode past her as if she weren't even there, his arms heavy at his side, his head bent heavy forward, shaking back and forth. Controlling her was like controlling wet cats. So much for mission control. To a stranger, he looked like he might not be able to stop, that this surprise visitor might just stride through the house and out the back door. Amber had turned around and now stood there, arms folded, and watched, a stone-still figure wearing her aggravation as he barged his way through her house.

Ethan was clear through the entry way and the living room, almost to the dining room before he stopped and turned. Slipping his hands into his pockets, he stared at her, rubbing the tips of his thumbs against his index fingers. He might hit someone if he took them out. There were only two people to choose from, and he certainly had not even the least desire to hit himself.

"We need to talk." The words were strong.

He looked at her. Her shock had worn off, replaced by a calm perplexity and the hint of humor. Even body language, not even the hint of a response. He had come to her home to be the reasonable one. Her calmness wounded him.

"I give." His head was still shaking, his dark hair a mess. At some point, his hands had left his pockets. Manic hands of his.

"I sat at Dave's for an hour, trying to put things together." He looked at her, pausing, like she was supposed to jump in or acknowledge that she understood, then went on. "You know how I am. Just think and connect. It'll come to you."

Another pause.

"That's all bullshit, Amber." He walked toward her—three long steps—his eyes focused away from her, his mouth mumbling about sitting in the car until he could get it right. Then he stopped and stared straight at this woman, the object of his disordered state. All the nights of wondering, all the aching—everything he had pushed down, it up and shook him with its memory. He didn't dare get closer, so he reverted to words, rushing them together as if he couldn't spit them out quickly enough. "I saw you that morning from the back, and I knew it was you before you even turned around. I told myself not to care. I could be pissed. I could be cold. I could be about anything. But I had better not care."

The heated look left his eyes. He just looked sad, like a little boy who's found out that his best friend was moving before summer even started. His eyes locked onto hers, eyes tempered by some flicker from the past. Still, he kept them locked as he moved toward her.

She stood framed in the doorway without moving. Why doesn't she move? Why couldn't she make one step toward him? His left hand went out when he reached her, touched her hair and drove it away from her face with his hand, his eyes still locked onto her. His other hand touched her face at the jawbone and moved up along her cheek. He didn't close his eyes. Not then. He just moved his lips to hers, brushed them, nipped at them softly as if to test their reality. Then, as he moved his body against her, both hands pinned her against the wall next to the doorway and deepened his kiss. Only then did he close his eyes. His legs against hers. His chest against hers. His tongue in her mouth tasting her. She kept her arms at her side, in the shock of it all. But her tongue met his and she returned that kiss, tasting and pushing at him with her lips and teeth and tongue.

When he backed away from the kiss, he still held her in with his body, his arms locked, hands against the wall. All the heat that he had felt so long ago, all the heat that he had denied endless month after endless month, all that heat tore through him now. Amber leaned her head against his chest. He felt the pump of his heart against her, inhaled her sweet need, knew in his gut she was ready for him to speak. Need cried at him, need tinged with a sadness for what they had lost. His voice was hushed, part purr, part prayer, all edged with a rasp. "I just don't get it, Amber. No matter what I tell myself. Nothing makes sense." The words spilled over each other.

"I woke up in a crappy dorm room with scratched up walls and broken screens, lying on a sagging mattress in a beat-up iron bed, thinking you were still with me, and all I knew was warmth and a gut-deep joy." His voice grew deeper, gritty now. "And then I realized I was alone, just me in that empty bed, but I knew that all I had to do was reach out and I'd find you." He stopped, had to stem the bitterness that rode in deep waves as he confronted this woman. He pulled away and brought her head up to face him.

"So tell me, Amber . . ." A slick wash of wetness covered his eyes, and he tensed in the anger of knowing that. "Why the hell did you walk out on me?" He was so coiled, he would break. "Tell me, Amber, tell me now."

Dinner with her parents had been unnerving. Lillian's comments had wormed their way into the back of her head and left cement in her shoulders. All she had hoped for the whole way home was a hot bath and a little peace.

Amber kept her body still, but inside she churned. Now Ethan was here. "Ethan, I don't know what to say. I . . . I don't have the words."

The taste of that kiss, the memory of his hands, his tongue were imprinted on her. She could feel the heat of the man, the heat of his question. Even filled with the knowing of it, she only had been able to summon the ghost of a smile and a murmur.

The hardness of his gaze stopped her. "That's not enough. I need an answer."

He had lifted his head and focused on the wall, in safety perhaps, eyes narrowed above a stiffened jaw. The darkness of his eyes deepened. They bore into her.

"You're right. You need an answer. I just wish I could give you one."

He looked away. She felt the wait in his body. Her hands reached up to his wrists and gently dislodged them, bringing them to his side. His head did not move; his eyes and jaw gave up nothing. She understood the deliberate choice of his action.

Once she had told her students, "To not make a decision is to decide." Now she lived those words. The brunt of tonight had worn on her. She was tired and confused and numbed. How could she give him what he expected, what he needed here—the whole of the past three years come down to an answer right here, in this house, in this room, in this space, walled in by a man possessed.

At another time, in another place where the day had not been so convoluted, they might have sat on her sofa, one at each end, a woman and a man each talking across the neutral territory of a sofa cushion, for the first time in three years ready for honesty. Words might have tumbled from each to be tasted and chewed and digested, enough to put pain to rest. In that lovely place of resolution, Amber would have made tea or poured wine or popped a beer for each of them, and the night would have worn on as two ex-lovers began a journey toward reconciliation.

Too bad.

Too bad Amber had just come from another bout with the parents who loved her in their own way, a way that strangled and demanded and fed a mother's milk of guilt. Too bad her skin prickled and throat tightened. They might have begun healing all right. Instead, Amber said, "You have to leave."

His jaw tightened but he didn't respond. He almost was able to hide the surprise in his eyes. She had made no apology, certainly given no explanation. She read his face but pressed on.

"This whole dance we've been doing, it's too much. Let's just be adults and go on with our lives."

They were two feet apart, neither of them aware that they had moved away from each other, each of them boxed and rigid shouldered. The words must have stung. His answer certainly stung back, his voice edged, so unlike the voice she had never forgotten.

"Adults?"

The word spat out like a curse. His chin and neck were so tight, Amber could see the muscle strain.

"Adults face their problems. Adults seek resolution." He backed away one more step from her, lowered his voice, cut her with his eyes.

"Adults are not children." He looked like a principal laying down the proverbial hammer.

You know what the guy says. "You can't fix what you don't acknowledge.' Before you supply me with any kind of answer, you'd better find a few of your own."

Amber's eyes, so tired moments before, darkened and her lips drew in to a pucker. "I'm not the one who barged in full of demands and . . ." She was sputtering. "I'm not the one who shoved someone against a wall and stuck his tongue down her throat." She shoved him away from her and then stood there, arms crossed. "You haven't changed a bit. You're still the same know-it-all trying to run the world your way." Her voice was sharp and her words way past self-control, blame falling from her mouth like froth.

"And while we're at this blame game, tell me, Ethan. If my running away was such a trauma, why didn't you come after me? How could you let me stay in Chicago all this time without a confrontation if I was this fount of joy? You don't let joy run through your fingers and seep away without at least trying to close the gap."

Ethan stayed quiet, watching her, his eyes cold, his whole body wooden. While Amber's foot tapped and she waited for a reply, he walked past her and left, the sound of his feet his only answer.

The bottom part of her face shook, her teeth clacking. Her neck was a rock.

Ethan Michaels had come back into her life all right.

Chapter 9

Wednesday morning. Ten hours after confrontation. The first day of school.

The halls that had seemed so empty this week filled with the din of teenage chatter. Kids swarmed, some in packs, a few by themselves, all leaving the scent of hormones and new beginnings as they pushed their way.

8:01 and all was well.

Outside her classroom doorway, Amber leaned back against the wall, watching the splendid chaos that unfolded every year. Ben Hennings, last year's star football player but less than stalwart academic, sauntered past, a mocking grin on his face as he turned toward her while he continued down the hall backwards, never missing a beat in whatever inner rhythm drove his gait.

"Yo, Ms. Helm. You are looking *mighty* fine. How could a sweet thing like you give me a D last year? Don't you love me no more?"

Amber grinned back, one finger raised and pointed in teasing banter. "*Anymore*, Ben. Could be one reason for the D."

Ben threw up his hands and turned back with a laugh, slipping his arm around a blushing sophomore as he steered her around the corner and out of sight, never missing a beat as he made his way.

"Miss Heeeelm. We're so glad to see you!" Three girls descended on her, their adolescent frenzy a kind of war dance complete with painted faces and costuming. Face glitter and bright orange were definitely in this year. They exchanged five minutes of information in thirty seconds, and then the girls moved on, hands waving in the air as they chattered, plastic bracelets bouncing up and down with each gesture.

Amber blew a laugh through her nose and smiled, totally

entranced with the magic of the first day of school. Seven months
from now she would be bolstering sagging spirits as the March
doldrums hit, but for this one perfect day, all students loved each
other and the halls rang with the heart of teenage serendipity in all
its hormonal glory. The wonder of adolescence.

The absence of Ethan.

The one minute warning bell rang. Lockers banged as if some
locker director stood in the hall waving a locker baton, and students
scurried off toward the lines of oaken doors on each side of the
hallway, shouting quick goodbyes, a few muttering that once and
for all, *this year* they wouldn't be stuck in tardy detention. Amber
whisked the last of her charges inside the room and closed the door.

Everything had been readied. Walt Whitman kept guard right
above the door to the room. Emerson offered words of wisdom to
Uncle Walt's left. For those less inclined toward the Romantics,
classroom rules were posted next to Emerson's portrait and words
on self-reliance. At the back, away from the action area of the
class, a fresh pot of mums sat on her desk next to her coffee cup
and cache of reference books. At the podium up front, armed with
the latest but certainly not the final attendance list, Amber took in
the room, swiveling her head like a slow-motion windshield
wiper from one end of the room to the other, the requisite no-
nonsense teacher look marking her territory, but just enough of a
smile to let the kids know she was on their side—mostly. One boy
in the back still attacked his backpack as if foraging for supplies,
but the harsh ring of the final bell brought him—and everyone
else—to attention.

School had started. All was well.

That was one of the great cosmic rules of teaching. Kids always
paid attention the first day of school. After that, it was anyone's
guess.

"Good morning. Hope everyone . . ."

Just then, the door swung open and a girl-child strutted in,
slight of build, almost boyish. Amber first saw the black, a shroud
of black hair, long strands dulled by cheap hair dye or choice, bangs
slitted and hanging past the eyebrows. The clothes continued the
shroud, baggy black jeans and a long-sleeved, ratty black t-shirt
circa Goodwill. Fingernail polish, even her lipstick.

But the girl's face and hands, they were the purest white Amber had ever seen on a post-summer student, china-doll white or perhaps the translucent white of parchment.

Her jewelry, a dull gray, fit as a merging of the black and white. Rows of gray studs and small circles lined her ears. A worn dogcollar studded with gray nuggets looked like it could choke that waifish neck. A single metal ring hung from her right eyebrow.

The girl walked over to Amber and handed her a pass, her dark eyes meeting the green of Amber's, her only sign of life, once she reached the teacher, a thrust of hip and arm speaking volumes of disdain.

Amber felt a flicker of shock but recovered quickly, her veteran teacher voice speaking to her loud and clear. Diffuse and plow ahead. She read the name on the pass but wisely did not extend her hand. This was one kid who did not want to be touched in public. Or maybe not at all. Too new, too angry, too much the rebel perhaps with a cause. She had the look of kids who had passed through the system in the three years Amber had been teaching, kids who saw no meaning in their lives or swallowed pain like razors. "Welcome, Jocelyn. Why don't you pick out a seat and we'll get started.

Jocelyn muttered a "Whatever," and moved to a desk in the very most back corner right next to the yellow mums. She plunked down her folder with a bang. Amber scanned the don't-mess-with-me body language, the slithering into the seat, the glare.

The girl stretched her arms tightly across the desk, fingers gripping the plastic ends, her black legs and army booted feet flung out into the aisles as if hoping to trip up anyone who dared violate her space. Amber held in any reaction for just a second. This was one hard case. Jesus could walk in with a bazooka and she'd just stare Him down.

So much for the positive first day of school. Back to square one. After giving a nod to the new student, Amber sneaked a peek at the clock. Sure enough, forty minutes left in the class period. She'd deal with Jocelyn as the need arose, but right now, the structure of the year needed attention. Smiling broadly, she walked over to the blackboard and grabbed a piece of chalk. Part ritual, part adventure, she scrawled a huge *Welcome*, then turned to the class, her entire self jazzed by the thrill of a new year. "So, what do we mean by "Welcome?' Let's take a look."

The kids followed her lead, settling to listen to expectations. She turned it into question and answer time. "Yes, you get to go to the bathroom. No, you can't stay there for twenty minutes. No one's bladder is that needy. Gum? Doesn't that stand for *Grammar, Usage, Mechanics*? If so, it's important."

Another ten minutes and business was settled. "Now let's start with what brings us all here. Learning." The year was on.

"I want to know about you. By the end of class, you will write a letter about yourself. Not just about what you do, and who your family is, although that certainly makes up much of your story. Let me know about you, the inside you, and especially how I can help you make this year a success."

She looked at a sea of faces, some startled, others already fixed with the look of wheels churning. They were her charges for the entire two semesters. Even this new girl.

"To get you started, I'm going to walk you through a strategy called Klinefelter's Meditation." The rest of the time sped by as Amber led her students through the activity, walking around the room as she spoke, occasionally bending down near a desk to give some advice or calm a fear. Everyone worked. That is, except for one figure clad in black who raised her head just enough above eye level to let everyone know she would never run with the herd but she might watch, her arms still stretched and taut across the desk, her knees locked and boots pointed upward.

The last locker bang and muffled sound of sandals shuffling down the hall ushered in the calming peace of a day well taught. Amber sat at her desk, shoes long kicked off, and let herself slip into reflection. Interesting day. Three students from last year had popped their heads in between classes to say hello and complain that Mr. Murphy wouldn't be nearly as much fun, and couldn't she just please teach 11th grade this year or they'd be bored to death and have to plant themselves in the closet or drop out of school or whatever. Four others had checked in to make sure that absolutely no one could possible replace them and weren't the tenth graders a bunch of morons this year. Then they ambled off to afterschool jobs, practices, and maybe a bout or two of hackeysack.

Now she was alone, finally ready to focus on the long journey of teaching her students. She spent a few minutes reading through student responses. Mostly they told of parents' names, numbers of siblings, all those safe things that students could share at the beginning of the year. Time passed as Amber jotted notes in the margins of a few of the writings, little notes of welcome and connection. Halfway through, she indulged in a few moments of idle spacing off.

A wisp of afternoon breeze nudged the papers on her desk and played with her hair, now damp and curling even more at the hairline and nape from the heat and humidity. Amber lifted tired arms to stretch like a cat, and then her hands lifted her hair while she let the breeze do its magic. A good day, for the most part. Her thoughts, however, couldn't help but turn themselves to a single student. The one who had let Amber know in no uncertain terms that she had nothing to share.

Amber would have to find Marti before she left for some information on Jocelyn Quint. This girl was just what Winston Churchill once had called Russia, a riddle wrapped in a mystery inside an enigma, but this time the metaphor described a child instead of a foreign country. Was Jocelyn's obvious dark pall a matter of personal choice or more a matter of defense? What was behind the defiance? The glint in her eyes and the taut stretch of her limbs demanded to be left alone. Amber let her thoughts be pulled into a haze of her own childhood. All children want to please.

Amber, dear, just do as your mother says. You don't want her to be sick, do you?

Amber, for God's sake, pull up your socks and pull down your dress while you're sitting here. You know you need to be a lady.

You're Mother's perfect prize. What would I do without you?

That's why I depend on you to make me proud.

Amber swallowed what had surprised its way into her thoughts.

Whatever instinctive throwback to more ape-like days, the instinct that warns us of intrusion, brought Amber back to the moment. Jocelyn was standing just inside the doorway, barely visible. She held a piece of paper in her hand, her arm hanging loosely, the white of the paper and the white of her hand against the blackness of her clothing. She was the picture of small.

Amber opened her mouth, but the words she would normally use to greet a student couldn't form themselves. Or maybe Amber just knew better. She only watched as Jocelyn approached her desk, slid the sheet down onto the desk with an "I did it" and walked out. That was it. An "I did it," and out she went, a sylph melted into the forest of the hall way. Amber picked up the paper. Finally a clue about this new student. Then she caught her breath as she read.

I dance on the edge of the abyss, a silly tap dance for fools, shuffle, shuffle, step, step, skirting closer to the rim now and then just to take a chance. What can a peek hurt, cast one eyeful there, silly dupe, believing that evil sleeps. Or maybe this time the lie will be true and she will act. I forget that evil smiles just before it swallows us, just before it gets on with things.

A shiver grasped her throat, then slipped down into her chest. She felt the tightness in her gut as anger took the place of the shiver. Tenth graders wrote about boyfriends or football games or alien cockroaches and laser guns.

They didn't write about evil. And they didn't write with such depth. "Evil smiling before it swallows us," the paper said.

What had happened to this child? Amber hadn't seen any bruises. But then, bruises heal. Then she remembered reading about battered kids, the ones beaten with words instead of fists. She forced herself to breathe, twice, before she noticed both her hands yanking at the paper as if she wanted to rip apart the nameless enemy who had victimized this child she didn't even know. She wanted to rush out and find this child, sweep her away from some unsaid menace.

Who would sell a child the promise of love and then rip it away? Kids believe too easily, too deeply. The wave of her anger kept rising, grabbing at the inside of her throat until she could barely breathe, so intense it rode her.

Never once, in all that anger did she stop to ask herself why this child, at this moment, had unleashed such a reaction.

She stood up and stalked out of the room, trying to unclench her teeth as she made her way to Maggie's room, her hands rolling up Jocelyn's writing into a tube. Someone else had to know that this thing existed. Someone else had to share this, had to know the pictures forming in her head right now, had to be her anchor and get her grounded so that she could do some good.

She marched into Maggie's room, the afternoon shadows hiding the rage on her face.

"Hey Babe, how goes the war? Any casualties yet?"

Amber just looked past her even though her eyes were physically directed in Maggie's direction, trying to get a handle on the emotion, the anger—no, the rage—she felt as Jocelyn's words kept playing in her head. She whacked her desk with the damned piece of paper, each slap a smidgen harder and faster. She was a teacher whose job it was to protect these kids, and, nothing, not a phantom face, not a parent who should be nameless—or dead— should be allowed to bring out that kind of bitterness in a kid who wasn't even old enough to drive, for God's sake.

"What's the point of being the class clown if I can't get anyone to laugh?" Maggie sat down, an arm thrown in mock desperation across her face, waiting for Amber's reaction. Amber just sighed deeply and fingered the tube, rubbing her fingers across the white smoothness, her eyes narrowing and her lips tightening.

"Okay, time's up. If your lips were pressed any harder, they'd be glued."

Amber played with the paper, this time turning it end over end. She had always vowed that, short of suicide, student confidentiality was a right, not a privilege. That was a given. But this child's anger had reached out from the pages and grabbed her. Something had slipped past her guard and she didn't like it, did not like it one bit. Her mind tried to chew it over but the darned thing chewed back and all she was left with was a soggy mess and a sense of needing to do something and do it quickly. If one of her students was in some kind of danger, and the message of this girl's writing surely indicated there was some kind of danger, Amber was legally responsible to act as mandatory reporter. Law be damned. She was morally responsible for the welfare of her kids. Her initial anger had softened to determination and questions bounced inside her head.

What the hell did dancing around an abyss and evil smiles tell anyone? Maybe the girl was just playing with fantasy, just like her whole appearance seemed to play with something dark. Or maybe Jocelyn was trying to call for help, her outrageous costuming and eerie writing response some kind of encrypted truth.

Where to start?

Maggie pressed on. "I thought we were all settled with smoothing panic attacks. What happened to 'I'll be a professional if you will?' A lost love is one thing, but Amber, this is getting weird. Do I need to give Father Harrigan a call to come here and sprinkle a little holy water? Exorcise the ghost of summer past?"

Amber finally responded, using the writing as a pointer, her voice edged and slow. " This isn't about Ethan." Maggie didn't say a word. It wouldn't have mattered one way or another. Amber was in her own zone of pure fury.

"You know, the trouble with parents is they don't know how to parent. Sometimes they don't even know how to be human." She studied the folded piece of paper in her hand as if it would somehow speak to her, let her know how to proceed.

"The bastards think that because they pass on a little DNA, they have the right to inflict any whim onto their kids. Like kids are just pieces of property.

Well, they're not, Maggie. You know that just as well as I do! They're not!" By now Amber's voice was shaking and her lips trembling.

Maggie just looked at her, absolutely still.

Immediately, Amber's face fell, and she backed up one step. It wasn't like her friend should be jumping from desk to desk, Amber following behind her, shaking that piece of writing all the while, both of them yelling like some crazed creatures unleashed and dangerous.

Amber did expect some empathy. They were teachers for god's sake.

"Maggie, you know as well as I do what happens to kids. They couldn't even arrest people who chained up their kids for child abuse 100 years ago because there were no laws on the books. They had to use cruelty to animals. They cared more for their damn horses than they did for their children."

Maggie watched in awe as something surged inside her friend. Amber felt the convolution, an invisible voice that came up from

Amber's gut to slowly make its way through her body, through her arms and wrists and fingers, beg her to beat the desk with that damned piece of writing. It drilled through her, in unknown places, places she couldn't see, couldn't touch, hadn't even known were there. The whole time it did its winding, Amber did not notice that Maggie had approached her, reached out to take her face in her long red-nailed hands. The touch of skin on skin brought her back.

"Amber. Reality check."

Amber tossed her head, as if Maggie's hand had been a hot poker. She shook, a single shudder, and sat down, ambushed by her outburst and seeking self-control. This was beyond ridiculous. She was an adult, a teacher for crying out loud. First, she'd flipped over an old boyfriend back in her life. She was railing like a maenad under a full spring moon over a piece of student writing. Some help she'd be. No one ever helped kids gain control who wasn't in control herself. Teaching 101.

"Sorry, Mags." Amber slowly unrolled the paper now wound as tightly as the woman holding it. "You just wouldn't believe what a day it's been." She tried a smile. "Today's supposed to be the one good day of the year, but it's been more than from hell."

Just then a shrill giggle from somewhere down the hall caught both their attention. Maggie smiled, even though her face registered concern more than humor. She gave Amber a firm hug and whispered, "Honey, they're all from hell. It's just a matter of which level."

Amber was tempted to give her friend the *So Why Are You a Teacher* speech, but she was too tired. Too overwrought. So overwrought, in fact, she hadn't even noticed the concern on Maggie's face while she'd delivered her tirade. Their usual good cop/bad cop routine over for stress relief was missing. When Maggie wrapped her in a girl-hug, Amber hugged back, then stepped back, her head lowered.

After a long breath, she looked up. "There's a new sophomore named Jocelyn Quint."

Maggie looked at her friend. "You mean the walking death girl with the dog collar? Ken Redalen told me about her. He put her in the front corner to help her get acquainted with Rachel Schiller and Kelcey Shepherd. Anybody can get along with those two and their mothering. She did the School Sucks slouch the whole time. Didn't say a word. Ken says she has eyes like razors."

"Did anyone stop to think . . . ?" Amber struggled for control. "Maybe there's more to this kid than a dog collar." She didn't even flinch as she held out the unfolded sheet, now curling as if caught in some bad habit.

"Read this."

Moments later Maggie looked up, her lips puckered and her eyes large. "I take it this is Jocelyn's"

Amber just nodded.

"Have you seen Marti about this?"

Another nod, this time a no.

"Amber, I know how you get into your save-the-world mode with your kids, but this isn't some girl with boyfriend problems or a kid needing after school tutoring. This could be pretty serious abuse. Or even worse, a sick fantasy bubbling up from some nasty neurons." She paused to let it sink in, even though a part of her knew better. "Let Marti handle it. You can set up a Care-Team alert, but don't go tilting at windmills before you know exactly what's making those windmills spin. Especially now when. . ."

Amber didn't hear her. At a level more deep than she could recognize, she was far away, back in a bedroom watching an ambulance take off, her stomach in ropes, tears welling in her eyes even after all these years. She was only aware of the now. Children needed protection. They needed to be heard. And she'd be damned if she'd stand by and let a child suffer that kind of pain.

Chapter 10

The bitch wanted her to write a letter. Get in touch with herself and share. Practice. Learn to connect. The good little kiddies did their best. Gotta suck up right from the start.

Jocelyn laughed. Guess I showed her. So Miss Helm, how'd you like it? The laugh was spent, a tensing in its place as she thought of her classmates penning that assignment.

She sat at her desk, derelict grabbed from the curb on garbage day, took up her pen. Little pussies. Writing about life. Life. What did they know about life. About writing. About anything.

I write because I must. I write because the very force of her pushes the pen forward—should the words spill in blood or the black of spleen? I write because if I don't write I will die. My words will weave the magic. The sound will not touch me and the mirror will tell us that we both are beautiful.

Liar.

Jocelyn Quint stopped writing. She had to. The paper was ripping from the sheer force of her pen as it tore at the yellow sheets of the legal pad. Too bad the paper wasn't her mother.

But the keening had stopped. For now at least. Evelyn Magee Quint was asleep, passed out actually, an empty vodka bottle testimony to her ability to swill with the best of them. She was such a sloppy drunk. Probably the Irish in her—or so said one of the many boyfriends who had traipsed through her life. That is, before the inevitable slam of the door and her mother's crying signaled another departure. Sometimes the men lasted as long as several months. Other times—they hardly lasted through the night.

What did it matter? The results were the same. The faded red hair on the floor. The thin line of drool spilling from a mouth once beautiful, now puckered and notched from too many cigarettes and too much booze.

And all that noise. "Jocelyn," she would wail. "Jocelyn, he don't love me. He's like them all—they all just use me. But you're my baby, Jocelyn. You'll always be my baby, and you'll always love me, won't you baby. Come here and tell your momma how you'll always love her." Not to worry. If Jocelyn waited long enough, she wouldn't have to answer. Evie would be asleep, daughter forgotten in the blackness of her stupor. But the daughter wouldn't forget.

Couldn't forget. She kept hearing that incessant sound, the banshee cry for love, a drunk's plea for grace without redemption. God, how she hated her mother.

Little girls are supposed to be coddled, read to, taken to the park where they could ride on swings, soaring to the sky, legs straight out and head back, their laughter a sure sign of trust and safety. Little girls were not supposed to lie in bed and listen to the hollow laughter that came before the grunting and the occasional, "Shh. If you wake the kid, she might come in." Before the snorting and the snores. Before the musty smell of the sheets she had to change the next day, sheets that smelled of booze and body odor and sex.

Oh yes. They all loved her mother. They all loved Evie before they left and Jocelyn had to hear the litany again. She looked down at the paper. Lines of square boxes moved across the page underneath her words. She couldn't even remember drawing them, those blue cubicles against the yellow. She'd read somewhere that people who doodled boxes felt trapped.

God, how she wanted to love her mother.

And how she wanted her mother to love her.

Fat chance. Here she was, new school, new teachers, same crap over and over. The English teacher looked like she might be okay, maybe the biology guy with the weird glasses, but then didn't they all—the ones who promised to reach out, and then dropped you like a snotted wad of Kleenex.

Schools changed all right. Too bad life didn't.

Jocelyn went to bed that night the same as every night, her arms cradling the baseball bat she had bought with the money lifted from her mother's purse. The bat kept her safe. The bat and the razor.

Chapter 11

Tuesday.

Not everyone has an office that greets clients with stuffed animals and jars of cherry licorice. Then, again, not everyone is Marti Butler, Clausson's counselor extrordinaire. The place was small—an eighteen-by-ten box divided into two cubicles by a brown partition scrounged from the music room. By itself, nothing to brag about. With Mrs. Butler, another thing altogether, the Last Stop Saloon for emotionally thirsty teenagers and bedraggled teachers alike.

In the outer section, college rep schedules lined the walls beside the entry, a pile of key rings with *School-to-Work Works for You* hung on neon plastic next to one lone copy of *Reviving Ophelia* casually tossed on the back table . . . just in case a girl might pick it up for a look. In the inner section, a stuffed dog fluffy enough to run for Miss South Carolina perched on a dorm-sized refrigerator well stocked with after-school colas.

The wall directly across from Marti's work area was covered with poster paper. Kids could use markers to write or draw what was on their mind. Usually the art work stayed up until the wall was covered. Occasionally, when the message got too personal, Marti took it down. Everyone knew that. Part of the rules. Mrs. Butler's rules.

The room had been student-ready two weeks before in-service started.

At this moment, barely an hour after the second day of school, the room was the home of anarchy.

The source of Marti's trouble was taped to the wall above her desk. This year's master schedule. This year's behemoth. Hi-liter in hand, the guidance counselor stared at the latest changes.

Pink for classes added—*Ms. Butler, Mom says I have to have a third language, can ya fit it in?* Green for drops—*I can't get algebra, it's nothin' but numbers and Mr. Stevens hates me.*

She had juggled the schedule at the beginning of each semester. She knew what to expect. Come the first two weeks of September, she'd start to mumble to herself and wonder why she had chosen this job in the first place. Count on it. And, of course, that was what she was doing, an hour after teachers were allowed to leave. An hour ago, outside her door, kids had howled and yelped at each other on their way out of school. Now all was quiet. Even the faint notes of jazz band practice had given way to an eerie stillness.

Martha Janine Butler, do not close your eyes and scribble, do not. You are a professional.

With a little bit of luck, you might be out of here by seven.

Another school year in full swing.

Marti reached over to her desk to grab the three-inch thick pile of class drop slips that had accumulated just today. She never failed to be amazed at how much paperwork could accumulate between eight and four. And she was sure those slips would somehow triple overnight if she didn't tackle them before she left for home.

The schedule is the problem, not the kids. Kids are kids, and they need to be with their friends. It's your job to organize anarchy. Keep telling yourself that, Marti. You can finish this off, and then get back to what you're really here for. Guidance.

Come on down, kids, we've got whatever you need for whatever ails you. Just listen, breathe deeply, and somehow we'll get you through this thing some idiot dubbed 'the best years of your life'.

"Is it too early for a nervous breakdown?" Marti jumped, then turned her head to look at the source of the interruption.

Amber. Amber leaning inside the doorway, arms folded, a cracked smile underneath blinking green eyes. The eyes were the giveaway. Amber's eyes turned bright green when she was in turmoil. They were two emeralds burning in a mottled face.

Marti smiled, an invitation more than a greeting. Amber face had been harried ever since that incident in Ethan Michaels's office last week. The woman in Marti was full of questions. *When had*

Amber and Ethan met? What note? And what about "not meaningless sex"? The expert won. Time for de-escalation. She paused for a second and then laughed.

"You, too? I thought I was the only one ready to gnash teeth and foam at the mouth." She motioned to the form standing in the doorway, manila folder in hand. "C'mon in and have a seat. Tell me. General anxiety or something specific?"

When Amber hesitated, drawing in air, Marti added, her tone softened, "Tell you what, kid, I'll kick off my shoes if you kick off yours. She pointed to a seat right across from her swivel chair.

Amber stepped inside, smacking the manila folder against her hip like a crop.

Bad sign number one.

"How 'bout an Oreo? No milk for dipping. Just cookie." The counselor watched as Amber looked toward the stash place, jerked her head away before plunking down in the chair directly across from Marti.

Marti kept the light banter going. "A little early this time of the year for student uprisings. I haven't even heard a prediction for Senior Skip Day."

Usually Amber would laugh at the joke and give back one of her own. Instead, she sat forward in the chair and closed her eyes. Holding the folder in her left hand, tapping it on her lap, she attacked the middle finger of her right hand, gnawing on a hangnail, the ultimate act of nerves for her.

Amber opened her eyes, looked at Marti watching her. She surrendered the biting and sat up straight. Hands neatly folded in her lap, she gave a stilted laugh and said, "I know. I know. My mother used to wrap bandages around my fingers to stop me. Didn't work. I chewed them, too."

She stood up and walked over to the wall and stared at an Army recruitment poster, once again using the file like a crop. She lifted the folder to her forehead for a second or two, then pulled it down before she did a crisp turn and sat down in the chair again. This time, she bent forward. Her right leg beat up and down in agitation, the heel of her shoe quickly tapping, the file keeping pace with leg.

"I want to beat on the walls." The words came out softly, Amber's lips barely moving.

Ah. Progress.

"Sometimes they need a good beating."

Amber looked at Marti's face, her leg and hand stilled, the file lying quietly in her lap. Her hand went to her mouth and she returned to gnawing, then stopped as she pushed herself further back in the chair and folded her hands. "Did you get my e-mail about Jocelyn Quint?"

Diversion? Marti thought about her morning's run-in with Jocelyn, the well orchestrated use of black, the mumbling and the well-thrust-out hip. And how for a fleeting moment, in spite of the symphony of disdain, she had caught a glimpse of fear in the girl's eyes, like a deer startled by headlights at the suggestion that her parents come in for an orientation, "Ah. The new student. The one with attitude du jour." But obviously, Amber well knew that or she wouldn't be here looking like melt down ready to happen with "new student" on her lips.

Amber's voice was apologetic. "I'm sorry, Marti. I know how busy you are. But this has me crazy."

Marti leaned forward and took Amber's hand. "I know. All I have to do is look at you. I don't know what to do for you except to listen." She paused to let the words sink in, then continued. "Deep breaths, in and out. Tell me what's wrong."

Amber's mouth was a taut line. When she spoke, she was rocking.

"What do we know about the new girl, Jocelyn Quint?"

"We don't have any records on her so far, probably won't have for at least a week." Marti sat back and took a collective pause before she leaned forward and continued. "But I have to tell you. That child takes alternative to new heights. And that paleness. She can't be healthy. She looks like the first fall wind will knock her down."

Amber opened the folder and took out Jocelyn's writing, now folded in half, set the folder aside. It was Amber and the piece of writing. She leaned back a little and took a deep breath. "You know I normally would never share a student's work without permission . . . " Then Amber started pursing her lips, and the red mottling on her face was back again.

The dam burst and the anger poured from her as she thrust the paper at Marti. "Read this." The two words were delivered with an edge of hysteria. Marti watched Amber rub the back of her neck, trying to collect herself. Her eyes were closed.

Amber shared her meeting with Jocelyn, the intensity of both the words and the slam of the student's hand on her desk. As she spoke, her head shook, and her voice was a strange instrument, quivering and rising until she finished.

The words seemed to exhaust Amber. She put her head in her hands and let her hair tumble, hiding her face. A few seconds later, she raised herself up again and leaned back, eyes fixed on the ceiling.

"Marti, something's really scary about Jocelyn. Maybe not about Jocelyn herself, maybe her situation." She brought her gaze down and looked at Marti, then leaned forward. "Marti, this is one troubled child. And she needs us. Now.

"I tried to talk to Maggie, but she doesn't get it, Marti. How could she not understand such an obvious call for help?

"All I can do is come to you. I know you can help."

Marti listened, careful to register patience and interest. If Amber wanted to talk about a new student, then talk they would. She smoothed the piece of paper in her lap and handed it back to Amber. When Amber took it, she stood up and began pacing, clutching the paper in one hand and slapping her other hand against her hip while she moved around the office and spoke.

"You know how we've talked about the pressures on kids today. We know that between divorce and drugs and the notion that virginity is a burden, kids are pressured and kids are angry. We see the anger every day. But Marti, this stuff goes beyond that. I saw rage in that child, a fury cold and boiling at the same time. I can't even begin to describe it. She was aloof and daring and yet something about her is so waif-like."

Marti watched the eruption with a professional eye. Amber was talking to the wall. Not talking. She was spitting out the words at sheets of blank paper not yet scrawled with graffiti. Marti had seen this look. Human contact could shatter her, she was so enraged. This was not just about a student. Amber loved her kids, all of them—the jocks, the geeks, the kids with pressure who looked at a *B* as failure, the ones who laughed off a *D*. None of them, however, had ever sent her beating a wall. Marti pictured Amber's face that

day with the new man, the battle to register the correct emotion—
shock, embarrassment, defeat.

Caution, Marti, this is the Amber you've worried about. The
counselor leaned forward, concern brimming in her eyes. Jocelyn,
indeed, was a student in need. But Marti's words and demeanor
were for the immediate.

"Hon', take a seat." She waited while Amber settled herself and
sat down, her hand clutching that folder for dear life. "First thing
we do, Amber, is get grounded ourselves." She shook her head, a
quick shake up and down and blew out a long stream of air. Then
her face smoothed into a benign Mona Lisa study of inscrutability.
"I've seen you stare down linebackers twice your size and wield
compassion like a fairy godmother. But Amber, I've never, in the
three years I've known you, seen you this upset."

Her chair squeaked as she stood up. "How about I close the
door and we really have a talk." Her voice remained friendly
although now there was an edge of concern in it. She pointed to the
refrigerator. How 'bout a cold one?"

Amber shook her head. "No, thanks. The last thing I need is a
caffeine high. She lowered her eyes to the floor, then abruptly
raised her head and looked to the right at Marti's *How are you
feeling today?* poster taped to a blackboard. The kids loved moving
the magnetic circle to the appropriate facial expression, usually the
one with the frizzled hair and the crossed eyes.

"So where do you fit? It's not just a question for kids."

The answer was pretty obvious. Amber was a porcelain cup on
the edge of a table, spinning to try to keep from falling, doing a
poor job of it at that. The fall might only shake her up. The fall
might break her to pieces. Marti's job was to catch Amber before
she broke.

She sat down in front of Amber. They had to be level, woman
to woman. "Marti, to say this has been a hell of a week is more
than mere understatement. I feel like it will be my epitaph.
Everything is just so wacked out, and it's only the first week of
school."

Marti shook her head and adjusted her glasses while searching
for the right words. Keep it cool. "We haven't talked about—what
was it, 'the note was a mistake; it wasn't just . . .'" Amber held up

her hand to stop her friend. What came out of her mouth was somewhere between choke and chuckle. "Marti, if you only knew." Her eyes rolled and she sighed. "Some day I may get into *that*, but for now my big worry is Jocelyn."

Looking across at Amber, Marti hesitated, her counselor hat on, her mind searching for the right words. Marti thought of Amber not just as a good teacher. No, she was a crusader wrapped in cotton candy armor. The red-haired teacher would go the length for the kids, but never stop to measure how long that length might be. "I don't know where I heard this, it was so long ago, but it's served me well, and I think it may apply to you."

Amber looked at her warily. "Is this where I say, 'If it's good for you, then it's good for me?'"

Marti laughed, then continued. "As educators, many of us, the best of us. . ." She looked straight at Amber and gave her a reassuring smile, ". . . are fix-it people. We want to cure all ills, and fill the world with love. Otherwise, why would we ever take on teenagers?" A pause filled the air as both women's bodies filled with the emotion of that truth.

Marti picked up again. "But here comes the insight. Chasing after perfection, trying to cure the world's ills, tells a tale."

"What ills chase after you?"

Amber's eyes stared straight ahead, a well of tears glistening, then she shook her head. "This has nothing to do with me." The words were firm, the next ones questioning. "I don't know what it is." She shook her head, went back to firm voice laced with a laugh. "I know there's no way I see myself in her."

Amber stopped and let out a sigh. This girl—she's so fragile and so angry at the same time. . . . I can't figure out how to even begin. All I know is that I have to do something." Now the tears fell, huge drops a rivulet carving white lines through her make-up, soundless drops that left her face and stained her silk shirt. Amber was rocking, her only sound an intake of air, three short breaths in, one long breath out. Her jaw quivered, but her eyes stayed open, locked on nothing outwardly apparent. Marti could only guess at Amber's inward sight.

She moved her chair directly facing Amber. "I only know what I see. But I see enough to know that this is not about Jocelyn."

Amber shuddered but said nothing. No denials. No asking for help either.

"Amber, a long time ago, I heard a great piece of advice. If emotional pain could be measured on a thermometer, we would not fail to take action at one-hundred degrees. The problem is, most of us live at eighty-five, miserably wanting to do something, but too afraid to begin." She paused to let Amber take this in, then took her friend's hands. "The hardest step is moving toward that eighty-sixth degree."

Amber's face morphed into a stoic mask, white and rigid, and she let go of Marti's hands to wipe her eyes. She sat up with all the posture precision a graduate of the Oakdale Academy could possibly muster and pulled herself up, her action forcing Marti to roll back her chair. Amber was a stone. She walked to the door without turning around, stood there to give her final words. "Thanks for listening. I know I sound like a middle schooler on too much Mountain Dew, but I'll be fine, and we'll both figure out what to do about Jocelyn. Please. Just keep me posted when her records come in."

Amber walked out of the office, leaving the guidance counselor biting her lip and shaking her head. Marti was sure that something had been unleashed. The problem was that she well knew that many more tears had to come, and that the teacup needed to fall. She hoped someone would be there to catch the cup before it broke into shards.

Amber had barely made it to the bathroom. She stood inside, pressing her body against the tiles of the wall, hoping to calm herself. How could her fingers feel so numb when her heart was racing? A sense of dizziness had engulfed her, not the pass out kind of dizzy, just a sense of being out of herself.

Get control, Amber. The tiles felt cool. Amber pressed her back against them, hoping for control, but the arc at her waist was a knot that refused to let go. She was sweating and chilled at the same time.

Damn it, Amber, you're such a fool. You can't even control yourself talking about a student. Not even the slightest suggestion that you're an adult.

What had she been thinking, marching into that office and making a scene.

Get hold of yourself, you're no better now than you were when—no, don't even try to think about that. One meltdown three years ago has nothing to do with today.

Push. Relax. Straighten that back. Come on, muscles, let go.

Her heart slowed to a steady beat, and some of the chills left. Now she was just warm. Warm, but at least whole. What had happened?

Her whole body had betrayed her.

But then, why not? The rest of her had pretty much done the same thing in Marti's office.

Thank God, no one had stayed in this wing and needed the bathroom.

The adrenaline rush began to subside, in its place a slow creeping of shame.

What was the matter with her? She turned and looked in the mirror, watched herself as she walked closer, then felt the cool smoothness of porcelain as she grabbed onto one of the sinks. Surveying the reflection, she felt her chest tighten. Her hair was a frizzed wreck, her eyes the eyes of a stranger, some old woman creased by too much life.

She was a fool, no more in control of herself than the girls who looked in the same mirror each day and hated what they saw.

She had wanted to help, was driven to help. Instead, here she was, stuck in a bathroom looking in the mirror at a fool.

She closed her eyes. Her body finally relaxed.

She was so tired, no more than a sad and petty failure who had thought she could save a child in only a day.

Chapter 12

Week two of school. Labor Day was over, students more or less settled in—the ninth graders even knew how to unlock lockers—if they could remember where they were. Seniors were sharing the first round of graduation pictures, and the juniors were countering with the first plans for homecoming week. Time for the annual Young Writers Conference, a time for sophomores from around the district to meet and share their work, pick up advice from professionals who remembered their own struggles.

Amber stood at the foyer steps of the Chicago Cultural Center and watched her students gawk as they made their way into the main room at the top of the steps. No surprise there. The building never failed to amaze her with its beauty and symmetry.

Two students were right beside her, watching with her, their faces solemn with the beauty, like two nuns at prayer.

"This is as close to a place of pure grace as any woman can know." She shot them a look and then smiled. "Or young people with the right sensibility, judging by the expression on your faces."

Others shared the vision with the three in their own ways.

"Miss Helm. This place is so cool."

"Look at those lights! Bet you could swing on those like Spiderman and sweep right across to the lake."

"Do we have to go back to school? Can we stay all day?"

Amber scanned the main room opening from the stairway. She felt its textures welcoming her. Mosaics filled its walls and floors; the ceiling, a sphere of perfectly pieced squares of tinted glass, waited for the notes from the grand piano to fill its space with equal grace. It was a building that was a poem needing to be heard and felt and lived clear to the marrow. If only they could stay.

She watched both students who were still awe struck. Craig Jensen had moved forward, one foot on a marble step, his hand gripping the railing. Sharon Sage stood by her teacher, a sweet smile on her face as her head swept back and forth. Some of the best teaching invited itself when the kids were ready.

"This used to be the public library. When the library moved, the city wanted to tear it down to make way for more financially productive investment opportunities."

Both kids looked at her and shared a simultaneous "No way!" Craig folded his arms and looked upward. "So what happened?

"Sometimes the good guys win. Eleanor Daley, bless her soul, would have none of that. Her husband, the mayor, might have been the head of the political scene, but 'Sis' had clout of her own." Amber stopped, put one hand on Sharon's shoulder and gestured widely with the other. "And this place of bliss is proof positive. It is to be cherished and experienced." Amber smiled to let them know that lecture time was over. "Let's go up and enjoy."

The kids raced up ready to explore more wonders before the conference started. Amber took her time, taking in every sensory experience as she walked up the stairs and entered the room that still took her breath away just as it had the first time she had seen it as a child. Her eyes actually ached with the beauty. Whenever she brought her students to the annual conference, Amber was struck with the desire to wave her hands as if she could touch the art deco light fixtures that hung from the dome, even though it would take a magic wand to reach that far.

Then she saw him.

Ethan Michaels was on the other side of the room. Ethan Michaels was staring at her as if she were a lizard in a Natural History Museum's exhibit several blocks away.

Good thing the room was huge.

Seven days ago, Amber had sighed with relief. Ethan's tenure at Clausson would not involve her, at least professionally. She was safe—professionally at least. While she watched Ethan, her voice snarled low while a sense of impending hysteria muddled within. "Duane—you dumb ass. The fall conference is my baby. The last thing I need is a train wreck waiting to happen." As if that could make a difference.

Duane had decided to have Ethan join her excursion, to help pump the senses, as he loved to say. And who could be more perfect as the primer of that pump than the lovely Miss Helm, herself. The students would be more motivated and Ethan would feel much more at home, Duane had assured her, especially since an old classmate accompanied him into the city. After all, Freston College had been their home together, if only for a few short weeks during their undergraduate days. Now it was time for Amber to help Chicago welcome Mr. Michaels while he helped her students.

You bet, Duane. The grandeur of this building had played a sick sort of parallel to the grinding sense that any minute now, her cover as competent teacher would come crashing down, and everyone would know all those secrets—her betrayal, her weakness, her failure to follow through with anything right. Part of her wanted to be able to trust Ethan in spite of their history, both ancient and recent. After all, he certainly didn't want any gossip. Juicy bits of their affair weren't very conducive to community building. But that fiasco last week—those insults they traded after that kiss—that memory was etched inside of her turning over and over, a fuzzy threat gnawing at the control she worked so hard to keep.

Right now, though, it was Amber, Ethan, and forty-seven tenth graders wrapping up a field trip. Let's hear it for control.

Students milled around, sharing their descriptions, their comments interspersed with an occasional giggle.

Three hours later, it was time to go. Control had won, at least for today.

Amber and Ethan did a head count. Everyone there except for one. Jocelyn. Of course she was missing. Why would she follow directions?

"I'll check the broadcasting museum. You take a look at the photo exhibit in the west hallway." Amber moved quickly to the first floor where the Museum of Radio and Television Communication was housed. The museum had three main sections: an actual recording studio where visitors could sit in the audience while radio shows were taped; an early television exhibit area with everything from Bozo the Clown to ESPN; a radio area with rooms decorated from the forties and fifties where motion-action detectors automatically set in play favorites from a bygone and golden era. Amber entered the museum and turned left, toward radio land.

A few minutes later, she found Jocelyn sitting at a chrome table in the kitchen exhibit, the sound of Don McNeil's Breakfast Club perky and nostalgic, hardly traits to describe the wayward student at this moment. Jocelyn's left forearm rested on the table. Her right hand supported her head. She was staring into space, a twenty-first century anachronism in a red and white kitchen straight from the fifties, complete with shirred fabric around the kitchen sink and a June Cleaver clone pictured on the wall, pert and smiling.

Her words were laced with bitterness. "That's right, Donny, old man. Get those daddies off to work and the mommies busy doing Mommy things." The bitterness in the words. No one should be that raw, especially a child.

Amber moved toward the exhibit, stepped up to gain entrance to the kitchen tableaux, her urge to chastise gone, replaced by a deep warmth of compassion for children left alone. She felt it in her chest and in the back of her neck, although if someone had asked her what it was, she would have been riddled to name it. She made a coughing noise to announce her presence.

Jocelyn didn't move, but her voice let Amber know she was aware of her. "Funny thing about tables like this. They expect families." The words came out as a mutter. Then Jocelyn sat up, gripped the edge of the table, and peered under. "Anyone got a spare mother?" These words were edged with sarcasm, but the voice held a sadness.

Amber's guard fell, that aura of professionalism that separated teachers from students and allowed for proper discipline. It had been shaken the moment Amber had entered the museum, one of her favorite haunts, cracked when Amber saw Jocelyn staring at a wall, seeing her own pictures, ones that Amber could only guess.

The sound of Jocelyn's voice and the choice of the girl's words demolished it for good.

What the heck. It was mostly facade anyway. This time, this moment was true. This was daughter to daughter.

"We could always check Jack Benny's vault on the way out. He might have an extra."

The words came out softly, an invitation to survey potential. Amber moved toward Jocelyn and smiled, a sisterhood kind of smile because both these daughters, separated by age and status, still had so much in common, even though they could not know that fully. At least yet. She took a seat at the table. Later, she wondered where the words came from, but for now, they just came. "The trouble is, there's never one around when you need her, is there?"

In the distance, someone had walked by the Lone Ranger display, activating, "Return with us to the thrilling days of yesteryear. With a hearty Hi-Ho-Silver, the Lone Ranger rides again."

Both of them looked up simultaneously, drawn by the pronouncement, then looked at each other. Jocelyn's face kept silent. Amber only said, "Oh kid, it sucks, doesn't it?" Then they sat there, each caught in her own thoughts.

Jocelyn was the first to stand. "Time to go, Teach. Ain't nothin' yesteryear about now." The faraway look in her eyes was gone, but so was some of the hardness in her posture.

Back with the other students and Ethan, those subtle changes turned miniscule and then disappeared. Jocelyn's mask was back on. But Amber had seen them. Jocelyn might strike a fearless pose, but the girl was as needy as Amber had suspected the first time Jocelyn strode into her room and plunked down a piece of writing like a glove inviting a challenge.

The doors had hardly whooshed shut before the high school din started. Students poked and gestured, choreographing the vocal dance of young people massed together and talking.

Ethan stood watching their return to school, once again amazed at the unleashed energy of adolescence. He jumped away as his bus lurched forward and he met up with Amber who was corralling the stragglers, her eyes intently seeking any would-be skippers.

I can't even imagine what they're talking about. Bet it's not writing.

"What's up with the missing student?" Ethan's question was muted. Just one teacher to another climbing the steps behind students fresh off the two buses that had delivered everyone back from the conference. His head was turned toward her, his face far more friendly than earlier at the center. She'd looked so pure in that setting, her face so serene. Instead of the expression of professional interest or congenial teammates, he had pictured her at the house last week, her face nothing but bitterness and spite. Funny how he had to prepare himself to even look at her. She pulled on him, making him wary of every move, every word.

She looked away and straightened the purse strap on her arm.

"Just a little bit of one-on-one with Jocelyn."

"Problems?"

"Nothing that I can't handle. She just needs someone on her side."

Ethan looked straight ahead. "There seems to be a lot of that going around." Then he moved past her and opened the door, went in. He held the door for her, a gentleman giving way for a lady. His face was neutral. He wanted to grab her and finish the fight they had started last week, put all his questions and frustrations to rest. Instead he nodded to her "Thank you," and they went their separate ways.

Chapter 13

Jocelyn had been dreaming of June Cleaver taking an ax to her pearls while the Lone Ranger hollered "Hi ho Silver." She laughed to herself even in her sleep, that is until a noise woke her, one far more familiar than those she had heard today in that stupid museum. This noise she knew. It first had wound its way into her room, a little worm of a noise resting near her brain, its earthy dankness wresting her from her sleep. "Wake up, Jocelyn. Wake up, girl and listen to your life." She heard it again. This time she knew. The clank of the glass, a thud, a bit of muffled speech and a sob or two, almost poetic in its narcissistic woe. Her mother was at it again.

She turned her head, looked at the moon outside hanging there so far away, pure and white and innocent. It promised so much, that silver ball hanging in the black night. Maybe she could reach out and touch it, glean some of that shimmering beauty and pull it into her life.

Fat chance.

She rolled over and looked at the clock on her nightstand. 3:18. Yup, the bar on the corner was closed, but her mother's favorite bar, Evie's kitchen, was open for business with its two best customers, Evie and Frank. Another sound, this time the rasp of a snore, made its way up the stairs. Great. The middle of the night. Mom's boyfriend's sound asleep, the goddess, herself, is in LaLa land, and I'm awake. Way to go, guys.

Jocelyn rolled back onto her back and tried to shut her eyes. She flipped over onto her stomach, pulled the pillow over her head and tried to make a deal with a God that was as remote as that moon outside her window. I won't go down there and use this friggin' pillow on her if you just let me get back to sleep. God obviously wasn't in the mood for listening, but then, why should He? She had made this deal so many times, God was either tired of listening to her whine or laughing at the futility of a stupid, sleepless girl lying there wishing she could touch the moon.

Getting the kids to write after the conference was no problem. Dealing with demands of feedback—another story altogether. Amber sat at her desk staring at the drafts waiting for her assessment. They stared back, taunting her. Come on, teacher lady, bring on the ink. Applaud us—give us those cute little stars by the good stuff. Tell us how to fix what's wrong—pile on those circles and dashes and margin comments. You know the drill.

Amber knew she needed divine intervention, preferably something with grammar check. Her fingers fiddled with her pen, turning it end over end, while her eyes stared straight ahead, unseeing, at nothing in particular. She brought the blunt end of the pen up to her chin, tapped twice and scowled.

It was 4:00, and she had accomplished exactly zero since her last class had crowded out of the classroom thirty minutes ago, glad to escape the heat and thankful for no homework.

Trouble was, Amber had homework, that as-yet untouched pile. After another minute of actively ignoring them, she let her eyes fall on the top one, a lovely tome, no doubt, judging by the fluorescent purple ink and significantly dotted i's. Two weeks into the school year and all the freshness of that new start glow that had buoyed her during workshop had fallen flat in a hurry. Lordy, sixty first drafts. At twenty minutes a piece she'd be safely ensconced in the home, dementia spittle barely drying on the final piece before she was ready to hand them back to the kids. She rejected purple gel, moving it to the right and glanced at the next contender, scowled at that one too. Who taught these kids penmanship? Jackson Pollack? She tried reading the first line again, deciphering the scrawl, looking for the slightest hint of intelligence. The draft refused to be intimidated by such unreasonable expectations and maintained its inscrutability.

The wall might read "Failure is only practice for success," but right now success loomed more distant than ever before.

Knock it off, Amber. You're as bad as the kids. You'd better start reading those bits of wisdom you posted on the walls of the room. Take the step, start the journey. Pen to paper, woman.

She looked up at the ceiling fan. It hung there, broken and still, mocking anyone who expected relief. Outside, September had crested for another day, but it was nothing compared to the heat in the room, fan or no fan. Amber's dress began to plaster to her body. Her hair, damp with sweat, was already curling along the back of her neck, and sweat had begun condensing on her arms.

What is wrong with you, girl? Girls have been blathering in purple since estrogen was invented, and boys have always written in code. It's the beginning of the year. Nobody's trained. And the fan working in September when we need it? What do you expect?

Maybe she needed a cup of coffee. Her shoulders sank with that thought. Not in this heat. How about a trip to the snack machine? Chocolate knew no temperature limit. She ran her hand up the back of her neck and through the unruly mop growing more damp by the minute.

Don't even think about candy. Get into those papers, woman. No one twisted your arm to make you an English teacher.

Something else was rattling around in her mind, beneath all that avoidance ritual, an unsettling image, one that had flitted and then settled darkly in the back corners, waiting for the day's tasks to have their say and then retreat where they belonged—into oblivion. It was no longer flitting; it turned grinding and demanding, kept Amber's scowl firmly planted, although this time over something much nastier than chicken scrawl. What was she going to do about the scars?

Slices on Jocelyn's forearm. Thin red lines that peeked out from under her sleeves, fresh ones judging from their color, a self-inflicted rosy tattoo of anger and helplessness. Amber had spotted them last night after school. Jocelyn had slipped into the classroom, moved so quietly and then just stood there, waiting for, how long? Amber almost jumped out of her skin when she lifted her head up from her computer and saw her, just standing, waiting. Then the girl raised her arms and splayed her fingers, like a mime pressing against a wall.

"I need to talk." That's all she had said. But the silent girl had started rocking back and forth, her breathing forced through her nostrils, her jaw trembling. That's when Amber saw the scars.

Jocelyn saw Amber's reaction, that sudden intake of breath before Amber had put back her teacher face, before Jocelyn had yanked her arms behind her body and left as silently as she had entered.

Damn. Amber should have known better. Ninety degrees out and the girl wore long sleeves to school every day. That wasn't some sort of angst-ridden fashion statement; that was fear hiding the truth. Jocelyn had fled before Amber could even completely take in what had happened. By the time Amber found her feet and rushed out, it was too late. Jocelyn was gone. And she hadn't come back. Not last night. Not today. The office had checked home since no one had called in that morning to clear the absence, standard procedure in an era of high risk absenteeism, but no one had answered. The office worried about truancy. Amber worried about a lot more. Had this been deliberate, the showing of the scars? Or was the mime's wall been a signal to Jocelyn to run from any attempt to find help? And what kind of help did Jocelyn need? What drove a girl to slice her arms? Child abuse training talked about deep-rooted anger in girls, but what girls weren't angry?

Watch, Amber. Little girls don't get angry. Anger is for those who have no control, and ladies always have control.

And you're questioning. Good little girls never, ever question.

"Bullshit!" Amber shoved her chair back and stood up, dug her fingers through her hair while she lifted her head and grunted, a deep and feral sound that was anything but what a good girl would make.

Marti had warned her about getting involved. "Amber, are you sure you know what you're doing? We all care about the kids, and we all take our jobs as mandatory reporters seriously. But Amber, you're letting this come from way down too deep. Who are you trying to save? Have you thought about that?"

She had thought about it all right. More, she had felt it. Let the rest of the faculty wait for records and eyewitnesses. She was ready for war. After all, fools about to rush in never bother with much of anything except that incessant pounding that urges them off the edge and into . . . whatever angels fear. That didn't matter. If Marti wanted to wait, let her. Marti would wind up mopping the blood and crying out her regrets. Amber would take action now.

Nobody hurts kids and gets away with it. Not on her watch. Even if Amber wasn't sure who was doing the hurting or why. The trick was, how to get the answers. She could try a home visit. "Hey, folks, I was in the neighborhood and thought I'd drop in to ask you just how and how often you drive your kid to cut herself." That would certainly fly. She drummed her fingers on her desk and looked around at nothing in particular while she brainstormed, focused on the pile of mail in the upper tray. She grabbed a flier from the top of the pile. Her Uncle James, literature professor at the college where she had met Ethan a lifetime ago, had mailed her a brochure on the Grace Remington Memorial Writers' Contest. Perfect. No one would fault a teacher dropping by with a contest entry, especially if the student had been absent. Can't wait on those things.

Can't wait, all right. Deep in the bowels of her gut, Amber knew two things about Jocelyn Quint. One—Jocelyn could write, far beyond the ability of any student Amber had met in her three years of teaching. Two—Jocelyn was a girl in deep and disturbing trouble. Trouble done to her, not trouble of her own making. That perception had reared and snapped and snarled, had punched at her heart and made her skin cold the first day of school. An angry writing voice was bad. An angry writing voice followed by despair was a looming disaster and Amber was not about to stand on the deck of a sinking Titanic straightening deck chairs. Jocelyn's second piece of writing, again slipped to her one day after school, but this time with a little less force, spoke of sorrow and the cold penitence of a whining voice too weak to even know she was a fool. "A dusting of remorse" Jocelyn had named it. Remorse for what? And from whom?

Amber didn't know. But she was damn-well on her way to finding out.

Chapter 14

This was not Lincoln Park at its finest. No Goadie's Coffee shop packed with latte-loving preppies. No restored brownstones, porches crowded with mountain bikes, definitely not a haven of the upwardly mobile. This was the other end of Irving Park Road where grass grew only in sidewalk cracks and houses wore faded gray shingles and half-broken wooden stairs. A place that nice girls like Amber drove through. Nice girls like Amber did not stop in neighborhoods like this.

Amber knew someone who did. Every day.

This was Jocelyn's neighborhood, if the address given by the office for Jocelyn Quint was correct, an area not yet reached by the zeal of those restoring Chicago's near North side. Amber parked in front of Delancey's Bar, itself a study of brown despair, a building of warped vertical siding landscaped only with weeds and fast food sacks discarded by too many people who just didn't care. Climbing out of her Miata, Amber's nostrils immediately reacted to the rank smell of discarded deep-fat cooking oil and used diapers left in the alleyway next to the bar, gone, but certainly not forgotten. She looked at the alley next to the bar. Two kids, not more than fifteen tops, were doing business. Money exchanged hands, for what Amber couldn't see. Drugs? A gun?

"No wonder the girl's angry," she muttered to herself. "If I lived here, I might cop an attitude myself." *Yeah, and you might even carve on your arms.*

Amber checked the address she had jotted down, scanned along the street, then made her way to 2411, the upstairs half of a double "family" dwelling her mother would have called proof that not all people were necessarily human. The structure itself was attached to an empty brick building that once had been a small grocery store, judging by the remnants of food flyers still stuck to the glass. *Call Kowalscowski Realtors* the sign said, but even the for sale sign, faded from sun light and neglect knew better. Her nerve melted, when, down the street, a car horn blared three times and the driver's epithet reminded her of just how road-raged Chicago could be. God, she must look like a dork out here holding her purse and a writing contest invitation.

Heated resolve had brought her here all right, to this place of odors and blight. Other emotions had their chance now, and Amber felt them all at once swirling around inside her like the litter that blew in the alley and tumbled along the curb. She pulled her purse into her chest.

What are you doing here, girl? Do you have any idea how much trouble you can get yourself into? Why don't you think before you act? When will you ever use common sense?

She pressed her lips together and shook her head, felt the pressure of her teeth clenched tightly in a jaw that was rigid. This wasn't about her. This was about intervention. A young girl held enough rage to mutilate herself, and Amber would find out why. Besides, she certainly wasn't the first teacher to make an unannounced home visit. Everything would be fine.

It still took Amber three long breaths to move her feet from the relative safety of the sidewalk and climb to the second floor. She made a deal with her body. The rest of her would follow her feet if they would just take that first step, and her lungs would try to remember to breathe. With breath one, she scanned the two windows for any sign of life, a futile search through a solid sheet of city grime, and she pushed her feet forward up those steps. Her sandals settled on the wood as her feet moved her forward. She only allowed herself an exhale on the third step. So far, so good. Only one little creak from a warped slab. Let's hear it for safety. *You're on a roll, girl.*

With breath two she sped up, finishing the stairway, and landed firmly on what might loosely be called a porch. An old stove squatted to her right, abandoned and rusted, its oven door missing, a collection bin for empty booze bottles shoved into its maw. Someone had stuffed a plastic pot and some ivy into a space that had once housed a burner. Urban gardening. At least it's a try.

Amber focused her eyes on the half-broken aluminum door, its screen mottled with dead flies and squashed June bug hulks.

Time for breath three. She knocked, trying to peer past the carnage in the screen.

A slow, gargled, "Yeah? Whadda ya want?" came from behind the screen along with the slapping sound of bedroom slippers. A forty-something woman with narrow eyes in a bloated face stared back at Amber. In spite of liner and mascara, sagging lids almost hid her eyes. Her mouth was a sunken coral rosebud ridged by lines that fought with her lipstick for control. Faded red hair, carefully teased and sprayed several days ago had fallen victim to the toll of wind and sleep. In fact, her whole mien seemed to have slid into the blight of heavy living. She was a blue-light special right out of Dollar Days Department Store, the best in faded polyester. She was also, quite probably, Jocelyn's mother.

"You selling something? I don't need nothin'. Especially if you're some punk tryin' to sell God."

Amber put on her best parent-teacher conference smile. "Mrs. Quint? I'm Amber Helm, Jocelyn's English teacher. I wonder if I may come in for a few minutes and talk."

The narrow eyes looked her over and the coral lips puckered, deepening the lines. The faded hair held firm.

"Helm? Jocelyn's English teacher." The woman straightened a little, tried to pat her hair, then swayed and Amber caught the scent of whiskey through the screen door. The screen door creaked and rattled, almost a death sound, as it opened toward Amber. She grabbed the handle and pulled while a bizarre image of a rusted gate opening outside the fog-enshrouded castle filled her mind, and Amber wondered for a second if she'd find Igor waiting inside. Inside the apartment, Amber took in the curtainless windows decorated with lines of caked dirt and peeled paint, warped wooden floors and faded furniture, boxes piled high and filled with old magazines shoved up against the walls both to her right and left. The air held a sense of deadness to it. Outside, the odors were sharp. Here, the odors coated the air, seemed to roll together and sap the oxygen.

To the left, a bit of black caught her attention, a pant leg hanging from the end of a pea-green sofa. She craned her neck and stared, eyes narrowed, trying to see around the closet that barricaded the rest of her view. The office records indicated that Jocelyn lived alone with her mother. The bare foot at the end of those pants was long and white, with tufts of black hair growing toward the toes. Definitely not Jocelyn's. A brother?

She forced back her attention, her cheeks flushed with embarrassment at the thought of Mrs. Quint watching her. Get on with it, Amber. You've got a job here. Trying to summon a few magic words for this moment, Amber searched the compartments of her mind. The stench of stale cigarette butts mixed with the sickening sweetness of old alcohol assaulted her. And the sight of that disgusting, puckered mouth. She looked at Mrs. Quint. Something about that mouth, shriveled and worn yet meticulously colored, caught her attention. A splinter of memory made its way into her thoughts.

Her mother's eyes, locked on the image in the mirror, voice expertly maternal, hand poised and ready to finish the beauty routine.

Lips, like hair, are a woman's pride. No matter what is on the inside, the lips must be your rosebud, soft and warm with hue.

A shudder made its way up her arms. Her mind's eye juxtaposed another image next to her mother, Jocelyn standing there in her classroom, dumbstruck by the thought that someone had seen her scars.

How apt. Lips and scars. Both red. Both puckered and rising from soft skin. Red lips may be a woman's pride, but Jocelyn's scars had been red and cold.

Amber moved her eyes to the right. Anything to stop looking at those obscene lips, but a ripple of fury raced through her anyway. She wanted to shake this woman, demand to know what the hell she thought she was doing to her daughter, and perhaps rip a few more wrinkles around those ridiculous coral lips.

Amber blinked away that notion, dredged up from who knows where, slowed down her breathing and focused. Parent-teacher conference maxim #1—every mother wants success for her child. She'd never find out anything if gave into the desire to take off Mother Quint's face.

The woman narrowed her eyes so that they seemed no more than slits. "For a teacher, Miss Whatever, you sure do stand there." She scratched her crepey throat with her free hand and motioned toward the dining room. "Have a seat. What's this about my baby?" Then she turned away from Amber and made her way toward the dining room table, a nightmare of chrome and scratched red veneer piled with newspapers, ashtrays, its centerpiece empty.

Budweiser bottles and a long gone fifth of Jim Beam lay on its side.

Well, Amber, you're the take-charge girl. Get in there and take charge.

Amber managed to follow Mrs. Quint and sit down at the table without turning down her nose at the intensified pall. She faced the kitchen, away from the entry. Her chair was the same dulled chrome, but the seat was covered with faded red vinyl. The edge was ripped, the stuffing missing. The chair seemed a gloomy metaphor for the whole apartment, and Mrs. Quint herself.

The two women sat at forty-five degrees from each other. Amber leaned forward, her hands clasped over the contest sheet and black purse that sat in her lap, her best professionally concerned face a hopeful mask to cover her sheer terror. "Mrs. Quint, I just wanted to stop by and . . ."

Vague resentment turned to hostility. The mother's face was a mask. Her brown eyes tilted to the right, looked down, and then came up again, narrowed. She tapped her fingers while she spoke. "Jocelyn woke up with a headache today, so she insisted on skipping school. I always told her how important her education is. She can't get nowhere without one these days, but that Jocelyn, once she gets it in her head she's gonna stay home, ain't nothing gonna change her mind."

Amber leaned forward. "No, no, I'm not here about Jocelyn being gone."

The woman's eyes narrowed even more and she sat back, arms folded. "You're not? Then what are you here for?"

Amber put on her best disarming smile. "I came here, Mrs. Quint, to tell you that you have a very talented daughter."

Mrs. Quint's body was square-shouldered and stiff, the mask still on, except for a slight softening in the eyes.

Amber's took that as a good sign. "I perfectly understand about Jocelyn needing to stay home . . ." Amber tried not to choke on the word 'home'. "This time of year, between the weather and the stress, we miss several students every day. Is she better now?"

"She's in her room, sleepin'. Probably has her music plugged in her ears. No wonder she has a headache, all that banging.

"Now what's this about Jocelyn and talent. You sellin' something?"

"Not at all. Every year, I encourage my best writers to enter writing contests —at no cost to themselves or their parents. The school pays the entry fees. I've read some of Jocelyn's writing. She's far beyond anyone else in her class." She's certainly far beyond the material for her writing. Amber gave herself an internal slap. No side barring.

"Let me tell you about the contest and then you can share it with Jocelyn—when she's up to it."

Gone was the mask. The mother's face actually glowed. She sat back in her chair and pointed her right index finger at Amber, girlfriend style, while she sought to smooth imaginary wrinkles from her polyester shirt. "Imagine that. A writing contest." She leaned forward, her body inviting more discussion. "You know, I always said my Jocelyn was one smart girl. Wait'll I tell Frank."

Just as she turned her head to herald the news, a voice came from the other room. "Hey Evie, I'm outta' cigarettes. You got some?" The words came steadily nearer as the mandate closed in on them. Amber turned her head around just as a man turned the corner and entered. He looked about thirty-five, 5'8", maybe 150 pounds on a truly dripping day. His black hair was slicked back and wet, but wanted to dry curly. Probably his pride. He had one of those ferret faces, pinched and pale, that made Amber immediately search for tattoos that promised to "Love Rosie forever." He wore a wife-beater tee-shirt and worn jeans, and was barefoot. He stopped shortly, looked at the two women sitting there, took in Amber while his eyes moved up and down. Amber watched him stop at her breasts and legs, his mouth turning a half smile. Then his whole manner changed. His brow furrowed, two sharp lines creasing the bridge of his nose, and he scowled. Someone had invaded his space. But not for long.

He walked over to Mrs. Quint and put his hands on her shoulders, kneading the rounded ends, marking his territory just in case the visitor needed to know.

"What's up, Baby?"

This was no brother.

Mrs. Quint whole demeanor changed. She turned into a sixteen-year-old, in the full tingle of a crush and well-wooed, all gush and muffled giggles. Her eyes glazed over and her mouth turned soft, or at least as soft as something that worn and puckered could turn.

Amber felt prickles rising on her skin, and her stomach tightened. She thought of Jocelyn's first piece of writing. *I dance on the edge of the abyss, a silly tap dance for fools, shuffle, shuffle, step, step.* This could be one really tense visit.

The middle aged love child sighed. "Frank, this is Jocelyn's teacher." She leaned forward slightly. "Honey, what did you say your name was?"

"Miss Helm. Amber Helm."

"Yeah, that's right. Miss Helm." Mrs. Quint raised her head and leaned back into Frank, no doubt more for her body's benefit than to precipitate conversation. "Frank, honey, Miss Helm's come to talk to us about Jocelyn. Miss Helm thinks she should be in a writing contest. Imagine that, my baby a writer. Isn't that something." She lowered her head but kept her body pressing against Frank. Amber made a mental note not to throw up.

Frank finally spoke. "Shut up, Evie." Evie slumped back in her chair, pouting but quiet, and pulled her head into herself like a turtle sensing danger. Frank smiled at Amber, his eyes narrowing and intent on her breasts again. "Don't give me no bull about no contest. What's the problem with Jocelyn?"

Hey, Asshole, there's nothing wrong with Jocelyn. But you two could keep country music lyricists busy for months.

Frank kept looking at Amber and rubbing the shoulders of the ever-pleasured Mrs. Quint who more and more looked like a fat, spoiled cat kept well in cream. The woman was a chameleon.

Amber pointed her attention to the mother. "Jocelyn was absent today, and when the office called your number, no one answered. I don't wish to intrude, but I had been looking forward to talking to her about a writing contest, so I thought I'd stop by and drop off this brochure and see if she was okay." She bent her head and reached for the piece of paper on her lap.

"I told you, lady, she don't need no contest." The voice was low and steady and full of contempt. It was also male. Amber's hand stopped. "And she don't need no pissant teacher coming here to check up on her." A blush crept up along Amber's neck and made its way toward her jawline. She raised her head, first catching Mrs. Quint's tight stillness. Then she turned her attention to Frank.

"Excuse me?"

Frank just continued to look at her, his mouth turned upward, deliberate and mean. In the background, Evie's new-found mewling served as a moronic chorus to the intrepid Frank. Who was this guy? He was a twit, a greased-up bonehead with the IQ of mold who thought he could rattle Amber. She returned his stare, head raised slightly, shot him an ageless look, the one that labeled its victim obviously brain-dead, a look fierce and steady and calibrated to put him in his place. Then she tilted her head downward slightly and fixed those green irises on steady. Hordes of teenagers had surrendered to this look.

Frank was no teenager.

He poked his fingers at her, and his mouth was a sneer. "Look, lady, what makes you think you can stroll in here and check up on Jocelyn like she's some lab rat you've adopted and can teach to run a maze. I've run into do-gooders like you, the ones who think they can walk into a man's life and make him dance.

You're all nothin' more than bitches who get off on thinking you can boss around hard workin' men, tell 'em to get off booze or they'll lose their kids, when you don't give a rat's ass about the kids in the first place."

The air was thick with more than cigarette smoke and booze now. Evie's voice cut through. "Oh, Frank, don't be so hard on Miss Helm. She's just trying to . . ." Before the poor woman could finish, Frank's hand gripped her arm, his fingertips digging into the soft flab and causing her to wince. "Evie, when I tell you to shut up, I mean, 'Shut your fat mouth!'"

Evie's face turned white. She sat still, sniveling, a film of water pooling in each eye.

Amber's mind went numb, then charged into fury. Who was this maniac? She forced her hands and arms still. Never had she wanted to hit someone like this. Her fingers actually burned with anger. Then a thought chilled her. The man was an ape, for sure, but apes could lash out. Jocelyn had not cut herself over something petty. Amber had cried to Marti about no one having the right to hurt a child and her determination to save Jocelyn. What had she accomplished by this home visit? She was up against a study case of spinelessness, a woman who had the mothering aptitude of mad-cow disease, and Frank, master of his domain. Her throat constricted. An invisible presence hovered over her, sapped her bravado. Her guilt compass was on full alert. *How stupid can you be, getting yourself into this bind?* Jocelyn's face burned in her mind. She was supposed to help. She was a fool up against the thing that made razors cut white flesh.

In an apartment, trashed with ignorance, Amber forced her head to stay straight ahead, her feet to stay planted while her mind whirled. Idiot. Get out before you do any more damage. If not to Jocelyn, certainly to yourself. She felt tears well, felt her throat tighten even more.

But the whisper of something deep and feral got in the way. Stay in there, Amber. You can pound the walls and sob your eyes out once you're back in the brownstone, but no way you're backing down to this little weasel. Commitment. The best way to handle a bully was to ignore him, so ignore him she would. He might even not kill her.

Amber focused on Mrs. Quint, still on the verge of tears. Not too far from her own state. Leaning toward her in the same "You know, girlfriend" pose the woman had assumed earlier, she put her left hand to her throat and oozed all the empathy she could muster. "Mrs. Quint, I know it's unusual for a teacher to visit, especially unannounced, but I've been so impressed with Jocelyn's talent, I might have let my enthusiasm outstrip my sense of propriety."

Lord, I sound like Duane now. What's next—selling tickets to the PTA Carnival? The image of Duane in a ticket booth calmed her. This probably was the dark side of hysteria, but it gave her an edge of calm. If a teenage girl could live through this, so could she. She returned to the schmooze. "Let me assure you, I'm not here to impose." She ignored the snort from Frank and kept her attention on the target. "And I know you want the best for your daughter." She paused and smiled, shaking her head, as if the two women were sharing stories about their toddlers. "Sometimes I think they just tolerate us while they go about their business, humoring us so we'll give them what they want."

The woman looked like she might sway toward Jocelyn a little, but Frank stood firm. Evidently he had education issues. Maybe one of his female teachers had tried to call him Frankie.

"Ev', you gonna let this bimbo talk you into some school shit thing?"

Amber turned to him, her voice like silk. "Mr. Quint, please. . . "

Before she could finish, Frank interrupted.

"I ain't Mr. Quint."

"Oh, really." Her voice dripped sarcasm like honey. "Then let me talk to Jocelyn's mother." The title of mother was said a little more slowly, enunciated just a shade more than the other words. Amber had her mission.

But so did Frank. His face contorted and he almost sputtered, but he snapped his jaw tight and gritted his teeth, his fingers working the back of Evie's chair like a grinder pulverizing meat. Amber could envision spittle foaming at the corners of his mouth. The man was mad, but then, so was she. No slimy hood was going to shut her down. She stood up slowly, her fingers wrapped around the straps of her purse and clutching the wadded contest sheet, put both hands on the edge of the table and faced Frank.

"Mister, I see little boys like you who confuse their swagger for manhood and sarcasm for intelligent thought. They don't scare me, and neither do you." Amber added a silent, *Please God, don't let him know I'm lying.*

Before Frank had enough time to process and walk over to deck her, she turned to the woman sitting there still terrified. Amber could find no sympathy for the woman. "I came here, whether you believe it or not, out of concern for your daughter." Her voice quivered, more out of rage than fear, and her lips tightened. "Perhaps the best way to see if Jocelyn is *all right* . . ." The words were spit out of her mouth. ". . . is to involve the authorities.

Truancy is against the law. So is neglect." She shot Frank her best teacher look. "In fact, any kind of abuse. Got it?"

Frank started for her before she could get away from the table, his fingers clenched, his fist shaking with the desire to hit something, her face his first preference, no doubt. He stopped and pulled his head back, his face and eyes lines of pure hate, his fist still twitching.

Amber simply snorted a breath of disgust and walked away, shoulders squared and posture finishing school perfect, eyes locked on the front door. A crash jolted her to a stop. She turned and saw Frank standing there. Instead of a fist, his fingers were wrapped around the top half of a broken beer bottle. He rocked back and forth on his heels, his eyes glinting, and then he started toward her, no more than ten feet separating them. Without thinking, Amber reared back, and just as he closed in, she whacked him with her purse. Thank God for cell phones and nasty cans of hair spray. The impact was enough to send Frank sideways toward the floor. His weapon spun out of his hand, and he stumbled, trying to recover his balance.

Amber beat her way toward the screen door, ran out, and tripped on the threshold, crashing toward the porch's front frame. Her left arm caught the wood and she banged her knee, but so much adrenaline was flowing, she didn't even wince. She just raced down those steps toward her Miata, Evie's cries of "Oh, Frank, are you hurt!" behind her. It took her about three seconds to grab open the car door, jam herself in, slam the door and lock it. Then she sat, shaking, her earlier sense of purpose squashed like the litter in front of Delancey's Bar, willing herself to calm down enough to find the keys in her purse before Frank appeared, cum bottle knife, intent on slashing her face to ribbons. After a few minutes of sobbing and gulping for air, she managed to fit her keys into the ignition and take off for the safety of civilization, knowing no more about Jocelyn's absence than when she had arrived, but infinitely educated about what made that poor girl nuts.

Chapter 15

The workout area was a godsend, a stripped-to-the-bones place in the brownstone's basement where Amber could exercise at whim. White walls, gray concrete floors, treadmill ready round-the-clock, all there to serve Amber at her convenience. Even now at 11:30, when sleep was elusive and the pain of the day threatened, the treadmill's narrow path of rubber promised Amber forward movement set at her own pace. Nothing veered. Nothing changed, not unless she pushed the button. Foot to rubber in the basement, the treadmill was her friend.

If she kept at it, the rhythm of one foot then the other, the snarl of emotion might leave her body, move from her throat, her gut, her hands, travel down her legs and through her feet to flow into the rubber and be flushed away. Her hands gripped the metal sidebars, palms pressed tight against the black grippers, fingers latched onto the smoothness of the hard cylinder. Her every exhale sought relief, the sweet fatigue that now eluded her.

Frank. That little ferret. She should have hit him with more than her purse. She should have whacked him with a two-by-four, dropped his nicotine-stained teeth down his throat. He was a foul-mouthed ferret.

Amber pounded her feet against the ribbed surface of the machine bed as if the pressure were an exclamation point, an echo of the fury within.

Nope, he wasn't a ferret. He was a rat. Frank, the rat. Eyes red and beady, nostrils twitching while he sniffed garbage with impunity. A slum-reared rat that scuttled in the darkness and spread disease.

A fresh surge of panic, whirling and raw-edged, rose up and pressed against her ribs. No one had ever talked to her that way, had ever steeled his beady little eyes and sneered at her with his tight-lipped arrogance . . .

She wiped her face with a face towel she kept on the side bar and focused on yoga breaths—deep into the abdomen, the diaphragm, then to the chest. Breathing steady as the pace on the treadmill. The routine started to work, but the thought of Frank as a rat kept at her, seeded in the primal part of her brain. *Some rats can't be poisoned, and they can't be trapped.* She had read about that in one of Jonathan Kozol's books. The New York rats, the ones near the river, the ones that came out even during the day. They were immune to the poison set out by the city workers and practically sneered at traps. They came out, and they went after the vulnerable, the kids, the babies. Kozol's words had hit her when she first had read them, and now, when they were so much closer to home, they out-and-out menaced. The sweat that had seemed so warm and reassuring turned cold. She touched the control and slowed down.

A cool down they called it. She felt frozen.

That son-of-a-bitch might have killed her.

One summer, when she was ten, after two hours in the swimming pool, blisters the size of tennis balls had spread across her back and shoulders, weeping on her red back when she had been foolish enough to put on a shirt. Her mother had been incensed. "We're supposed to shop for Aunt Ruth's wedding. How could you be so stupid, staying out on a June day, roasting yourself when you knew we needed to find you a dress." Amber had wanted coolness to soothe her pain, an end to the headache that rode her. She had not wanted Lillian's voice reminding her of yet another inadequacy.

The same voice that spoke to her that long-ago summer surfaced from memory, words laced with vinegar.

Well, what did you expect, silly girl? You jumped into a completely dangerous situation without any kind of plan and absolutely no protection. Only by the grace of God did that cretin not kill you. I don't know who's more of an idiot—you or that beer-ladened boor who couldn't even keep his balance. I've tried and tried to make you see, but no, you turn around and barge your way. It's all about you, little Lady Amber who wants to save the world

*but can't even take care of her own self. When will you
ever learn?*

Amber slammed her finger onto the off button. "Oh, shut up."
She grabbed her towel and wiped at her head and hair, elbows on
the treadmill control panel and palms supporting her head. Great.
She had just told the critic in her head to shut up. Out loud. It wasn't
bad enough that she talked to herself. No, Amber Helm, future
resident of Bedlam, had to answer her imaginary evil twin. Nearly
midnight, in a basement in Chicago with her windows wide open,
she was a woman freshly pitted out and still standing on a treadmill,
having an argument with her alter ego like a couple of bent-out-of-
shape sophomores. Good sign.

She grabbed the towel and stepped off the treadmill, the
breathing routine that had once been so forceful now broken, her
jaw quivering from the emotion that held her. The scent of cigarette
smoke hit her, just the faintest tinge of tobacco wafting in from
outside, through the open window. She jerked around. She was
alone, down here in the basement, alone. Who was out there?

Settle, girlfriend. There's no smoker. Maybe someone illegally
burning leaves. Nothing at all. The smoke was in her mind.

So much for the good news.

Now for the bad. She was alone, down here in the basement,
all by herself, a-killer-outside-the-house-could-grab-her-alone. The
silence that had seemed so soothing now filled her with eerie
disquiet. The nape of her neck tingled, and her back muscles
tightened. Something creaked. She bolted for the stairs but stopped
short at the first rung.

Damn, it was a long way from that first step to the top. And the
door was shut. What if she got to the top and Frank was there
waiting for her?

Knock it off, Helm. Breathe some more and move those sweaty
buns, you big baby. You're just doing the wee hours of the morning
baby-sitter thing, sure that if you turn around the axe-murderer in
back of you will take home half of your skull as a souvenir. No
one's up there. Just because your legs are quivering and your
coping skills melted doesn't mean the danger is real.

Yeah? Tell that to Frank. No doubt, she had forgotten to lock the
back door and Psycho Frank was standing right inside on the

landing, armed with his broken Budweiser, ready to slash as soon as she reached the top. Why do they put basement stairs by the back door, anyway?

Amber squeezed her eyes shut. Who was the grownup here anyway. Stop your whining and get moving, and keep your head forward for crying out loud.

Oh yeah. That's how they get you, those boogeymen. You let your guard down, and slash—you're nothing but blood.

Upstairs. Now.

Hands shaking, she finally made her feet move.

The steps creaked and her gut lurched. She stubbed her toe. The pain was a welcome distraction while she finished her climb.

Thank you, God. I'm not dead.

Yet.

Of course, she still had outside to worry about. Her fingers grabbed at the bolt on the back door, then she hobbled through the kitchen and living room to secure the front door, the whole time wondering if Frank could climb up onto the second story and cut open her bedroom screen without the downstairs neighbors noticing.

Climb? He could probably scurry up the drain pipe without moving a hair. The porch light was on, but it couldn't promise safety. The flower boxes and wrought iron fencing that seemed such romantic touches during the day sent shadows scurrying toward her as she stood watching for ghosts and gathering the chaos of her fear.

Hours ago, she had spat, "They don't scare me, and neither do you" at the weaving Frank, that boil on the neck of manhood. But he had scared her, continued to scare her. Here, she had gone to protect Jocelyn, and she couldn't even protect herself. Some hero. Here's the problem, Amber girl. You've been chasing the bad guy all by yourself, and all by yourself obviously does not work, even with the best of intentions. You need some allies. Some gathering-around-the-campfire-ready-to-kick-ass partners who can sort through this mess and figure out how to save Jocelyn, and maybe even keep you from getting yourself gutted by a bottle-wielding maniac.

So who? Amber pictured Maggie sitting on a trussed-up Frank, threatening to geld him if he made a move. Marti would sit nearby offering him an Oreo and asking him about his stress level, but eventually get around to the subject of consequences. They were for-sures. Duane was out. He'd wipe his brow and worry about lawsuits.

She went upstairs to her bedroom where she called Maggie, only after locking her bedroom door and checking the closet just in case. After five rings, she heard a muffled "'lo?"

"Maggie?" Amber's voice was edged with tears and a disjointed intake of air. "Oh, Maggie, I am so dumb. I am so, so dumb."

A bewildered "Huh?" sounded on the other end of the line. Amber could hear Maggie breathe and feel her trying to make sense of the call. "Whoa. Whoa." She paused. "Amber? Honey, is that you?"

Amber held the phone away from her ear while she untightened her lips enough to answer. Then she sputtered, "Who else would call you in the middle of the night, totally hysterical?"

"Amber. Slow down. It's Maggie. Whatever's wrong, you're okay, and I'm here. C'mon Sweetie, tell me about it."

"I went to Jocelyn's after school tonight."

"You what? You went to Jocelyn's?" Maggie's volume had just tripled. Then after a lag, a quiet sigh set up a more civil tone. "I thought we agreed to take it easy and let Marti start the process."

"Never mind the *process*. Just listen. There's a live-in boyfriend there, and I made him mad. I really, really grated him. He came after me with a broken beer bottle, and I barely got out of there with my face intact."

"Jesus, Mary, and Joseph!" Maggie was definitely awake.

Amber's voice began with no more than a whisper, shook with the trembling of her jaw as she formed her words. "It was so crazy. That poor girl. She has to live with those psychos, live with that disgusting woman and that animal. Go home to them every night, wake up knowing he's still there."

The silence on Maggie's end, laced with exhales, ended. "Amber. Tell me about this guy." She sounded like a rape counselor, her voice low and calculated to comfort while she sought information. Amber, in turn, poured out the events, her explanation tumbled and disjointed, punctuated with forced breathing, a steady in and out to calm her while she explained.

Maggie cut in with questions. "Did this guy threaten to come after you?"

"No."

"Good. Does he know where you live?"

"He probably doesn't have enough brains to remember my name, much less find out where I live."

Another release of breath carried across the phone line.

"Even better. Now, this is very, very important. Think hard before you answer."

Amber's eyes widened. What did Maggie sense?

"Amber . . . did you really knock him on his ass?"

The spin of Maggie's tone took the head out of what fear had driven Amber to the phone in the first place. After one last shiver, she felt a sudden giddiness—the image of Frank's legs flung upward, Evie's arms coiled close by, her mouth making little slurping movements like a carp out of water trying to capture air.

By the time Amber finished an elaborated description of Frank lying sprawled beside the bewildered Evie, both women were laughing. Frank was a bully on his turf, no doubt about that, but he was a bully on his own turf only. Amber had left his territory; she had run. Victory was his; his male honor had been restored. Besides, he was probably passed out by now. When Maggie offered a sleepy, "Do you want to sleep here?" Amber just replied, "No, I'll see you tomorrow. Sorry. I'm just being paranoid." Just before she hung up, she even managed an extra laugh and added their favorite line, "Don't get jealous because they're only following me."

She yawned, a huge yawn that stretched the muscles of her jaw and neck and felt good clear down to her belly. She reveled in the fall of her shoulders, the creak of her back, the easing of all those muscles that had so clenched in fear. She had wigged out over nothing. Sure, she had flirted with danger today, set herself up in a situation through sheer stupidity, but that's all it was, a situation. That was then, and this was now. And now was time for bed. Tomorrow she'd meet with Marti and figure out a game plan for Jocelyn. She glanced at the clock by her phone. 12:02. Good lord, it *was* tomorrow. Good thing the tomorrow was a Thursday. That made it Friday Eve. Doable.

Yawning again, she made her way to the bathroom, took enough time to run a washcloth over her face and neck and shoot herself one critical look in the mirror. You are one piece of work, Amber Helm. Teacher of the year—gone amuck. Get to bed before those bags under your eyes cement into permanent luggage. She clicked off the light. Thank God the bathroom was right off her bedroom, the sink no more than ten feet from her bed. Eleven may have been too far. She hardly had the strength to shrug off her clothes and pull down the covers on her bed.

What a day.

Half-awake, she murmured a quick prayer, thanking the universe for Maggie. In that place between awareness and sleep, she Maggie's laugh lulled her, wrapped around her, swaddling and soft. What would she have done without her. Yes, a girl could count on her friends, couldn't she. What a buddy, that Maggie.

As she drifted off, her mind tumbled in that weird way when years of thoughts collided with each other in a new pattern that had been there potentially all along. Maggie was the familiar. Another thought half chased her, a thought that lived deep within and drove her hope, whether or not she wanted it to, or even knew that it was there.

What about the other one you know you can count on, the other one who's proved himself so far, the other one who swears no pressure but who long ago held you and promised to slay dragons if you would only trust him? He's walked away, says it's over, but you know better. What about him?

The strength of that thought brought to full awareness. She lay in the bed, her duvet pulled up to her chin. On other nights, Amber would have called this snuggling, the last ritual before a good night's sleep. Tonight, it shocked her with its truth. Eyes closed, she prayed for the blessing of sleep. Instead, she lay awake beneath the protection of those covers, her sleep robbed by two men. One made her glance at corners, sure of a cigarette butt still smoldering in the gutter, a dark-haired man ready to climb and slash her for trying to help a girl. The other made her restless in ways she could not let herself remember.

Chapter 16

The dream was intense. Amber had finally slipped into sleep, but now her body lurched against a swath of images made of gauze.

Fog. Swirling from the warm ground, eddying in a circle. Tentacles of fog. It blocked out the row of forsythia and blurred the steps to the front doors, this mist of cold and silver.

It almost hid the body.

Almost.

But there was her mother, lying on that gurney outside their home in Lake Forest, her eyes wide and staring in death, her chest spurting blood, the bottom half of a beer bottle wedged in the middle of all that blood.

Frank was off to the side, his voice a tinny ghost wrapped in wetness. *So Miss Hoity-Toity, guess you're not so special. Want Jocelyn to write about that in your precious contest, how a rich bitch teacher who can't keep her nose out of other people's business got her mother killed. You didn't get the job done when you were seven, but looks like you sure did now. How about I come on over and grind with you awhile? My bottle's sharp as ever.*

Amber woke up crying, too startled to even release herself from her hunched position, her knees pulling into a fetal position, a weakness in her chest as if she had been a small child sobbing in the dark for hours. She gulped air, one gulp after another, fast paced yet rhythmic—take them in, Amber, one, now two, that's right. No one had killed her mother. Not Frank. Not her. No, not her.

She managed to sit up and flip on the bedside light, then grabbed at the phone as if it were a lifeline and dialed information, oblivious to the clock's red digital 3:00 that glowed like a demon.

"David Petrie. Lincoln Park. Diversey Street? Must be."

Another gulp of air and then a shudder. A simple "Thank you."

She hit the numbers. The pads of her fingers stung with the pressure of her panic. Hours crawled by. Surely hours while Amber waited for the sleepy and confused "Hello?" "Ethan. Put Ethan on the phone."

While she waited, more hours passed—surely they were hours. She could hear the pad of David's feet as he carried the portable phone into the other room. He hadn't even asked who it was.

A sleepy "Hello?"

"Ethan—he was going to cut me!" Amber gulped more air, but now her voiced was choked with sobs. "Frank. He was going to slice me. He laughed. He was going to kill me, and he laughed! That bastard laughed!"

No answer from Ethan. Not even a recoil of surprise.

"I should have listened to you. But I had already almost killed my mother. I couldn't let her die, too. You've got to believe me. I'm so sorry. I'm so sorry." By now all she could do was swill the air in between sobbing, her chest heaving.

She couldn't even hear the startled "Amber?" that tried to cut into her keening. All she could do was grip that phone and listen as her teeth sent chattering noises courtesy of Ma Bell.

"Give me twenty minutes. I'm on my way."

His words warmed her as she sat in the silence, her fear cold and heavy. Amber put the phone back in its cradle and sat there, zombie-like, her eyes staring, the edge of her focus on the phone. Her upper torso rocked in a steady motion, and she closed her eyes, trying to erase the dream. As she caught a rhythm, her rocking slowed as did her mind, slowed with the movement until she was nothing but that comforting sway. She stilled herself and stretched her neck, one side and then another, immersing herself in each blessed creak. She was such a fool. She felt her disgrace—the shame and the fear, and at the same time, the wounding of her pride. That bastard had laughed at her as she ran.

A strong man was coming. A safe man.

She knew she could stand up, could even get dressed. A pair of sweats and an old shirt later, she was downstairs waiting, the panic ebbing in her stomach, her legs, her shoulders as she let the thought of Ethan quiet her.

Those hands. The substance of his warmth.

Her mind's eye was so intent on convincing herself that Ethan would calm her, she didn't even notice her own hands, the right one clasping the left, her thumb brushing across the palm and middle finger of the other, a dazed attempt to connect the years through some sensory motion. Ethan was coming. She could wrap herself in that thought and feel him through the memory. She could shake off the night.

Frank . . . yeah, Frank was toast. A dragon turned to no more than a slimy scale or two and beer-breathed fire.

Not long to go. Ethan was coming. God, she was tired.

Time had crawled at a snail's pace while she waited to hear Ethan's voice on the phone; now it passed in a flash. The door bell announcing him—one, two, three rings so close together they were one sound. She stood up and went to let him in, then stood at the door, too terrified to even check who had done the ringing. Her mind kept telling her, "Of course, it's Ethan, you fool," but her body would not let her look out the peep hole, much less open the door.

"Amber. Are you okay?" A voice deep with concern. Such a beautiful voice.

Ethan. Thank God.

She stepped back, opened the door and waited, arms at her side, eyes straight ahead, a cadaver patiently waiting to be picked up and delivered to the morgue, somehow still standing in death and ever so cooperative. All her blood, she was sure, had settled into her toes and fingertips. She had never been so achingly tired in her life.

He had the same disheveled look that had so disarmed her that summer three years ago, hair dark and tousled, eyes almost black even now when they were clouded over with sleep.

She started sobbing and shaking, this time absolutely tearless. All her tears had been shed. All she could do was stand there sniffling and shaking, bringing in air through her nose in little gasps, then exhaling while her chest heaved and her hands shook.

He opened the screen door and let her fall into him. Just his presence changed the tone of her panic. Moments ago—wasn't it just moments ago—sheer panic had sent her pounding digits on the phone. It had bled her dry, emotion sucking at her like an Anne Rice wraith. Now it had sent her toward his chest, panic in check, but pain still obviously in control as she continued to shake and exhale an occasional sob. She would not have to face tonight alone. Ethan may have steeled a wall around himself for protection all those days since he came to Chicago, no one could blame him for that after what she had done. But that wall had not claimed him. He was here.

She wanted to wrap her arms around that hard body and find security as his arms would find their way around her, but three years still exacted a toll. So, instead, she leaned into him, fists in a ball supporting her head, perhaps out of guilt, more out of the fear of guilt. "Ethan, help me, Ethan. I can't sleep. All I can do is see her dead. She's dead, Ethan, and I killed her. I'm so tired. I've got to sleep. But Ethan, she dead, and it's my fault."

His vows of never letting her hurt him again had been left at the door, didn't have a prayer of winding their way in here and giving her more pain. Amber's sobs had quashed any sense of self-preservation. Her need had moved him as vengeance could not. He led her to the couch, shushing her with "That's all right, baby. Shh. You'll be all right."

While he sat with her, she was a frightened child in his arms. His strength flowed into her emptiness, his fingers stroked her hair with all the compassion they had so long ago. Funny how he had forgotten the paradox of Amber, the hull of confidence, armor that covered a darkness, a deep-rooted sense of being unlovable, an unwillingness to even ask for what she could not name yet sure that she could save the world. She lay on the couch, her head in his lap as those fingers continued their sweet soothing. He continued to stroke her hair, wanting to soothe her. Wanting to stroke away her fears, share his strength.

"Just try to tell me what happened." His words sounded so far away. Were they low and hushed out of sympathy? Or did they sound so far away, like words drowned in water, because she was so empty and yet held down by this awful ache that wound around her?

Somehow she managed to sit up. She felt as pale as the thick candles on her fireplace mantle—and just as likely to melt. She stared straight ahead, too ashamed of thoughts unnamed to face him.

"I don't know where to start."

"The beginning is often a good place." His voice was low, warm.

"The beginning." She begged herself to be able to turn to him, to let him lock onto her pain. But that worm of shame choked her movement. All she could manage was an exhale and one long breath in before she began. "I love my parents. You have to know that. Love the very thought of them. Daddy's a banker. Remember?" Amber's face stayed tense, her focus still on the wall, but in the midst of shame, she felt a gentling in her eyes as she thought of better days. "He was always so busy downtown, but he found time for his little girl. He gave me my first writing journal, read every entry until I was ten. One summer, when I was only four, he rented a pony and led me through the neighborhood.

Mother tskked about the neighbors watching, but she followed us coming up the drive and smiled. I can still feel the wind in my hair and the wonder of it. Daddy with me on that pony, and Lillian's smile."

The warmth in Amber's eyes turned cold; her tone changed, now deep and unforgiving.

"The dream's my pound of flesh for letting them down. I killed her. Dumb girl, I killed her with need for a star."

Her whole body stayed glued toward that wall. She could talk if she didn't have to look at him. If he touched her, she would break like glass.

Ethan drew her closer, kissed the side her face once, a soft kiss to let her know she could go on. "Okay, it's a dream that has you scared."

He tightened his arms around her ever so slightly. "Let's start with you killing someone. Whom did you kill?"

Whom. He was always such a stickler for grammar.

"My mother." The words came out child-like, barely a whisper and yet so matter-of-fact. Just the saying of it moved within her, and she let a light laugh escape her—how the hell a laugh had survived this night she'd never know, not to mention the suitability of laughing at the terror that had held her-- but that one small action let her know that just maybe even she'd survive this whole thing.

His silence was calming. So far, no branding. She could continue. She could let it out. She could.

That half-smile of his, it warmed her even if she didn't see it.

"Funny how we still share the basics," he said. "It was a fantasy of mine, you know."

Amber felt the soothing of his laugh, and took a chance. She let herself turn and look at him. Yes, the smile was there. It gave her the faith to go on.

"I just couldn't let her suffer anymore. I had to do something."

"Your mother?"

Each word was an echo of itself, fading and more full of sorrow. Amber mouthed, "No, no, no," while her head tried to sink into her shoulders as they lifted to protect her. She took a chance and let herself look at him.

"I went to Jocelyn's house. I had this plan . . ." His arms grabbed her shoulders. He wore his shock and anger.

"You went to her house? That's crazy! The girl's a nut case. Who knows what goes on where she lives."

Amber felt a wave of emotion rise in her, a broken promise. He was supposed to understand. She stared at him, waiting for him to take it back.

"Don't you know? That child is in danger. I had to do something."

"That's the point. Danger." His fingers tightened. "You went there alone?"

She shrugged away from his grasp and turned, her back toward him, arms folded. "Jocelyn wasn't there, but her mother was." Amber's chin quivered, and her teeth rattled at the next thought. "And Mom's sleazy boyfriend." She shook just saying the words. "That poor child. You can't believe those people."

He softened his words with a gentle massage, his thumbs pressed in, his fingertips brushing her upper back, once, twice. "I can believe pretty much anything about a girl who's a poster child for anger mismanagement."

Amber shook her head and pressed her lips before she spoke.

"I remember a time when you took a chance. You thought I was a worthless brat, but you helped me."

"You were my writing partner, for crying out loud. Of course I helped you."

Amber turned back and looked at him straight-on. "You came to my house, the house where I was staying with Uncle James, our professor's best friend. Pretty ballsy for a guy working for the college.

"That's not the same."

"It is the same. You took a chance. And you kept taking chances with me, prodding and caring while I learned to come into myself."

"As I recall, it was well worth it." His smile spoke of lush August nights, a sky strung with white stars, the feel of her. He pulled her close and kissed her temple, a soft kiss, light-lipped and tender, his lips grazing, his right hand still caressing her hair, that caress spanning so much time and space in such a few moments.

Amber could have lived in that hold for hours, let herself slip deeper and deeper into the warm. Safety. Protection. Instead, she took a chance.

"Remember my letter to you that summer?"

As if he could have forgotten. "Yeah." A very abrupt, "Yeah."

She backed away to look at him, then took his hands and held them gently. "I told you how I needed to handle finding myself, that all the garbage with my parents was something I needed to take care of, that I couldn't be a lover until I was an adult." The words came out stilted and broken as she walked her way through them, each word a piece of glass ready to cut her.

"I felt so sure when I was with you. It was so easy. Break the umbilical cord once and for all." She squeezed his hand, then backed away.

He dropped his arms to his side. "Why did you call me tonight? Why me?"

Her turn to be strong, even for just the moment.

"After I woke up and felt the panic pressing on me, even when all the filth swirled and smothered me, I could see your face down deep, and I knew I was safe. I know that sounds crazy, but your face—it promised safety."

She sighed and her pitch dropped. Her voice was low and husky, almost a whisper. "Ethan, I told you how you were my best friend and my lover and I would never forget you. Ethan, that was the truth. Please believe me. I would never have lied to you."

She waited for the *Then why did you walk out on me?* that had hung between them. They had danced around it since his first day. But the question never came—except for a flicker in his eyes and a tic in his jaw muscle.

His voice. His touch. His very presence urging and comforting. An inner strength she could never admit to herself, the one that had kept her sane—at least until this moment—washed over her, drove her as she spent the next hour telling him what made her try to save children like Jocelyn, how a little girl who so loved her parents had watched an ambulance drive away with her mother, how the hushed household and the condemning eyes drove her demons ever deeper until they could only be seen in her dreams. She talked of years of knowing that she had failed at pleasing the beautiful woman, the one who dangled smiles just often enough to give hope, and then dashed it with contempt for a child who could never live up to her expectations. And of that poor contemptible child who could—and would—kill her mother if she ever demanded what other people took as birthright. Freedom from the control of those who had given her birth.

She talked until the pain that had sent her keening spent itself, her head up toward the ceiling one minute and then in her hands the next as she twisted her hair and rubbed at her forehead. When she fell quiet, her legs and arms had curled tight, and she had rested her head in Ethan's lap so his fingers could work their magic at the nape of her neck and in her hair, fingers stroking and comforting while they both wondered what the hell they were going to do. Her senses felt heightened and calmed all at once. This moment, so fragile, so tenuous, sent warmth to dark places that had been so cold.

He had the hands of a worker, this writer who spent his summers working outside, yet his touch was soft as he stroked her arms and hair. She wanted to seize the fingers; she wanted to flee from what was growing so deep inside her. But the touch of him, the rhythm of his caring as he cradled her.

With a touch as soft as a murmur, he bent toward her and kissed her.

Amber was still, had to be still. If she moved, he would be gone, this beautiful, beautiful man who surely was here only in her dreams. His lips stayed close to her ear. She could feel the breath on her, feel the warmth of his breath down to her neck.

Ethan couldn't take away the horror of Frank, the pain of herself as a child, but he slayed something within her with the softest of touches, with his very presence in the wee hours. Lying still while the minutes ticked toward the inevitable confrontation of the workday dawn, Amber continued to replay their summer, turning each memory over in her mind, feeling the tension from a vantage point of safety, that awful tension of wanting to know each other and the worst tension of finding the knowing and then wanting it even more, a wanting more deeply mixed with the rush of hormones and something too stirring to even be named.

The darkness lay around her, granted her its grace to let the images become more real in her mind. "What do you want, Amber, what do you really, really want deep in your gut?" he had once said as a writing exercise. It had become a mantra, mixing with the days and nights they had spent moving toward love, hovering over the petty questioning that defined her. It had grown awesome, but the days were spent too quickly to let it penetrate all those layers that Amber had built, those irritations that were no precious pearl building in an oyster.

She lived this memory, embraced it, let it seep deep within and warm those cold places so besieged by guilt. Possibly, just possibly, there was room in this world for some peace, some essence of love of self that she had denied herself for so long. In this darkness, she could let the echo of his question settle, like fine ash burrowing into tiny cracks, let it dispel all the things that had made her so guilt-ridden.

Amber reached to let go of something dark and unnamed and heavy that had weighed on her for so many years. It nudged within her. She felt its first hairline crack.

As the minutes went by, she let the sensation of Ethan fall over her like a blanket, and she slept.

Chapter 17

"There are no coincidences, just occasions of opportunity." Today's bit of wisdom, courtesy of central office. Amber considered lifting her head. Bad idea. Too much work.

Where was a Saturday when you needed it?

Right now she was cached behind her desk in her cushioned roll-away chair, feet planted on the floor for balance but arms dangling limply at her side, head tilted back against the head rest. Occasional muffled voices and an even rarer locker slam or two floated by her room like echoes from a parallel universe while she took full advantage of the last minutes left before the first hour bell.

Please, dear Lord, let me just rest here and focus on the back of my eyelids for another hour or two. She took in a deep breath and exhaled slowly, let the breath travel through her throat, into her chest and out again like a prayer. Her eyes each weighed far too much to consider opening them, and as for her fingers, why they had, no doubt, been so numbed by the force of lead weighing them down, she'd be lucky to hold a piece of chalk by lunch time. She knew that she had aged at least a century since the same time yesterday.

Intellectually, she was ready to teach. But her emotions—they had sucked her dry. She had always known that catharsis was good for the soul, but no one had ever mentioned feeling like a hollowed out shell. Besides, she was going on two hours of sleep and a pot of strong coffee. She might as well have been in college again after a forty-eight hour finals marathon.

She had enough energy for one smile. No problem there. The smile stretched itself across her lips, warming her mouth. Ethan had come to her apartment. He had sat there, cradling her in his lap and listened, then held her while she slept. Her fuzzy mind brought up a picture of them in her living room, her lying there on that couch in that drugged state between sound sleep and consciousness, him anchored at one end, one arm straight across the back, the other loose, occasionally touching her hair while she drifted off—at least she thought he had. She saw all the soft shadows around them, even heard the gentle buzz of her refrigerator. She remembered him placing his finger on her lips and whispering, "Not yet." Then he had simply kissed the top of her head. But when the clock alarm buzzed her back to the reality of another work day, he was gone. He had left her. He was gone and she was there on that couch, a pillow under her head and her afghan around her, tucked in like a child, only one question hovering in the early morning.

Where did that night, and his disappearance, leave them?

"Picked up any serial killers lately? Anybody sending you love letters in a bottle?"

Amber had prayed for silence. Obviously, God had a sense of humor this morning. In walked Maggie, coffee cup in hand, primed to deliver one of her early morning wake-up calls, the lighthearted small talk etched in acid, meant to pull the perpetually sleepy Amber out of her daily morning doldrums. Today, it was verbal salt rubbed into wounds the early bird Maggie couldn't even begin to imagine.

In fact, today, while Maggie's words rode in on the air sure of a receptive audience—once said audience woke up enough to respond in kind—the words simply swirled around the front of the room, decidedly amazed at the lack of reception, and limped toward the back, nothing more than mere echo by the time they reached the body strung out behind the desk.

Amber opened her eyes halfway without so much as a millimeter of head movement. Her right hand limp-wristed a feeble wave of dismissal while her head fell toward the desk and onto her left arm. Camille at her best.

"Whoa, girl friend. Cheap theatrics is my bag." But Maggie's voice lost some of its bite as she walked in and made her way toward Amber, then stood over her friend, looking down at Amber's face. Maggie gave her best Cheshire cat grin. *All I want from you, at least for now, is a sign of life—if nothing else, a twitch or two.* She patted Amber's head twice and then gave her one soft mothering stroke. "I thought we were over this Frank thing. He's too much of an idiot, a clumsy idiot at that, to be much of a threat."

When that failed to elicit a response, Maggie took her hand away and kneeled beside Amber, her mouth a few inches from her friend's ear. "Or is it something else? I know—it's your love life." Amber froze. The possibilities scared the hell out of her, or would have, if she'd had the energy to be scared. No way could Maggie have guessed about Ethan's late night visit. Amber could hardly believe what had happened herself.

"Did he come to you in the middle of the night?" Maggie let just enough sibilance caress her whisper to make the question come off as an accusation.

Amber let out a growl and managed a glare, but didn't move.

"Ha! That's it!" Maggie on a roll was a thing to behold. She lifted her eyebrows and turned her voice even more lecherous, throaty and diabolically low. "Duane climbed your iron trellis in the middle of the night in his polyester Batman pants and had his way with you. Oh . . . your panties are still wet even thinking about him!" By the time she had finished that piece of fantasy, Maggie was caught up in the sheer idiocy of that thought, cackling like an old crone.

Amber was tired, not dead. Even post-traumatic shock couldn't stand the onslaught of a Duane-as-Batman image. Amber turned her head enough to shoot Maggie a most prim I-am-about-to-be-right look. Furrowing her brows just for emphasis, she spat, "You've finally found out our secret." Head still resting on the chair's neck, she did manage a wink and continued. "But Mags, he lets me ride his Batmobile and leaves me Catwoman glasses." She paused while she pulled herself up to seating position and crossed her arms. "With real rhinestones." With a little purr, she widened her eyes and sighed, a smitten vixen rocking back and forth in a fantasy of he own making.

Maggie's cackling was history. She simply shook her head. "You are one sick woman." Raising her eyebrows in mock alarm, she gave Amber a smirk out of the left side of her mouth. "However, you did have one hellofa scare, and hysteria will often bring out the worst in us."

That put a damper on Amber's progress. That and the fact that she had just expended the little energy she had mustered thus far. She sighed and gathered her thoughts while Maggie waited, radiating tolerance for her morning challenged friend, the benign smile of a morning person blissfully in tune with the rise of the sun.

"I will admit, last night I was a little . . . vexed." Vexed. Good word.

On that, Maggie almost doubled over. "Vexed? You think you were vexed? What is this? Vocabulary day? How about 'ired'? Or perhaps 'importuned'?" She raised her right hand, fingers flipped in the air toward an invisible speaker. "Oh yes, madame, we had a bit of a tussle with a madman brandishing some kind of weapon, and absolutely refusing to mind his pints and quarts. But things are under control again and Mum can rest her fears." She pursed her lips. "I'd rather deal with the thought of Duane and his batmobile."

Amber managed to sit up. "The point is, I'm fine now."

"Oh, gag me. And by the way . . . " Maggie set her hands on her hips for emphasis and looked straight at Amber's green eyes for any sign of wavering. ". . . just because some *thing* . . . and I don't mean a liaison with Duane. I mean the real wettin' your panties thing that you *still* haven't dealt with . . . ." She worked the word *thing* like a thespian, her tongue playing with the word to clip out a tone of emphasis, " . . . just because a *thing* falls apart, my dear, doesn't mean the pieces can't jump up and bite you in the ass." On that she gave her friend a wink, popped up, and spun out of the classroom in true drama queen panache, tossing her head and swaying her hips.

Amber returned to lethargy and dropped her head. "Oh, Maggie, if you only knew just how much you've nailed my whole life." By now Amber had her head in her hands again, her elbows propping her lower arms, her fingers trying to massage some life into her scalp, maybe even wake up her deadened brain. Where's a snow day when you need it. So what if it's early September.

"Yo, Miss Helm, what's up? The dog eat your lesson plan book?" David McPhearson's voice startled Amber into a self-imposed alertness. Time for the show. No way could she let the kids see inside her, let them in on all the rips and ruptures that had cracked her cement, releasing emotions that had rumbled so furiously and then left her drained. Acting was often the best tool of a teacher. Amber looked up, forced a smile.

"No, David, he's acquired such a taste for your homework that he absolutely refuses to even sniff at anything of mine." Three rips for early morning small banter. But why, oh lord, on a day like this when everything was in a haze.

By second period, the need to crawl inside her eyelids was still very much a presence, but Amber had some modicum of control. The secret was to stay moving and keep the windows open. Luckily, a high pressure front had moved in and the weather was no longer in monsoon mode. A dry breeze kept the air circulating, ruffling on Amber often enough for her to welcome the sensation while she met with individual writers who were spread out around the room tackling Haikus. An imaginary poem had wormed its way onto the legal pad she kept on her desk for between class notes to herself; this one, set in the too-near future, summed up how she envisioned the afternoon when she would face Ethan again. The news from the unconscious was definitely not an upper.

> *Footsteps echo near.*
> *Petals sigh on fragrant breeze.*
> *Lover knows her fear.*

Hey, those Asians sure do know how to wield a few good syllables into truth. Another whiff of breeze passed over her neck, a sensual whisper announcing the inner critic.

Face it, woman, you're tired, you're insecure, you're in this thing all over again. But this time that critic was stopped by an awareness. In the wee hours of this morning, the cement had dissolved from her shoulders and neck, left a new lightness in spite of the draining all those fissures of emotion had caused. More than her relationship with Ethan had changed. While tenth graders searched for Haiku syllables, Amber lifted her shoulders unconsciously and drew her head back. The sound of the intercom startled her.

"Miss Helm, you're wanted in the office. Mr. Borski will take your class."

What? No one ever took over a class unless someone had died—or was about to. She knew it. The kids did, too.

Amber forced a smile and the tone of objectivity while she grabbed her purse.

"Sam, you're in charge until Mr. Borski gets here.

"Everyone else, keep writing."

Chapter 18

Officer Donald Evert Calavari didn't like having to go into Clausson High School. For Calavari, the hallowed halls of any school blistered with memories of a bitter youth spent dreading the clientele of secondary education. Bottom feeding slugs had coasted the halls of Mount Xavier High School, their scowling presence a knot of secret fists lowered so the teachers couldn't see the punches aimed at the hapless in general, Calavari in particular. Not all harassment had been physical. Reptilian tongues had unleashed a storm of humiliation aimed at badgering a skinny Italian kid not yet into his growth spurt and cursed with the tag, Donnie E. By the time he had grown into his shoe size and could whip their pimpled asses, Senior Prom was on the horizon and the morons were all caught up in fantasies of flinging more than spring. Twenty minutes spent in a high school hallway sent him back to days of yesteryear that weren't much for remembering.

He did manage a chuckle at today's twist on terrorism in the public sector. The sign on the front door of the high school had advised, "Visitors must check in at the front office. "That was smart. Turn off the good will and make the crazies laugh. *Oh, I gotta check in the office before I blow off my kid's head. Better go home and think about it.* Another stirringly intelligent choice by the good guys. Calavari just loved authority. It always made him laugh. He made a point to nod in homage to the gods, though, just in case. He had his mission after all. And the office was Mission Central.

"Aggravated assault on a parent," he muttered as he made his way along the hall. Back in the seventies, when he had gone to high school, Mr. Steinmann would whap a kid or two with a ruler, but no one ever left a bruise. This one—what was she, an English teacher? And a beer bottle. She must pack quite a wallop the way that Quint woman had looked. A black right eye and a swollen lip, not to mention the crack on the head that had sent her to the hospital. Jeez—a teacher. His partner Bellini was sure she was a lesbian who took her butch role too seriously. "Hey, she's white and she ain't a hooker. That means she's gotta be a lesbo." But then Bellini was pretty much an imbecile. Trying to find insight in Bellini was like trying to build houses out of hair gel.

Still, Calavari had a picture forming, courtesy of Bellini. By the time he reached the office, he had it sketched in tight. Black crepe-soled shoes and black socks—they always wore black socks—below really hairy legs, thick hands and lank hair, inscrutable eyes watching for the slightest error. Childhood days best left forgotten were etched in Calavari's long term memory, Bellini's theory notwithstanding.

Once in the office, all nostalgia was forgotten. Calavari was, instead, contemplating "sore thumb" as in "sticking out like one." As soon as he had flashed his badge and introduced himself to the principal, the looks had started. Not obvious ones necessarily. Secretaries were great for working one-eyed while the other scoped him out. That was standard in his experience. But a cop in a high school might as well be riding a broom writing "Surrender Dorothy" in the sky and lining up winged monkeys when it came to the student helpers who stood at the counter, any thoughts of helping the guest annihilated by his West Oz presence. He chuckled and scratched his chin. Couldn't he be Glinda just once? Maybe not. Somehow, stepping out of a bubble and waving a wand didn't fit his image. Bellini would have a field day, laugh his ass off with that one.

He turned to the administrator. "Thank you, Dr. Aaron. If you don't mind, I'd like to speak to Miss Helm alone. He opened the door, stepped inside, and almost forgot to close the darned thing. The figure seated on the sofa at the far end of the room was a drop dead gorgeous redhead. Well, gorgeous except for eyes lined with black smudges and lips tightly pursed. And the stare. The stare was cutting in spite of her obvious misery. This was the bottle-wielding lesbian?

While he stepped toward her to take a seat, Calavari's cop compass spun. Except for the signs of stress, this woman belonged on an ad for Chivis Regal instead of an arrest list.

Watch it, Calavari, the last time you let a gorgeous face psyche you that fast, she turned out to be a high cost call girl who extorted her married clients. Calavari's momma didn't raise no fools. Gaining composure, he became a cop again, a cop with a mask of pure genial kindness and a mission to rationalize the games he would have to play. Two decades of the same dance had served him well. Don't challenge. Hold back. Let the opponent take the lead and then demolish him—or in this case, her—and smile the whole time.

He took a seat across from her. "Miss Helm, I'm Detective Donald Calavari. "I want to thank you for letting me take you from your class." Right, old buddy. Scare her out of her mind and then say 'Thanks'.

Let's a have a talk." Turning toward her, arm extended in invitation, he surveyed the suspect, watching for a reaction, especially focusing on her eyes. Appearances could be deceiving, but a perp's eyes told a lot, especially at first contact. Liars usually couldn't look you straight up unless they were sociopaths.

They each took a seat at the round conference table, choosing to sit across from each other. Amber's eyes were clamped on him, straight forward, irises normal. Calavari's cop compass spun double. She was either very good or very innocent. Trouble was, he didn't know which.

He took out his notebook and pen, scanned the details he had already sketched out, more a matter of setting the timing than searching for information.

Eyes still seemingly tied to the notes, he kept his head down, his voice neutral. "We've heard from a . . ." Calavari paused for the affected perusal, the 'oh golly, I don't even know the simplest little ol' detail.' "Let's see here, yes, an Evelyn Quint." He looked up. "You know Ms. Quint?"

A Chicago cop does not pay school visits just to hang out with teachers. Five minutes waiting for this man had sent her into fight or flight mode. And now he wanted to talk about Jocelyn?

"Yes. She's the mother of one of my students. Jocelyn. Jocelyn Quint." The words came out with a calmness that felt foreign, given the circumstances.

"Ms. Helm, according to Ms. Quint and her daughter, you paid a visit to their house last night. Is that right?"

Amber definitely had her hackles raised by now, trying to gain some sense of the shifting of the wind here. Her "Yes" came out even. She forced herself to sit back, told herself to relax, that this was nothing. Nothing. This was nothing at all.

Just don't fumble or hesitate or do any of the dumb moves that television fabricates when the character needs to look guilty. Art just might imitate reality. And you are the good guy here, after all. You have nothing to worry about.

Sure.

Oh, my, yes, I paid a home visit to the Quint's. I am a professional after all. Just love to keep home-school channels of communication open. And oh by the way, Officer Cavalari, I was attacked by a psycho boyfriend who probably still wants my face carved like salami. Could this perchance have anything to do with your visit?

Definitely do not go into Frank territory.

"I don't usually make house calls, but Jocelyn had been absent, and I wanted to drop off some information about a writing contest." Calavari's face remained impassive. Amber continued to play good citizen in spite of a few Frank-zapped nerves wanting to have their way with her neural system. "She wasn't there, or at least I don't think she was." The image of Jocelyn in that apartment forced a shift in Amber's focus. Her awkward self-preservation gave way to panic. Jocelyn. What had happened to Jocelyn?

"Officer Calavari, is there something wrong with Jocelyn?" Her adrenaline had kicked into overdrive. She might have run from Frank, but by God, she wouldn't run now. If Jocelyn was in trouble, she was a mandatory reporter, and now was the time to report, loud and clear. She sat forward, hands resting on her knees, and gave Calavari her best teacher look, or at least the best she could muster under the circumstances and the growing sense that nasty things had taken up sudden residence in the pit of her stomach and were plotting havoc. "Surely Chicago's finest did not drive over here to chat about home visits." She felt a knot growing in the back of her throat. "Please. Is there something wrong?"

Calavari's eyes narrowed. Amber watched him for some sign, allowing herself to be pulled toward a sense of trusting that had certainly not been earned, perhaps wasn't even requested, but needed to be there for Jocelyn's sake.

"I have to be honest with you, Ms. Helm. I'm here because Evelyn Quint and her *daughter . . .*" He emphasized the word daughter, then hesitated. "Both of the Quints, plus a Frank Copenchek, informed us that last night, during an altercation at the Quint home, you inflicted grievous and aggravated assault on Mrs. Quint, an assault that put Evelyn Quint in Cook County Medical with serious injury."

Amber didn't know which was pounding worse, her head or her heart. Evelyn Quint was in the hospital and three people accused her of putting the woman there. Her jaw dropped, and she had to start three times before any sound came out. She felt her tongue trying to jump start a reply. She also wanted to get out of that office even if it meant rending her clothes and succumbing to terminal palsy.

Instead she merely sat there and stared, her mouth opening and closing like a freshly landed fish, gulping for air and a sense of what had just happened.

"Officer Calavari, I have *no* idea. . ." Her sense of shock grabbed hold again, and she looked away, trying to force some sense of reality back into the situation. "Look, I went to the Quint's, just like I said, to see if Jocelyn was all right, and to drop off information about a writing contest." *Steady, girl,* she warned herself. *No more information than is necessary.* "Other than that, I don't know what you're talking about."

Donald Calavari took a moment to align his cop compass. "Why don't you come to the precinct station with me. Maybe we can sort this whole thing out." He stood up and waited. "Ms. Helm?"

"Absolutely not. I have classes to teach. A test fifth hour. Two sections of peer revision to coordinate."

"What you have is my request. Later, I may not be so affable." He let the words settle for effect, then went on, business as usual. "Your principal has already made arrangements for your classes."

"What? Liz knows about this?"

"She knows, and she's in charge. Don't worry." Calavari motioned for her to leave, even opened the door for her.

Amber walked through the door to the main office. She paused long enough to look at the principal waiting there, stoically facing her except for her eyes. They were guarded—almost condemning. Amber tried to be calm. She crossed to the main counter that separated the office staff from the rest of the world, took the pen and wrote a note on the note paper kept there for messages, then turned to her boss, her hand still on the message. "Dr. Aaron, please get hold of Maggie. Tell her to call this man. His number's in my rolodex on my desk." Then Amber moved forward toward the door. Just as she reached the threshold, she stopped and turned. "I'm sure I'll be back in time for my Lit class. The tests for the other classes are on my desk. "Be sure to let Don know—and thank him for me."

Summoning as much courage as her shaking legs would allow, she turned and walked away from the office, followed by the policeman.

Chapter 19

Everything was gray. The walls, the linoleum worn thin and faded by the scuffling of endless feet, the metal mesh that separated her from whatever officer would come to lead her to the interrogation room, even the hard wooden bench she sat on. Oh yeah. And her life. That looked pretty gray right now.

Bit by bit, she tried to reconstruct the day, but the sheer whirl of her fears closed in on her. She should have been able to calm herself—she hadn't done anything—but the more she forced herself to reason this out, the more chaos pounded at her.

Something sharp clanked behind her, jolting her attention away from the sense of doom that chewed on her. What was it? A jail cell door?

Hers?

She looked at the bare wall across from her. Cement blocks. Dirt and grease had left its history, marks of others who had waited there just like her.

What next? Will they fingerprint me and snap my picture? When do they read me my rights? And who has my kids? What does the school know? What will they think of a teacher who talks of "character first" and winds up in this room of gray grease-pitted walls? The questions circled her while her hands opened and closed in agitation. The muscle in the back of her head was a knot, its pressure reaching down her neck and into her shoulders.

Sitting there in that gray room, Amber swallowed hard and waited, palms and fingers numbed by panic, fiddling mindlessly, her thumbs rubbing each one at a time in a rhythm of agitation.

Enough. She slapped her foot like a petulant child, her questions turned to a single vow. She would not cry. Not even a

300-pound matron with a strip search kit in her hand would wring so much as one tear from her. Inside, though, guilt had a heyday.

Nice going, Amber. Look what you've accomplished. You had to do it, didn't you, had to jump in without thinking, just jump in like the nitwit you are. We've tried and tried, told you over again to have some self-control, to think before you leap. But no, you have to have it your way and barge in. It's all about you, isn't it?

She swatted at the critic, her mind looking for a little control in what seemed like an Alice moment, but she was her own Mad Hatter. Amazing, the power of guilt, how it lives to suck away any hope, how it races the heart, brings on the tears of shame that sting and bite and refuse to listen to any plea to go away.

Amber felt naked shame with the exposure of her fear and ineptitude. She shivered quickly, bent over, her head in her hands, her thumbs now rubbing outside her cheekbones.

Steady girl. Think. Her thumbs kept at her head, as if they could shake lose some kind of answer to this mess she was in. She sat up, blew out a breath, and stared at the wall while her mind focused on her dilemma.

Jocelyn.

Jocelyn had accused her of assaulting her mother. The mother Jocelyn hated, or at least accused of being evil. A question formulated, the kind of question that surfaces once demon panic has been swept away, more a nagging than something fully developed, like the last images of a dream before wakening. It tugged at her, this thought. *How do you know the evil is her mother?* Amber swatted at it. Of course the mother was the evil. Evelyn Quint was a polyester-clad slug, a wormy thing, something squishy and white and dank, something that sucked out love instead of giving it, keying on her fading charms, limited as they might always have been, and the booze that nourished her fantasy.

Her thumbs were going full throttle right now, circling as if to conjure up an answer to this mess. The evil that Amber assured herself was Evelyn Quint, the thing that had driven Jocelyn to mutilating her wrists just to relieve some pressure.

One of those demon thoughts resurrected itself. So, Amber, if the mother is so evil, how come she's the one unconscious right now? She's the one lying there in that hospital room. And who made her that way? And why would two women, one a girl and one a half-beaten middle aged has-been, both of them victims, why would they blame a teacher who had only tried to help? Why blame Amber?

This was insanity. From the moment Calavari had informed her of their accusation until now was part blur, part psychedelic nightmare. Jocelyn's mother was in the hospital, unconscious, might die in fact, and the police thought she had done it.

Amber brought up her conversation with Calavari like files on a computer. Yes, she had visited the Quint's home last night. Yes, there had been an altercation, but it was entirely verbal. The bruise on her arm? She had done that while running out the door, afraid for her life, thank you very much. Calavari couldn't have been very impressed with her commentary. The fact that two witnesses, one Frank Copenchek and one Jocelyn Quint, had sworn in written testimony that she, Amber Helm, had assaulted with deadly force the presently unconscious Evelyn Quint, contradicted that claim and looked pretty downright foreboding.

"Miss Helm?" Officer Calavari was standing in the doorway looking quite officious. "Let's go into the conference room and see if we can sort all this out."

Conference room. Cute. Not interrogation room. Not "place where they keep drooling police dogs and secret caches of truth serum and manacles and . . . ." Knock it off, woman, keep your wits about you. You're innocent and Chicago isn't Nazi Germany. Still, she found herself scanning the halls for monocled little men dressed in black trench coats and maniacal smiles. Calavari ushered her into a small, windowless room lit by long fluorescent lighting hanging from the ceiling. Instead of the gray of the waiting area, the color of choice in this room was brown. Brown metal chairs, two of them next to the wall and two on opposite sides of a brown table bolted to the floor. That spoke confidence. More ugliness. Tan walls streaked from water damage and smudges from who knew what. Linoleum, squares of mottled brown and black and a weird maroon that looked a little like dried blood. The lighting, or lack of it, cast shadows in the corner but clearly lit up the table and the scowl on the face of the plainclothes detective seated across from her.

"I have to tell you, Miss Helm, that you're in a lot of trouble."

She looked at him, not seeing anything except her plight. Trouble? I'm in trouble?

Of course you're in trouble. Why else would your stomach be grinding. You and the cop. So far you're on the same side. Veritable teammates.

Be cool. He's the one with the grimace, but you haven't done anything.

"Why am I here?"

"Aggravated assault is a felony, and with three witnesses, one of them the victim herself, the only thing that keeps me from reading you your rights is a need to hear why a teacher would attack a student's mother in her own home." He leaned back, arms crossed, evidently waiting for an answer.

Assault? Felony? The bruise on her arm ached, its purple stippling screaming her guilt. Calavari had noticed the bruise as soon as she had come into the office. She had seen his eyes lock onto it, caught the tension in his face. But she wasn't guilty. She had merely hit herself on the way out.

"She doesn't have to respond to that. Unless, of course, a couple of my favorite amendments to the Constitution no longer apply here in Chicago."

Warmth swept through her. That, and surprise. Good surprise. The cavalry was here. Not some middle infantry soldier. No, the general himself in the form of Robert Dobron, lawyer extrordinaire. Robert's bullish form had entered the room, his bass voice the trumpet of horn and charging hooves. The lawyer had been a linebacker at Michigan and regarded anyone posed against a client a potential quarterback asking for a sacking.

"If anyone's guilty of attacking anyone, it's the Chicago Police Department who has publicly humiliated a Gold-Star teacher by hauling her from school in front of her peers and students on some ridiculous accusation by two women obviously too afraid of the real perpetrator to tell the truth." You go, Robert! You gotta love a guy who can whip out that many words without stumbling. Amber was so relieved by the august presence of her father's lawyer, she didn't take in any of the message.

Oh, maybe a little bit of the amendments, and the nice touch about last year's award from the governor's counsel, but the significance of "real perpetrator" missed her entirely. Thank you, thank you, thank you, Maggie. Good job, Amber, for keeping the rolodex up to date. Family lawyer here, family doesn't know. Perfect. Okay, boys, you can put away the cattle prods.

Calavari was on his feet, his body seemingly relaxed but his eyes glaring, his right hand holding the top rung of the chair tightly enough to choke it. He was smiling, but Amber bet the smile didn't go very deep. Robert walked toward Amber, slowly, almost an amble.

"My dear, you look well, considering. How are you holding up under this outrage?" He shot Calavari a look of pure disdain, sort of an "And how is the child molesting business doing?" eyeballing.

"I don't call three eye witnesses 'ridiculous,' Counselor. We have a statement from the victim, the daughter, and the boyfriend that your Gold Star teacher here knocked Ms. Quint to the floor—without provocation—where she sustained life-threatening injuries. Sending a mother to the hospital is not exactly the same as sending a gum-chewer to the principal's office." Robert Dobron stood there, registering only stoicism as Calavari went on. "In addition, Miss Helm admits that she was at the house last night, and she did engage in an argument with Ms. Quint."

"Oh, I see, a home visit by a teacher now suggests assault. Sort of gives 'No Child Left Behind' an ominous twist, doesn't it?"

Amber had the strange sensation that she was at Wimbleton taking in a tennis tournament, but that she was the ball.

The detective had the next move. "Look, Mr. Dobron, you can put whatever spin you want on this for your own ego, but Ms. Helm needs less acclaim and more answering. She may have very well been education's answer to Mary Poppins, but the fact remains that I have a victim in the hospital and forty-eight hours to chat with this young lady before I decide"—Amber couldn't help but notice the emphasis on the I—"what this home visit suggests, and if it warrants an arrest.

Not with Robert here, it won't. Now that her family's lawyer had taken the edge off of her own panic, Amber's original source of fear returned. Jocelyn, the speaker of evil, the girl whose own scars screamed of anger and fear and enough pent-up rage to warrant her own self-mutilation.

"Look gentlemen, I hate to interrupt this sparring match . . ." Both men turned to look at the source of their confrontation, the woman they had begun to ignore while they spat legalese at each other. Robert broke in. "Never mind, Amber, this so-called match is over." He turned to Calavari. "I'm taking Miss Helm home now. You can reach her through my office." He cast a disparaging look at the detective. "I'm assuming, though, that you'll find better ways to use your time. Like in the pursuit of the truth of this matter." He gently nudged Amber upward. "Come, my dear, let's get you home so that you can return to your life."

Amber stood up and walked ahead of the lawyer, reaching for the door knob, a firm metal promise of freedom on the other side. While she turned it, a strange sense of calm pulled from some deep reservoir settling where panic had owned her earlier. No doubt this newfound coolness was Robert's presence, or maybe, what the hey—the calm before the storm. She couldn't help but mentally kick herself for choosing—yes, the choice had definitely been hers in spite of all kinds of warnings by her friends—choosing to walk into danger totally misguided by intentions that stemmed from emotion rather than any kind of sense. If she hadn't been so self-righteous about being the heroine, she wouldn't be here listening to two men battle over her like she was the turkey leg left over on Thanksgiving. Every time she let guilt traipse through her, another thought seemed to ride on its back.

What had happened to Jocelyn?

Robert's hand reached ahead of her, turned the knob and pulled the door open. He guided her out while leaning in to whisper, "Don't worry about a thing," then let his hand maneuver her along the hallway and past the front desk. Calavari followed, a scowl printed across his forehead in the form of knit brows. "Don't forget, Dobron, the rich may know how to buy their lawyers, but they can't buy away the truth." Both Amber and Robert Dobron ignored him as she gladly left the precinct, so relieved they didn't pay attention to the reporter sitting across from the main desk. The reporter who heard Calavari's parting comment. The one who particularly caught the word "rich" at the same time he recognized the name, Robert Dobron. The one who made his way over to the desk with a smile, a twenty dollar bill, and the knowledge that a story might well be brewing.

Chapter 20

While Amber was in the throes of her legal dance, the outside world carried on as normal. Students at Clausson High School—at least those not privy to Amber's state—were doing the pre-noon wiggle, squirming and checking the clock, as if anything much had changed since they had glanced at it fifteen seconds ago. A few teachers at Clausson gave in and let the students talk the last few minutes. Some were more stalwart . . . or full of naive hope. Like Mr. Michaels.

"And that, in a nutshell, is milieu ala Tolkien." Good thing he was wrapping up, he told himself. Keep it up until the end, but then let them run. Lunch time meant break time. Nothing like sending them off with swamp images and whirling ghosts. Ethan smiled and pointed at the door as soon as the clock hit 12:15. "Have fun with the mystery meat." With that ominous reference to federally funded school lunch, Ethan watched his fifth hour students move out into the hall and lose themselves in the swarm headed for the cafeteria.

Keep telling yourself those last two don't look like hobbits. Ethan shook his head as he eyed the two boys who sat closest to him in the front row but somehow were always the last to make it out the door, black backpacks swinging, mouths usually engaged in some talk of the latest in video heroes. You gotta love 'em. They all wanted to be Aragorn, but looked more like Sam or Golom.

Hey, Hotshot, you weren't exactly date bait when you were that age either.

Harsh but true. Projecting on kids who suffered from terminal puberty was hardly professional. He lifted his head back and stretched. A weariness had started settling after second hour, nudging at first and then spread as the morning plodded on. Frodo and his swamp had nothing on him. Ethan was totally worn from very little sleep and a middle-of-the-night expedition that had left him disoriented and wondering. He sat down at the writing table that served as his temporary desk and opened the top drawer, allowed himself a smirk while he grabbed for the peanut butter and jelly sandwich he had stored there this morning. Who said he was over being a kid.

Who said he was over all sorts of things.

You'd better concentrate on the peanut butter. The other will be there in full force after school.

A din from the hall broke that reverie. Great. Just what he needed. A lunch time brawl. Ethan set down his sandwich and headed for the door, expecting a cat fight.

What he got was . . . Maggie?

She was towering over Duane, who could do no more than flatten himself against the wall and sputter, her hands firm against the wall to keep the department head from escaping, a tirade rushing from her mouth, her body language stiffly hostile even though Ethan couldn't make out the words. Duane kept shaking his head back and forth like a wobbly-necked toy robot, but Maggie looked resolute. Ethan found himself checking her head for snakes and wondering if poor Duane was about to turn to stone. He could return to the room and his peanut butter, but what the hell. Chaos was much more fun than a power-resting lunch. Why not wander by and catch the fun.

He walked toward them slowly to keep from being noticed, not that it mattered from the look of things, then stopped short when he could make out Maggie's words.

"You little twerp, don't give me that political crap. What are you going to do for her?"

Trouble with a student, Maggie? What did the little whelp do? Out-zing one of your quips? Run off with your fluorescent pilot pens?

Duane's reply, delivered tight-lipped and abrupt, stopped Ethan in his tracks.

"I am not at liberty to discuss Miss Helm's plight with other teachers."

Miss Helm's plight? The statement registered, and Ethan found his feet. What the hell had happened to Amber?

By the time he reached the two teachers, Maggie's hands had lowered to Duane's shoulders, and she looked ready to beat the poor man. Any questions about Amber would have to wait until Ethan pried Maggie off of the guy.

"So, how about some lunch?" Ridiculous question—sort of like throwing water onto a dog. "Anyone for peanut butter and jelly?"

Maggie stopped long enough to shoot Ethan a stare. No one had to tell Duane to go. He scurried away, his mumbling in tune with his pace.

Maggie stayed, hands on hips, eyes snapping. Evidently Ethan's attempt at humor did not amuse the plucky Miss Witkowski. The tight-lipped slash of her mouth left and her words spat out in that controlled tone usually reserved for students who had just set fire to the classroom.

"Your room. Now."

Seconds later, after he had closed the classroom door and moved toward the table housing his lunch, he turned to the irate teacher. She stood across from him, her left hand clutching the back of his chair, the right hand balled up except for her index finger pointed at him. Her lips were back to that nasty slash, and she was quiet. Maggie quiet was really scary. Her eyes, nasty and dark, bored into him.

"Listen carefully, Writer Boy."

Ethan could feel Maggie drawing in her breath and exhale as if she were trying to fire up an internal engine. His next thought was only a little less civilized. *I will not shove my sandwich into her face, nor will I make her eat my tie.* He forced as much of a smile as he could muster and, grabbing his sandwich, raised it toward her. "Bite?" Just to make sure, he looked at his hand and added, ". . . the sandwich, not my hand."

The woman just didn't have a shared sense of humor at the moment. Maggie ripped out her words, low, controlled. Her tone could have razored steel.

"Amber was hauled off by the police less than an hour ago. Chicago's finest seems to think our Amber is some kind of vigilante pounding the hell out of wayward parents. She's at the precinct as we speak, hopefully soon to be in the presence of her lawyer."

The weariness that had him slumped into his chair just minutes ago was gone, was replaced by a surge of adrenaline. Jail? Amber?

"What happened?"

I'm not really sure . . . and guess what. I don't have to be. I'm her friend, and that makes me in one-hundred percent." The tone was still there along with the look. "So I'm going to ask you plain and simple. Are you ready to help her?"

The possibility of a "No" did not exist. Any idea as to an accompanying plan of action was just as remote. "You're sure she has a lawyer?"

"Robert Dobron. Amber was hollering his name while the local Gestapo escorted her out the door. I found his number in the rolodex on Amber's desk. He said he'd be there within thirty minutes, traffic god willing." Maggie folded her arms. I don't know what's between you two, and right now, the Holy Mother herself couldn't make me care. All I want to know is, what are you going to do?"

Ethan was deadly still. "I don't know."

Leaning toward him, Maggie hissed. "Well, you'd better figure out something by the end of the day." She punched out air in one harsh burst. "You're the only one around here short of the janitor who doesn't have some tie to school politics. That means I actually have to depend on you."

She made that sound like an insult.

Ethan put his hand on her shoulder—self defense never hurt at a time like this—and leaned his head down. "I can't take this all in, much less make a decision ten minutes before the kids come back from lunch." He felt Maggie's shoulder muscles tense. "That doesn't mean I don't care, or I won't help. Let's cool our jets and finish the day. I'll meet you after school, and we'll do some brainstorming. If Amber's called her lawyer, the worst of today is probably over."

Maggie had calmed down some by now, or at least her body seemed less tense and her eyes less panicked. She'd probably listen to him. "Let me know where we can talk. By this afternoon, we should both know more—maybe even a few facts instead of rumor mill suppositions." He turned and looked at the door, his arm still on her shoulder. "If the police came to the school, the kids will be hearing the pounding of serial killers past every locker." He stepped back from Maggie and put his hands in his pockets. His voice sounded gentle. "We both care. I promise."

He let that settle. "We have to go on as normal to keep the gossip mongers at bay. Just stay calm until after school."

Maggie bit her lip. "You're right. Here, I'll give you an address." She grabbed a pen and a slip of paper out of her vest pocket, scrawled quickly and left the paper on the table. Then she left, much less maniacal than when she had come in. She seemed to lope away like a wounded animal.

Ethan looked at the sandwich still waiting in one hand. He tossed it into the waste can next to his desk and checked the clock. Eight minutes until the kids came back. He ran his hand through his hair and sat on the edge of the table. Just last night—this morning in fact, he had calmed her and helped her sleep. Now, the ghosts of the night had paled in light of what Maggie had told him, and he was clueless. He felt a knot grab at his neck, and he tried to rub it away before it turned monster, as if his movement would untangle this mess and take them all back to the early morning.

Chapter 21

Maggie, at her most incensed, was a lamb compared to Jocelyn. Three hours after Duane had almost shriveled at the hands of a black haired harpy, school was over and Jocelyn had slammed the door of her apartment and stomped toward the kitchen, muttering a litany of obscenities. The sound of her boots against the old floor mixed with the usual creaking of the wood. She made it half way through the dining room before the muttering exploded in a full onslaught of shouting.

"Frank, get your sorry ass out here now!"

Last night had been one thing. Last night she had to save her mother, sell her soul to a creep even the devil wouldn't want. She had played to the unctuous boyfriend, allowed herself to be swept into dancing the same dance she had learned as a small child. Step, one, two, smile and kowtow even when you wanted to rip out a throat. Back, three, four, protect the mother until this one grew tired of the dance and moved on. Different boyfriends, but the dance had remained the same.

Today, things were different. Today, the school had buzzed with news. Miss Helm had been hauled in by the cops. The gossip grew in proportion to the time spent discussing it in the halls, in the lunchrooms, between bathroom stalls. By the end of sixth hour, word had it, Amber had been handcuffed by a three-hundred-pound ex-Marine and led away, accompanied by the brute and three equally loutish partners.

Kids who knew her talked of innocence and police brutality and demonstrations. Those who didn't know her made up their own fantasies. It made most media frenzies look like prayer vigils.

Jesus, kids were freaks.

So who's the freak that got a teacher fired?

Jocelyn knew the truth. After Amber had left last night, Frank and Evie had started in. She had to give her mother credit. Evie had spent almost forty-five seconds defending her daughter before caving in. That had been enough to set Frank exploding. By the time he was done, Evie's nose and mouth were bleeding, her left eye was swelling in record time, and she was headed for the floor, unable to avoid the sharp corner of a bookcase. The corner of the room looked like a blood-colored cubicle.

Frank refused to take the wounded woman to the hospital until Jocelyn promised not to turn him in. He had made her choose. "I'll take Evie in if you promise to keep your mouth shut."

His eyes, already bloodshot, turned feral, and he closed his lids half-way. He looked like a nightmare ready to spring.

What choice did she have? She wanted to wrap her hands around his throat and squeeze until those eyes popped out, find his slithering tongue and yank it out of his mouth while the rest of him twisted in a death throe. But Frank just stood there watching her watching him, smiling, his fingers playing with a cigarette that he twirled and broke in two.

She thought that was the worst. It wasn't.

He moved toward her, the broken halves of the cigarette forgotten, the smile still playing, his skinny body swaying to a golden oldie that sounded from 104.5 AM. Bet Dick Biondi didn't know that somewhere in Chicago Land a woman lay unconscious and bleeding while her boyfriend moved in on the daughter, swaying to "I Love Rock 'N' Roll."

"Wanna' dance, little girl?" The slap of his shoes made the lizard image complete. He was all slither and hiss. She could feel the threat of him from six feet away, his grim delight as her eyes glazed with fear in spite of her bravado.

"Not tonight, Frank. Think my mom's got a headache." Jocelyn wanted to vomit, felt her throat start to close. She kept her eyes on Frank. He was ugly, but not as ugly as a bleeding mother.

Frank paused and laughed. "You're pretty funny, aren't you." His hand reached toward her face, as if she were inches instead of feet away from him, and he gyrated his hips, dancing once again. He stroked the air. "Don't forget, little girl, I can get you any time I want to."

Jocelyn had tried to look him down. Really she did. But reality had enclosed her into her shell and she moved away. The three of them left for the hospital. The three of them lied to the staff.

Jocelyn had sold another piece of her soul.

But that had been last night. A million years ago.

Now she was home today. Home. What a cosmic joke.

A thin voice from the bedroom broke her trip down reverie lane, took the kill out of her anger. The voice was thin and insipid and all too familiar. "I'm in here, sweetheart, good as new." Jocelyn's skin crawled, and for a moment, she discovered the depth of her contempt. She just wasn't sure whom she hated the most of the three of them. Probably herself.

She managed to straighten her face by the time she walked into the bedroom. Her mother was lying on the bed, her face a collage of purple and red and black that only a demented Picasso could love. Yet Evelyn Quint had on a new nightie, a cheap pink thing picked up at some super discount place, the lace forming an eerie border for the bruises that meandered down her body.

"Come sit down, Baby, and have a talk." Evie patted a place on the bed next to her.

The rest was anticlimactic, mostly replay. "Frank's the best we got, Sweetie, and Jocelyn, baby, I love him so much." She always loved them. "He didn't really mean it."

They never did.

"He promises he'll never hit me again."

They always promised.

The "baby" did it. Jocelyn felt despair and revulsion, and a sad resignation that her whole life had come down to this moment, sitting with her mother in a ratty apartment, chatting with a woman decked out in cheap lace and a wealth of bruises, frozen in a fantasy world that just didn't stop.

And who was the bigger fool—the Evie or the daughter who had believed that her mother could change?

Chapter 22

While Jocelyn was busy with Evelyn, Ethan sat on the edge of his bed, sorting through the day's events. No wonder he had a headache. Funny how the best laid plans get plowed under. An image picked at him—two goofy men in an comedy classic.

Well, Ollie, a fine mess you've gotten us into.

Too bad this wasn't Laurel and Hardy do Chicago.

Days ago, Ethan had stood in a teacher's lounge wondering if professional courtesy was possible given that demented urge to either strangle Amber or turn tail and run. He had told himself he might be a dead man if he even acknowledged one ounce of feeling, that he'd best serve his time and run. But old hopes always trespass on the best of intentions, even the ones that might keep us safe. He had moved up to good old boy in charge of comforting, barely managing to get out with his pride intact. Now he had been summoned to figure out how to get her finely formed ass out of jail. He was really going places here. Fast.

Was he an idiot? He had finally thought he was over her, and then wham, here came the cruelest of ironies.

The last three years ran through his mind, playing like the flashes caught seconds before the car hits the wall. Yeah, hit the wall, that's what he had done, all right. Hit one big wall, a wall that hit back.

At first, right after she had left him, he saw her everywhere. She was the one who walked away, but for months she'd sneak her way back, brushing his fingertips with the memory of her skin, toying with his mouth with her taste. He'd deny her right to invade him, shut her away, but she'd creep back. Wanting shook him every time she slipped into his memories; the most primitive recesses of his brain warned him to run from any thought of her, but he wasn't strong enough to forget the smooth vanilla smell of her, the way her eyes changed, those eyes, always green but the green taking on a life of its own when she was. . . . Don't go there, buddy.

She was not an easy woman to love. Never had been. Impulsive. Self-righteous, either so damn right she'd face the devil himself and not give ground, or worse—when she failed—beating herself like a medieval monk flaying his skin in atonement.

She had broken his heart. She would do it again. But for now, he would battle demons themselves for a chance to taste her one more time.

He ran his hand down his throat and laughed.

You've just offered to save the spider. You might even be helping her weave the web.

What the hell. He'd been a fly buzzing around waiting for disaster before. Why stop now?

One of the defining things about life in this section of the city— besides the brownstones with fabulous bones faded to a Katherine Hepburn kind of beauty—was the atmosphere in coffee shops like Mr. Peasley's. Old millwork, a tin ceiling, scuffed wooden steps that led to elevated levels for reading or conversation over a mocha whatever and a bit of briotta. Perfect place for a poetry reading.

Too bad. Ethan felt like a Pict warrior asked to high tea, tucked away in the second level's back corner, poking at a raspberry tart that seemed to go with the place. He put his fork down and drank his coffee. The stuff was bitter. He was more used to sports bars or Irish pubs—hardly knew what to do without twenty television sets paying homage to ESPN. Besides, an artsy coffee shop was hardly the place to figure out how to help Amber.

How the hell did she get caught up in this mess? When he'd gone to her house last night, she'd run on about some guy named Frank, mixed in images of blood and her dead mother, her eyes scoured with tears and swollen. He hadn't even given much thought to the content of her ranting, he was so caught in trying to calm her, let her get some sleep.

He looked across the upper level, irritation nipping him like a ditzy toy dog. Where was Maggie anyway? He was on his second cup of coffee and no sign of her. At this rate, he'd be so wired on caffeine, he'd probably wind up in jail with Amber. He had to calm down, get focused.

Dammit. Where was that woman?

Just as he was about to stab his tart crust in frustration, Maggie stormed across the narrow floor, slid into the booth across from him, and smacked down a latte-to-go. "Sorry I'm late. I was talking to Amber."

Ethan set down his fork and fingered the crust on his plate while Maggie took a sip of the drink, shook her head and grimaced. "God, this is hot."

She set the cup down. "What the hell, so am I."

Ethan waited for her to begin, watched her relax her expression while she pushed her cup toward Ethan, then pulled it back.

Instead of talking, Maggie pitched her head backward and gritted her teeth, drawing in air, a fuming in that rolling-your-eyes kind of churning, part anger, part question. Her mouth puckered, then she picked up a spoon and tapped it on the table, once, twice. By the third time, Ethan was ready to slap her, but finally she spoke.

"How could that little bitch accuse her? Why would she say Amber punched out her mother?" Ethan turned her question over in his mind, as if the act of them repeating it would bring on an epiphany.

Maggie continued her tirade, spilling out her frustration in the tone of her voice, the swaying of her head, the whole problem bullying her.

"No way would Amber hit anyone. Especially a parent. Give her some grief and she'd sit the family down and read everybody a story, or else make them write about their feelings." She rolled her eyes for emphasis. "And then she'd check their journaling for voice."

Ethan gave Maggie a wry smile. "They'd be there because she'd slapped them with a detention. She's a manic do-gooder, lets herself get worked up over some cause and then kicks herself when she's in trouble." Ethan caught Maggie's look. Her eyes had darkened. Too bad. He would still have his say. Maggie wasn't the only one who knew Amber. "The Amber now is the one who invented pluck. The one I know is the Amber who plays tug-of-war with herself. If she were a terrorist, she'd have an apology for causing distress. That and a triple dose of guilt."

Maggie leaned forward, watching the table, her long index finger tracing the rim of her coffee cup, her lips tightening. Her words came out like bullets. "Great, boyfriend. That's just what Amber needs. A little more criticism." She paused and looked up, her whole face bent in hostility. "And where do you get off thinking you know her more than we do?"

She shook her head but at least leaned back out of fight position. "How's about we figure out how to get her out of trouble instead of trashing her."

"Look, no way am I about to trash anything. And I sure as hell don't mean to stomp on your friendship." His words turned slow. " I don't know how much Amber told you about us . . ."

On that, Maggie's eyes widened and her lips loosened—in amusement? Ethan's intensity dropped several notches. "I guess she told you . . . ?"

"Only enough to know you as the stimulus for some intense chocolate indulgence and at least one very bad St. Patrick's Day night full of green beer and drunken tears."

Maggie pursed her lips and her voice turned serious again. "Look, Amber's in trouble. Who cares about your sex life." She tried her coffee again, her face neutral.

He shook his head. "I keep having this feeling that our history, all that has brought me here as some kind of expert on Amber, has taken on a life of its own and is pushing at me, trying to get me to figure out what makes Amber tick . . ."

He leaned in toward the silent Maggie still sipping. "The first time I saw her, I thought 'preppie brat'." That brought the coffee drinking to a halt. Ethan wasn't sure whether it was the coffee or the conversation. But then Maggie nodded her head, the kind of nod that says, "I've seen that."

They had a link started. He could even laugh, not too much of course—he didn't want hot coffee in his face.

"She was sitting in the front row of our writing classroom, front row for God's sake. She sat there for the first three days, taking in everything as gospel, her back straight while she wrote down every word."

"That's our Amber. Get those notes down and get them right. She still takes notes during department meetings." Where Maggie had been giving him side looks of distrust, now she nodded in agreement. "Drives me crazy," she said.

Caught up in the story, Ethan leaned forward. "When she finally read one of her own pieces, it was pure junior high. I actually had to check the sarcasm when it came time for my feedback." He gave an easy smile at the memory.

Maggie's lips tightened and she furrowed her brows. Amber and criticism were no match.

Ethan read her look. Like it did any good. "She came unglued, stood outside our classroom, rigid with rage, sure of the justice of her wrath and the injustice of my words. Probably not the Amber you know and love." He sat up straight and cocked his head. His words sharp, they echoed the anger of a retort still remembered.

"Oh, really? I'm insipid? What I am is surprised that you know the word. You obviously don't know the rules about critiquing. Save your cheap shots for the PE complex."

Maggie backed away, just a slight movement, and weighed what he had said, the tone, the words themselves. "Unglued, I can see. Insipid? That's an Amber I never met. Amber's smart, and it's a smart full of insight, central to her core. She knows more ways to get kids writing than the rest of the department combined."

Ethan shook his head. "But to her, back then as a student, the insight was bottled up and the experience of writing with a voice nonexistent. You see the grown-up end product, the teacher, safe and in control. I saw the novice, the girl in the making."

"No wonder you coming here flipped her out." Maggie grinned like a Cheshire cat. "You've seen her naked, my friend, very, very, naked, the nasty, inside-your-gut-naked that isn't much fun. Amber does not like surprises, especially ones that make her feel vulnerable." She paused. "The other kind of naked, that might be just fine . . ."

Ethan tried to smile, but it came out too tight-lipped to be friendly. Maggie was getting too close. "The point I'm trying to make. . ." He stopped to collect himself. "Just like you said, Amber is smart." Something nudged at him. Hadn't Amber said something about grade school last night? What was it? Part of him searched for the answer while the rest of him continued to talk "She hates looking stupid. She's too afraid to step outside of herself to make any leaps or critical judgment."

"She's also a fixation ready to happen when she's on a mission. Why do you think the school chooses her for its pet projects?" Maggie's tone said a lot. This was concern, not a compliment.

"That's just it. When the project is outside herself, she's a terrier with a new bone." He paused, looking for the right words. His forehead tensed, and he glanced at Maggie waiting for a response? How much could he reveal, even to the best friend? Too bad they couldn't just throw some runes or cut open a chicken and read the signs. "Let's just call a truce and start over. Have you heard from Duane since. . . ?" A half-smile finished the question.

"No."

"Any political rumblings?"

"No, but in an age of phobias, anyone might call for Amber's head."

"I just can't believe things will get that far."

Maggie put down her cup. "Maybe not in Iowa, but this is the big city. Everyone's looking for molesters and abusers wherever public officials lurk. Schools are very paranoid about bad publicity." She took up her cup again, as if the caffeine would send her insight, like electricity moving through ceramic instead of metal.

"I called her lawyer." She lifted her eyes toward the ceiling. "Of course, I can't say what I called him." Her voice held that panicked edge of those who look to humor for comfort in times of crisis. Ethan found himself starting to relax, to even like her. "So she has a lawyer, probably a pretty darn good one given the family connections."

Maggie's voice dripped sarcasm on the last two words. Ethan understood that revelation. They shared more than a concern for Amber. Both knew of the family dance.

He took over. "The big concern will be to keep this all quiet. If the police don't press charges, it should all die down for now. At least until the mother is out of the hospital. How much do you know about that?"

"Not a whole lot. Amber's had a burr up her butt about this Jocelyn Quint since the first day of school. She can't just be a fireman and get kittens out of trees. Not our Amber. No, she has to tilt at windmills . . . she has to knock the damn things down over stray kids. If only she weren't the misplaced saint of impossible dreams." From her tone, the words were a compliment.

"Well, Don Quixote notwithstanding, the family lawyer will be able to smooth things out for now and give us some time to help. We just need to keep a lid on the gossip and make sure as few people find out about all this as possible." He ran his hand through his hair and chuckled. "Although I've got to believe that the rumor mongers will have a heyday with this one. Teacher escorted from school by police."

Maggie turned white and let out a list of expletives that might just possibly shock a Marine. Ethan grabbed his coffee mug and backed away, unconsciously. A lot of blue words had passed by him in his lifetime—he was no prude, for crying out loud—but Maggie was something beyond beholding.

"Don't give me that stoney look, Mr. Ethan Michaels. She's my best friend and her ass is about to get hung up on a meat hook."

Ethan looked at Maggie, watched her finger pointing at him like he was some junior high miscreant. He leaned forward, inch by inch, like he was trying to approach a wounded animal, wanting to help but wary of losing a hand. "Look Maggie, I hardly think the Chicago Police Department will hang Amber on anything."

Maggie shook her head. This guy was dumb. He was supposed to know Amber. "I'm not talking about the police, Ethan. I'm talking about Amber's parents. If Robert Dobron is the family lawyer, then the family is going to find out about Amber's little trip to the precinct. Do you have any idea what Momma will do when she finds out her daughter's been taken in for questioning? The bombing of Dresden will look like a wiener roast next to that moment. It doesn't take a brain surgeon to see the kind of choke-hold Lillian and Charles have over their daughter."

Ethan looked at her, taking in the eyes that waited for a response as she sipped her coffee, then he leaned back slowly, his back pressed against the chair. Oh yes, how well he knew their choke hold. He couldn't help a small laugh of irony at this point in their relationship. The Helms' lawyer would keep Amber covered, at least until . . . . Hell, Ethan had no idea where *until* led.

Chapter 23

Amber's exhaustion this morning had nothing on how she felt by 5:00 that evening. Every part of her ached—her head, her back, her legs, even her toenails. If mood could be a color, hers was a dark shade of sludge. Robert had suggested she turn off the phone—no big surprise. She could only imagine the speculation that had buzzed through the school as she was escorted out and placed in Calavari's car. At some point, she knew, she would have to start answering to the curious, but right now all she could think of was a shower's powerful water kneading out the knots in her neck and shoulders.

She dumped her purse on her bed, then pulled her dress over her shoulders while she used her toes to edge off her sandals. Underwear dropped next, added to the pile. Funny how the usual twinge of guilt over clothes dumped onto the floor didn't bother her today.

Guess a few hours in jail did that to a girl.

While she waited for the shower to warm up, she leaned against the bathroom counter, testing the depth of her anxiety while the water heater did its thing. She started playing with her nails—an old habit—noticed a cuticle that needed trimming and turned around to rummage for a nail clipper. She stopped up short when she looked at herself in the mirror.

And scowled.

What absurdity. She had spent several hours at the Halstead Station Police Precinct accused of aggravated assault, listened to the family lawyer spit out instructions and a host of recourses for the "what if's" that hadn't even occurred to her while he drove her to her house, and now she was standing in front of a mirror, tired and naked and worried about a hangnail. She would be lucky to not find *Our Miss Felon* scrawled on the board tomorrow morning—that is if she even had a job tomorrow. What was the penalty for a trip to the slammer anyway?

Twenty minutes later, she was in her living room towel-drying her hair, clean but scruffy in buffalo plaid flannel shorts and an old gray tee-shirt when the doorbell rang.

Great. The phone was out of commission for a while, but a door bell was forever. She made her way over to the door, still toweling her hair—hey world, in the criminal realm, what you see is what you get—and looked through the peep hole to see Dr. Aaron and Duane Murphy standing there. She stood there, motionless, eyeing them, trying to frame their presence into some sort of sense. Any meeting with Liz Aaron had been at school, comparatively relaxed, humor popping in strategic places to deal with a budget crisis or an impossible timeline.

This visit held no promise of humor. Liz's face was completely stoic, pure professionalism, and Duane's face was, well it was Duane's, a tight smile and tight eyes on a head that bobbed up and down, no doubt in anxiety. Duane did not like confrontation, and Amber was sure that the two of them were not buzzing her for a social call.

She opened the door.

"Liz. Duane. What a surprise." Ushering them in, her right hand held the door, her left one slapped the towel against her leg. Her mind thought *What the hell*. She tried a little humor out of habit, nervousness, or survival instinct. Who knew. "I'm afraid you've caught me at my worst," she said, rubbing the damp towel against her head as proof positive.

Damn hair? Not as bad as handcuffs.

Never one to let rank or propriety curb his movement, Duane moved ahead of Dr. Aaron and entered the hallway, at the same time taking Amber's hand and squeezing, oozing support like a best friend who's just found out the most damaging gossip. "Miss Helm, don't you worry a bit. We're all behind you one hundred per cent." The principal maintained her perfect posture and professional demeanor, her hands folded while she suggested, "Mr. Murphy, Amber, why don't we have a seat in the living room and try to sort out today's events."

Amber wished she could wrap the towel around her entire self and fold into it. She had known this would happen eventually—this reckoning with the administration—but she had pictured herself a little more rested and certainly not standing there dressed like a waif, hair wet and frizzing by the minute, hand holding a towel instead of a faculty handbook outlining her rights. And by the way, what were the rights of a teacher accused of a major felony? Teachers had been fired for showing R-rated movies in class, even if they cut out the controversial parts. What chance did she have, even if she were innocent? Little bug feet of consternation crawled up her arms while she murmured, "Certainly. Have a seat. Anyone care for something to drink?" Hemlock perhaps?

The amenities passed quickly. Liz Aaron was not one to chitchat, especially about something this serious. "Miss Helm. . ."

Great. She was Miss Helm, not Amber. Bad sign.

"Mr. Murphy is right. We have absolute faith in your professionalism, and thus, your innocence. The idea that you would strike a parent. . ." She shook her head as if to let the statement speak for itself, but she sat back against the sofa, a definite bad body signal. People on your side sat forward. The principal folded her hands and tapped her thumbs, then, as if remembering lessons on body language politics, sat forward, her hands placed neutrally on her knees.

"This afternoon we had a call from Mr. Copancek, who it seems, is upset that . . ." She cleared her throat and swallowed hard. "We are still employing a woman accused of assault on a parent." Liz's face softened and she closed her eyes before the return of her professional face. "This whole thing is so unfortunate, but our hands are tied. We can't ignore the demands of a parent."

Parent? Calling Frank a parent was like calling Attila the Hun a tourist. The pieces fell into place, all the questions about how they had found out the details. Amber had assumed it was the police. So much for assumptions.

"I'll be suspending you with pay until this situation is cleared up." The administrator paused, whether to let the words sink in or to search for her next phrase, who knew. Who cared. "I feel awful, but I must follow board procedure." That delivered, she sat back, a softening on her face.

Amber looked at her, saw the parts of her body, the colors she wore, and yet, she could not put together a whole. Suspended? She felt a wave of nausea well up in her, and she tried to find her voice while she waited for something to alter the jolt of what Liz had just said.

Duane spoke up. "I'm sure you'll want to contact the union representative to find out your rights." On that, Amber almost gasped. Her rights. Suddenly, gossip and the piercing stare of an Italian detective seemed child's play. She was about to be fired.

Then they were gone. Amber sat huddled in her chair, the cashmere throw around her, trying to find her mind.

They'll fire me. I've all but lost my job. My kids.

What do you expect? A certificate of appreciation for embarrassing the school, maybe even involving them in a lawsuit? If you're really lucky, Frank and Evie can waltz into your classroom and give a Power Point presentation on teachers who are fools. You'll gladly help them, of course, since Frank can barely talk much less run a computer. But what the hell, you're good at extricating yourself from screw-ups. You've had so much practice.

Your mother can watch. Maybe Ethan too. Lillian can see you tripping all over yourself to make things right, shake her head before she turns away.

Hell, let's invite the whole world.

The detritus of her life, all the sad and inept things that haunted her and made her small, paraded in front of her in a quick swirl while she waited for the judge, jury, and executioner to make a swipe.

Amber woke with a startled gasp still in her throat. She'd always hated that, waking up with that moronic half-snore still lodged in her throat. Might as well drool and make the picture complete. A fuzzy half awareness of some dream buzzed in her head. That and the knowledge that something had awakened her from a nap brought on by exhaustion.

The doorbell. There it went again. Just what she needed. More company to watch her crumble.

Amber shook her head and stood up to answer the door. I'm not asking for much. Be the pizza boy with the wrong address. Be a couple of guys dressed in really bad suits trying to save my soul. I can shut the door and say "No, thank you." Don't be anyone I know. Don't be. I've had enough stress to make me look like Grandma Wentworth snorting in her chair and denying that she had slept a wink. She ignored the gloom that hung in the room. Get goin', Amber. This won't be the last time you have to face someone. Can't play ostrich and hide in the sand.

She looked through the peephole in her front door. No pizza box. No duo dressed in sanctimony carrying a Bible.

Ethan.

She opened the door. He was posed ala John Wayne straight out of an oater, his arm rested on the doorjamb, his big hand supporting his form.

Too weary to fight, Amber felt the pull of him. It was a gravitational pull whose center had begun years ago, resurfaced just last night. Was it only this morning she had wondered what to say to him about his trip over here in the middle of the night? She closed her eyes just as the thought of her innocence forced them open to reality. Never say things are at their worst. It's an invitation.

"Evenin' Ma'am," he drawled. "Anyone in need of a friend?" His voice sounded relaxed. His eyes searched her.

How lame to respond with clichés. She did it anyway.

"Gee, we have to stop meeting like this." Her eyes started an upward roll to keep it light even though her body was made of metal. She sighed, her shoulders slumping, and motioned Ethan in with a "Sorry, my humor is caught in trite mode right now."

She let out another puff of air, just a short one. "In fact, come to think of it, my humor is pretty well spent. Just like the rest of me."

Embarrassed, she raised her chin and managed a smile. "Really. I'm always glad to see a cowpoke willing to leave the range. Come on in."

The push of knowledge startled her, but in such a good way. Some of the aches even gave up their hold. Ethan's presence. It outweighed the quicksand of all the realities that surrounded her, sucking away her endurance.

Together, they walked into her living room and sat down, each of them facing each other on the ends of her couch. Ethan's easy smile kept on her, waiting. But what was that in his eyes? Sympathy? Disappointment? He was under her roof again, this time uninvited, laid back like a shrink waiting for the patient to start. What had unleashed in her at his sudden presence now ebbed. What was she supposed to say? How could she even begin to talk out her dread?

"How about if I start?" The words made her give an involuntary jump even while they told her he wanted to help. He kept the warmth of the smile while he told her about his meeting with Maggie, who sent her love, by the way. Then he calmly listened to Amber give the details of the her visit from Liz and Duane. He smiled, frowned, shook his head occasionally but let Amber do the talking.

Finally she was quiet, clear down to her body language.

"How many times have you beaten yourself up tonight?" Some question. All the possibilities they could choose, and Ethan chose that one.

Smart Ethan.

"Come on, you know I know you. And I know you've hauled out those whips and chains and that one nasty hair shirt. So let's get to the bottom line. List your sins one by one so we can take a look." He leaned forward and spoke more slowly. "And then we can put most of them away and deal with the ones that count."

He was so calm. He was always so damn calm.

Calm and frantic could never mix.

Amber shook her head, her lips tightened, and her fears spat out through her voice, surprising even her. "Who the hell do you think you are? You always think you've got all the answers, don't you."

Ethan stayed still, his face cool, posture waiting. The whole world had changed since he had rushed over last night. She leaned back and closed her eyes. "I don't know what drives me more crazy. That you think you can come in here and tell me what's what . . . or that you're usually right." She covered the top of her face with a pillow, trying to ward off his words. She hated people who were right. She scoffed once, put the pillow aside and sat up, an act of sheer courage. "Okay," she said. "Let's hear it."

Ethan had been silent, watching her. Now he gave her an half smile and held up his index finger. His words held the gentle sarcasm of one friend trying to coax the other into friendly submission. "You drew out a student who has been locked in pain for years." Amber sat there, her face a mask. Ethan's middle finger went up. "Next, you cared enough to put yourself at risk to help her, at risk only after you sought help from other sources. You took the time to make a home visit for a positive reason to help that student. Yeah, I'd say you're a screw-up. Teachers aren't supposed to care after all, just get those reading scores up."

"Easy for you to say. You're not the one about to go to jail and get canned."

He let down his fingers. His voice deepened, let go of the chiding. "You can be angry with me if it helps." She watched him searching her face. His voice softened. "You look so stressed."

"Stressed?" Amber laughed. "I am so beyond stressed I could howl at the moon." She looked down at her hand. The laugh turned to a whisper.

"Why are you here?"

Ethan shrugged. "Last night, you couldn't wait for me to get here. What's changed?" He reached for a stray red curl that had fallen onto her face and moved it back.

She shook her head and pulled her hair away, a sure sign of early meltdown. "Last night, the bogeyman let loose. I needed a strong guy like you to chase it away."

"And tonight?"

Amber leaned her head against the sofa, her head in her hand, fingers massaging her temple.

"Different bogeyman. No blood. No knife." She sighed. "Just a pink slip and the end of all my dreams."

Ethan pulled her toward him. She felt empty, lying there with her head on his shoulder, like a scarecrow without the straw, his body warmed her, his chest, his hands. She felt the heat move through her, working toward her back. It gave her strength.

He expected sighs, a few tears, not the closing off of her body after such utter slack, the strength of her voice. Not the way she sat up and gave him a smile. But then, she had been surprising him since they'd met.

Once, he had been no more than a writing partner and a burgeoning strength for a girl sobbing in his arms. Now he was a man wrapped in a mission holding a woman, one who surprised him with this sudden resurrection.

She sat across from him, wrapped her hands into his.

"Enough pity party. You came to play cowboy? Wrong game. Tomorrow we get to play detective."

Her smile was tight and determined. "No one takes away my kids. No one."

Chapter 24

Amber's breakfast was one of those egg sandwiches that fed America on the run, great grease, the only cleanup a crumb of biscuit that had spilled onto her shirt. She swallowed the last bite as she pulled into the parking lot outside the law firm of Robert Dobron, her soon-to-be savior, then licked her fingertips to finish off the meal.

She tasted more than grease. She tasted hope.

This would be a turnaround day. Had to be. The sun was shining, its warmth edged by a cool breeze. Great omen, that sun. Only two people had run red lights, and no horns had blared any road rage.

Yeah. And nobody's come forward to help you either. With a shudder, she acknowledged the moment of her fear, then plucked a crumb off her shirt and flicked it away, taking the time to practice a sense of control. Last night she had committed to success. The old Amber was gone, the one who ate her dread. This was the new Amber, the resolute Amber. No matter how hopeless her situation seemed, no matter how futile last night's vows might become, no matter if she suffered from the worst case of self-delusion in history, she had to stand firm. Again, her fingers flicked her shirt where the crumb had laid—three times.

She raised her head, took a deep breath, and got out of her car. As she slammed her car door shut and headed across the parking lot, Amber thought of Robert's deftness with the detective yesterday and smiled.

She had Robert Dobron on her side. That and her pit-bull determination to reclaim her job.

Amber looked at the door to Robert's building. Robert G. Dobron ESQ. and Associates. The words etched in black spoke of hope—at least of a chance. Another good sign. Even the door wanted her there. She pushed the outside door open wide, walked ahead of the swoosh as it closed. Inside, it was like moving through class, lemon polish in the entryway greeting prospective clients, the line of photographs of important people who had moved through the lawyers' lives, the lines of awards garnered by the firm, all these assuring those who walked there of the firm's professional best. By the time Amber reached the oak door leading to the main offices, she felt downright heady with security.

As she took the bronze doorknob in her hand, she turned to look at the last picture, one with Robert shaking hands with the governor, and said, "This is it. We've got the bastard." She nodded at Robert's presence, his powerful handshake, his determined face and felt downright powerful.

By Monday, no doubt, she would be well on her way to reclaiming her job.

It was about time.

So far, the morning had sped by. Robert had called her at eight-thirty. "I need you to come into the office today. We have the research done on Mr. Copencek, and it's pretty interesting. How about 10:00?" Amber's elation had mixed with the black of even hearing his name as a bit of the past wormed its way into the thrill of the news. Sitting cross-legged on the bed, she had raised her head and shut her eyes, repeating her mantra until his presence was history. "No way, buster. No way. You are definitely worm food." She'd moved through the sentences, playing with words. "*You* are worm food. You are *worm* food. You are worm *food*." Funny how a speech exercise worked at home to calm the spirit.

Now she sat in the outer office. To an outsider, she was a young woman reading a magazine, flipping through the pages without a care. Inside, she was an avenger, reveling once again in the morning words, ready to wipe away the scum from her life and reclaim what was hers.

"Miss Helm. Mr. Dobron will see you now."

The lawyer stood up as soon as she entered. Instead of a formal, "Take a seat" directed to maintain a formal distance between client and professional, Robert said, "Pull that chair up close. I have some very interesting news about our Frank."

Our Frank. You betcha, Robert. Might and Right armed to the teeth.

"First, the good news."

"What do you mean, 'first'? It's all good, isn't it?"

"Frank Copencek has been picked up for all sorts of mischief ranging from petty larceny to assault."

"That's wonderful! I knew he was a criminal."

"He and his cronies have made quite the name for themselves on the South Side. I'm surprised Detective Calavari hadn't heard of him."

"Don't the Chicago police have a system to track criminals?"

"That's part of the problem. The system is based on convictions. Ergo, the problem. I'm sorry, my dear, but we've just entered the realm of bad news. As much of a slime Mr. Copencek seems to be, he's never been convicted."

Outside, the sun kept its blessing, and the traffic was still relatively civilized, but Amber's firm spirit sagged. To hide that annoying urge to dance her right leg in a nervous tic, she crossed her legs at the ankle and sat with her best private school posture, staring at Robert while she tried to gain composure. All that training dissipated while her throat turned dry and her whole body shrank inward. Her head ached.

"That's it? He gets away with it?" Her voice turned shrill. "Robert, he's a monster!"

Robert gave a gentle shake of his head and reached across to take her hands. They were large. Warm. He squeezed gently, just the slightest squeeze, one of calmness and reassurance.

Amber forced out the tension. Her voice was even.

"So where does that leave me?"

"Where does that leave us, my dear." Robert's voice was the voice of a friend, a lifelong friend, his presence at her home more often than not an informal meeting of minds between Robert and her father.

Her family. Robert Dobron wasn't her lawyer; he was the family lawyer, a lawyer and friend who would feel obligated to go to her parents with the sad news of their imbecile daughter. While she rode to the station with Detective Calavari, pictures had whirled inside her. She had set them aside during the rush of panic that had followed, but they had found their rightful place once again. Her father's sternness, posture military perfect. Her mother's tight lips, how she would rub her forehead with three fingers as if willing the stress not to engulf her. *Daughter, how could you disgrace us so. Have you no decency? Stupid, thoughtless girl.*

"Amber . . ." She looked up. Somehow, her head had wound up in her hands and her right heel was pounding the floor. Robert was talking to her, his hands no longer soothing hers, instead gripping the arms of her chair as he hovered close to her. The images of her parents still weighed on her and she stayed crumpled from their burden.

The old Amber was back.

"Robert, you've got to promise me. You can't go to my parents. I would rather fall off the ends of the earth than face them. Please, Robert." Her voice was a rasp, her words spilling in a plea.

The lawyer stood up, backed away, hands in his coat pockets. He kept his voice even.

"Amber Elizabeth Helm, you are my client. I promise you all the confidence that my profession demands." His manner relaxed and he wore the warmth of a friend. "Remember, my dear, not only do I know you, I know your parents. They are my friends, but I repeat . . . I know your parents. If they find out about this predicament, it will not be from me."

"And you can take that to the bank." He smiled and his voice deepened. "As long as it isn't your father's bank."

She sat back in the chair, her head resting on its back, her neck rubbing against the nub of the fabric. Her throat was tight. The strain of her throat pulling reassured her. She was alive, capable of action. She could feel.

No way would Frank win. She would make sure he was behind bars for hurting that child. Whatever it took.

Chapter 25

Some Roman guy said his life was a song, its melody scribbled on the wind. I heard that somewhere. Hey, Mr. Roman, meet me, the girl whose melody's scratched in shit.

Thursday night had been filled with dreams only in black and white. Even her dreams had been too depressed to have any color. The day seemed destined to go the same way. Another morning in Crazy Land. Time to get up and see who we can screw up today. Hell, it was Friday. The week was almost over. Let's get moving.

Jocelyn sat on the edge of her bed, a low growl gurgling in her throat as she let today play in her mind. The little bitch she had threatened to eviscerate yesterday afternoon had called a conflict management meeting for today, whatever the hell that was. Conflict management. What a bunch of crap. All the schools she moved in and out of had some sort of gimmick to get kids to sit down and talk. All things, of course, could be solved with a little talking, then maybe a quick round of Kumbayah.

Great. My mother's living a sot's prom with Frank, and today, Amber Helm starts her suspension. All because of me. She pictured the cozy scene that might play out in the guidance counselor's office. Sure, I'll talk. What'll we talk about? I know. Gee, Ms. Butler, I'm a little edgy today. Old Frank put Mom in the hospital the other night and made me swear that the one decent person who ever bothered to listen to me or even notice me somehow went berserk and pummeled her, sent her crashing to the floor for a really good skull crash. I could tell the truth and keep her out of trouble, but oh yeah, then my boozer mother's boyfriend will carve me a new asshole and probably fuck me when he's done. And then there won't be anyone to take care of Vodka Momma who's on a mission to kill herself anyway, and probably could care less if I'm dead as long as she gets to keep on slogging down that booze with her loser boyfriend.

Yeah. Hellofaconversation we can have over that.

Loser mother's loser boyfriend puts mother in hospital.

Loser daughter puts teacher in jail.

Jocelyn grabbed her pillow and held it to her, wondering about Amber all right, but it was a wondering that was gray with futility. Her body didn't have the will to summon up a decent tightening. She had a metaphoric gun to her head, could feel the coldness of the barrel snaking its way down toward her neck. That was her reality, that and the knowledge that a lizard held his finger on the trigger and would love to pull while he laughed at the fun of it. She was alone. So what was new?

Clouds hung low in the fall sky trying to threaten rain but just too tired to let loose a downpour. Students slugged from class to class, bored looks broken only by an occasional, "Look out, asshole!" when somebody bumped the wrong person. A few freshmen and the standard school weirdoes made some noise, but that was to be expected. Only a visit by God could get them to be quiet. Overall, the mood of the school matched Jocelyn's.

She stood just to the left of the second floor steps, wedged against the wall. Nobody noticed, those insects on their way to more bullshit in their pitiful lives, hurrying off to nothing before the bell rang. And rang it did. A few idiots worried about tardies ran for doors that would swallow them. She didn't care. She had her wall.

People talked about being a bug on the wall when they wanted to be nosy. She was a bug all right. But nosy? Not on your life. Here she was, rear end and head next to the boiler room door. Pretty appropriate, doorway to the bowels of the earth. She slid over, nothing more than a shadow in the hallway, pressed her back against the door, wishing she could rearrange her molecules and become part of its gray metal. She leaned in harder, hiding from the hall patrol that ferreted out kids like her, the ones who made skipping an art. Or maybe she just wanted to feel the hardness of the wall.

Lunch was still an hour away. No problem. Even double pizza and a couple bags of Cheetos couldn't tempt her. Only one thing baited her, called out like a banshee wailing on a moonlit night. Butler's office. God knows, she'd spent enough time there this morning working out her *conflict* with Bimbo Barbie, yet here she was thinking about that place again. Butler got under her skin, that little smile and those eyes of hers that looked so soft and understanding. Her life was full of soft eyes and lying promises.

Even Miss "I understand your plight, I'll save you Helm."

Especially that bleeding heart. Just another teacher with a bigger lie. She came to the house, marched in to save poor abused Jocelyn. Big save. Another do-gooder in her life that bucked and ran.

What the hell, what did feeling ever get her anyway, just a load of crap from a string of men, and another sob from the gutless bitch who had borne her. She was a lump, a fundamentally gutless kid, unlovable yet longing. She was a fool.

Mouthing all that anger gave way to the deepest fury. The dull hunger of her wrath pushed through her veins, and she pushed out air to clear her gut. She felt the heat in her face and the harshness of her breathing.

They were just like her mother. When she was drunk or wanting. Jocelyn would have walked over hot coals for her mother's look to be that real. Eyes closed, she struggled to pull her shell over the hurt, cementing it once again. It had always been easy before, this compression of longing within her. Smash it into smithereens before it grew into hope.

She slid down to the floor and sat there, student without a classroom, sinner hunched over, while behind classroom doors, students pretended to learn. Maybe a few suckers even cared.

Her mind played the litany of the previous night like a mantra. Her mother wanted a lawsuit. A freakin' lawsuit. She kept the image of her mother like a brand while she willed herself not to feel.

Nothing. The hall kept its silence while her misery deepened, the loathing that pressed on her, the loathing mostly for herself.

Jocelyn, the tough one, the one who never let anything get to her—not the inane jawing of mindless classmates, not the bullshit authority figures who babbled their own inanities, not the steady pounding of others' betrayal. Jocelyn could not summon numbness.

Her eyes closed and she fingered the chains on her neck. A pipe clanked on the other side of the wall. She jerked at the sound. Her mind took a turn and a voice came from somewhere deep, started as a niggling worm working its way into attention before it grew strong enough to make her grit her teeth and shake. She could feel it, masses of feeling, wet and growing like flotsam fighting its way to the surface.

She came to your house, idiot. So what if she ran. You'd run, too, if someone came at you with a broken bottle and a leer.

The image of Amber fleeing the apartment gnawed at her. Her stomach roiled and an intensity hardened in her neck and chest. The truth swirled in the back of her head. Her eyes hurt, and her mouth tasted like sandpaper.

Not everyone has screwed you over. Not everyone wants to use you and throw you away or make promises made out of cotton candy. And if you don't do something, if you don't have the guts to rise above the assholes, then what are you anyway?

The pipes started up again—as if signaling to her to take action. She sat there for a moment, clinging to her books, a lump in a deserted hallway as guilt wrung tears. Then she forced herself upward and wiped away the bitterness. Pity party's over.

So what are you waiting for, Goth Girl. Get in there and tell Butler the truth.

Chapter 26

All kids understood the geography of a school—where they were welcomed, where they were no more than a headache. Welcome trumped headache every time. That's why kids milled around the guidance office during lunch or after school—or best yet, during study hall. At least the normal ones.

Thank god only one was there right now. Jocelyn slumped in her chair, a knot of indecision, far cry from kid on a mission back around the corner just a few minutes ago, the one who had kicked herself with a need to spill the truth and set things right. Her eyes ached from last night's lack of sleep and today's lack of courage, and a whole slew of guilt that had pounded at her all night and led her here. The kids all said Butler could be trusted, but what did a woman who kept stuffed animals in her office know about life with Frank and Evie?

Mrs. Butler was sitting in her chair waiting, had already called the main office and asked them to hold her calls and any drop-in appointments. It was just the guidance counselor and the kid in need of guidance, a couple of chicks hanging out and gearing up for a chat. Right. Posters spoke of self-esteem and life choices. A jar of cherry licorice sat on the desk. And, of course, those fluffy creatures on the file cabinet just waited to be hugged.

Jocelyn kept rocking in the chair Marti had offered her. She hated herself for the need to keep moving. Cozy scene all right.

The first words seemed calm. Jocelyn had even leaned forward in the coolness of her intent. "Look, before I try to sort all this out with you, I want . . ."

She stopped there. What Jocelyn wanted didn't count. What she wanted had landed everybody into this mess in the first place. She shook her head and held her lips tight. "It's all my fault. This whole freakin' mess."

Marti didn't so much as move. Her words came out soft and even. "Okay, tell me about it. Why don't you tell me what the mess is, and we'll worry about the fault later."

Funny thing about dams. Once the cracks have weakened it, once those cracks turn to holes, the whole structure falls apart. Jocelyn's first words had come so self-assured. The dam she had erected wanted to stay tight, but the force of the flood behind it was too intense, and had been weakened—this time, too much to hold. The words poured out, sometimes incoherent, often mixed with tears and a level of profanity that spoke of anger and genius and a background no child should own. With the flood came a strange sensation, a tingling like fingers of electricity running up and down her arms, and then her legs, and then all through her like once the words came, feeling came, too.

The anger rose along with the feelings. Such a fury. It roiled in her, taking on a life of its own. In fourth grade, some doofus had told the class about a woman hung upside down to release a tapeworm thirty feet long. The thing had wound itself around her intestines and needed to be lured out with a bowl of milk. Jocelyn had her own thing wrapped inside her, just as parasitic. It slid up through her as she reconnected to feelings long dormant.

In the back cubbyhole of Marti's office, hidden from the world, Jocelyn let forth a wrath that would make the gods jealous. She pounded the walls. She threw the seat cushion. She threw the magic markers and books stored in the bookshelf. When she had spent herself, she sat on the floor, doubled over, and cried silently, huge sobs of boundaries broken and pain swallowed.

While Jocelyn was in the back room working out her grief, Marti started the process. She called the Department of Human Services. Yes, they could send Gerri. No problem. She and Marti had plugged holes and worked miracles before. Maybe one was due now.

Luckily, first hour was Maggie's prep time. Marti called her next. No privacy break there. Jocelyn's story had included permission for Ms. Witkowski to act as the bridge in helping Miss Helm.

Once the calls were made, Marti went to the back room, turned out the lights and sat with the child like one friend helping another survive the pain of a wake.

Chapter 27

Jocelyn had waited out the remainder of the day in the nurse's office. Two days earlier, if anyone had told Jocelyn Quint that she would spend her day moving in and out of sleep in a nurse's office, the girl would have given her best "Are you nuts" frown and walked away.

Yet here she was, her mind half-drugged from the roller coaster ride that had begun her morning, taking in the stillness of a school building on a Friday thirty minutes after the bell had rung. Not a soul around, except, of course, for Mrs. Butler. Jocelyn would spend the weekend with her until plans could be made on Monday.

The DHS worker told Jocelyn that she could stay with a friend. That was out. Jocelyn had no friends. Or, she could go home if she wanted. Leave it to a social worker to suggest that bit of heaven. That left Jocelyn and Mrs. Butler planning for the night.

"My husband's out of town until tomorrow night. How about a pizza?"

They had wolfed down a pizza at Giovanio's and were indulging in a mutual pepperoni high when Marti grimaced.

"I left the DHS papers on my desk. We need to have them filled out Monday morning." She rummaged through her purse, pulled out her keys and shook them. Her face looked stressed, but her eyes were soft with apology. "Sorry. We have to go back and pick them up. Knowing the government, we have about an hour's work ahead of us. We can grab them and make it back to my house in less than twenty minutes."

Jocelyn was so buoyed up by tomato sauce and satisfaction that she didn't mind the trip back at all. Anything beat the Frank and Evie show right now.

When they reached the parking lot, they both noticed the light on in Amber's classroom. Marti squeezed Jocelyn's hand. "I bet Miss Helm is enjoying what your courage has bought her."

A chill grabbed her, slowed her down, the grip of her emotion stuck in her mouth like so much cotton—but only for a step or two. Strangely, her hands felt especially warm. Mrs. Butler's next words wrapped around her. "I know, sweetie. I love her, too. Now let's get those reports before it's too late to eat ice cream."

Once they were in the office, however, it made sense to just get business finished, especially now that the school was quiet. "When we get to my house, you need to relax, not worry about filling out forms. The ice cream will taste that much better." The smile was all knowing. "Why don't you take a little walk while I finish these up."

Damn, that woman was smart. She knew that Jocelyn had unfinished business in a sophomore English class that had almost lost its teacher. Maybe she was even too smart to leave papers on her desk. Maybe she set up coincidences so that they could happen.

The classroom, itself, waited in semidarkness for the students to return on Monday. Low flung light seeped in from the hall, and the security lights outside sent eerie shards through the room's three large windows. Desks, neatly lined up by the janitors, looked like lonely tombstones lit by the rays of a white moon. Amber sat there in the back, out of the light's range, hooded in the dark, the whirl of the ceiling fan like music, its coolness a balm even in the evening's coolness. Closing her eyes, she let the sound run through her. She was in her room.

Her room.

An awareness spooled within her, keeping time with the faint beat of the fan. She was reclaiming the very thing she loved, the job that, in her heart, was hers as much as her breath or a single pulse.

Running her hands along the length of the desk, she let her mind follow the track of the day. Maggie had called at 11:00.

"She told the truth. You're back!" The school had called. "Miss Helm, you may report on Monday." One had buoyed her, the other—she wasn't sure what she felt.

Strange. Her first reaction to Maggie's call had not been for herself. She had pictured Jocelyn's life, frame by frame, seeing the cheap and the horrifying, the sum of neglect and danger not reported in the child's cumulative file. Maggie's reaction to her questions about Jocelyn surprised her—just a little. "I know, sweetie, she's safe."

Safe. Jocelyn was safe. It felt like one of those perfect moments, a first snow, the brush of a kiss, so tender was the joy that spread through her as she let herself feel the news. Then the two friends whooped and cheered, each of them carrying on like junior high kids over the new boy at school.

"I figured you'd be in here."

Amber's head snapped up. She could see the darkened image in the doorway. She knew the voice.

"Jocelyn." Her arms flushed with the touch of awareness as she rose. She wanted to run over and hug her savior, but her feet held firm. "Come on in."

Jocelyn edged closer. "Are you sure?" Her tone was low, the sound moving across the space between them the only break in the dusky room. "I figured, well with every thing's that gone on today, with all that crap about—you know—I might be the last one you'd want to see." Her words hung there, waiting. DHS is letting me stay with Mrs. Butler tonight. Tomorrow . . . ." Amber heard the catch in her throat and the sad silence, then reached out to the child with her words. "Isn't it great that there is a tomorrow." She rose and moved forward, closing the gap between them. She was there, hugging Jocelyn, hardly aware of the trip across the room. Amber's body warmed as Jocelyn's arms fumbled and then met her. She felt the child's shaking as she cried out her story.

"I should've told the cops right away. Frank—he said he'd let her bleed there, he said he'd hurt me, he's such a prick, I'm so stupid and gutless. . ." The litany went on without a breath between the words.

"You're right. Frank is a prick."

Jocelyn's stiffness melted.

Amber let her talk out her pain and guilt, all the while holding her, giving her the emotional swaddling to keep her feeling safe, acting like the mother Jocelyn had always wanted.

She felt the flow of Jocelyn's trust, in the tremor of Jocelyn's chest against her, in the stream of Jocelyn's words as they soaked into Amber, finally, in Jocelyn's simple whimpering when the girl was spent. Trust is a beautiful thing, the beginning of grace.

They sat there in the back of the room, a woman and a woman-child secure in a couple of dumpy recliners, calming ghosts.

The past finally buried, they looked to Jocelyn's future.

"What am I supposed to do now?" Jocelyn's recliner creaked. It had needed oiling for the last year. Now it was an exclamation point.

Amber made her answer as steady as her voice would let her.

"You'll have to be strong. We'll both have to be strong."

"Strong hasn't worked for me so far."

Amber reached over and patted Jocelyn's hand. "That's because you've always been alone." She held on for good measure. " You're not alone anymore."

"You're wrong."

Amber's throat tightened.

"I just thought I was alone. That's the point. I had to know you were there for me. Alone is when you don't know someone's there."

Jocelyn had been leaning back in the recliner. She thrust herself forward pulling her hand away, laid her head in her arms. "Miss Helm—I don't know how you did it. . ."

"Did what?"

Jocelyn bought up her head and looked forward.

"I don't know how you came and faced Frank like that. He's a weasel, but he's a nasty weasel. And then the cops—how did you get through letting the police take you away, and how did you face jail and. . . ."

Amber's laugh broke through the sluice of words. She squeezed the girl's shoulder. "You make me sound like some kind of hero."

Amber felt Jocelyn's look through the semidarkness of the room. "You are. You're the bravest person I've ever known."

Oh, Jocelyn, if you only knew.

Amber squeezed her hand. The recliner creaked again as Jocelyn's leaned forward to squeeze back in trust."

Chapter 28

Friday night. The universe had balanced itself—with a little help.

Jocelyn would stay with Marti. Evie could visit, if she wanted to and if she could keep from hassling her daughter. Marti would make sure of that. Frank was either on his way to jail or there already. Altogether not a bad couple of days for the good guys.

Tonight was party time at Gilley's. Where Amber—like most teachers—looked at the first day of the work week as a day of yawning, Amber now celebrated the pleasure of Monday—and all the many Mondays awaiting her. The beginning of the week used to bring on a groan. Now it lay there in her body, warm and wonderful. Funny how the chore of lesson plans seemed trivial and oh so sweet now that Amber's job was secure.

All that day, colleagues had phoned to assure her that they had known all along that she was never capable of such atrocious behavior, that they would have eventually stopped by or leaped to her aid. Some of them had probably even meant it. A few kids had stopped by early to welcome her back with smiles, some overt, some cautious and shy; a couple had shown more obvious signs, thumbs upturned, a couple of low fives. In fact, they promised her a glorious future with not so much as a single gum popping to test her.

Oh, those inexhaustible hoops people built for jumping. All you had to do to merit one, or a dozen, was be falsely accused of a crime.

Gilley's was its usual self. Barflies and bar stool jocks hung out at the Budweiser Central, fixated on the exploits of the team du jour, slurping beer and replaying decades of past games as if their comments would make a difference. Upstairs in the loft overlooking the main room, other celebrations were in order. A knot of teachers from George T. Clausson had gathered to celebrate a victory of their own. Good had triumphed. Frank, the evil witch of the west side had been smote, downright melted, and Amber, good witch of Clausson High, had reclaimed the ruby slippers and made her way home. Maggie was looking especially saucy. She had on her favorite tie-dyed crinkle dress, a lanky flow of red and orange and green that swayed with her dancing moves, a special Maggie dance as much born from victory as the effects of the two Blue Moon beers she had imbibed, because, "What the hell, they come with orange slices and I need my vitamin C."

Even Duane was there, promptly arriving at 4:00 before the rest of the group dropped in two or three at a time. His bald pate glistened with wisps of perspiration even though the air conditioning was running full bore, and he made his way around the three tables pulled together, eye-to-eye with each of his peers, clucking in his very special Duane manner.

Yes, this was a party. Except that the guest of honor had not yet arrived.

Right at 5:00, Amber walked in and let her gaze wander upward. She could hear the crew of them, even see them through the oak slats extended past the stairs as a token divider. Twenty-some total? Everyone loved a winner. And for tonight she was the conqueror, not the victim. Tonight, and many nights to come. She walked through the lower bar, remembering the many TGIFs she and Maggie had shared with the faculty, how many times Maggie told her to shoot her if she ever got as loud as the coaches who inevitably still played the wins and losses of games long gone.

Another thought tugged at her. Would Ethan be here? Before she could even decide whether that question was one of dread or excitement, she heard a voice call out, "Well, it's about time. What's the point of a victory party without the victor?" Leave it to a coach to holler that. Her smile brightened, and she found herself aware that she was carrying herself a little more stately, that her senses were attuned to the sights and the smells and the sounds that surrounded her.

"Hey girl, how's it feel to be free and sure of gainful employment?" Maggie raised her eyebrows and looked at her friend. "That smile on your face from beating the bad guys or you got a new girlfriend at strip-search central?" A few teachers looked shocked but most grinned.

Duane piped up, his tone chiding. "Now Ms. Witkowski. You know better than that. Our Miss Helm is saving herself for a higher calling." Just as Maggie was about to chug on that line, Duane smiled innocently. "She's no doubt offered the good Detective Cavalari to partake of some bonds of her own." Duane paused, his smile beatific. "After all, Miss Helm is a romantic."

Maggie almost choked on her beer. "Duane, you are amazing. Simply amazing."

Amber spent the next two hours replaying what could be said and bantering with the crowd. When anyone offered to buy her a drink or slip a beer glass into her hand, she gave a friendly, "No, thanks. I'm so high on excitement, I don't need anything more than you guys." And she was. The irony of being the center of attention and the only one not drinking amused her. But then, pretty much everything amused her tonight.

By 7:30, most of the crowd had gone. Only Maggie and Ethan stayed with Amber. Ethan had his arm draped over a chair and sat back. Maggie cradled her head on her hands and purred, "I don't know if every night should be Friday night, or I should be happy that I only have to do this once a week." She stayed in purring mode, and when no one answered in agreement, lifted her head.

"Okay, if you guys are going to be party poopers, I may as well go home."

Ethan grinned. "Want to have me follow you home and protect you against any cops with nothing to do but pick up wayward teachers?"

Maggie's purr deepened. "Sure, you can take me home. I need someone to tuck me in."

She didn't even bother to check for Ethan's look of surprise. "I'd even settle for you, Writer Boy. I'm too tired to move."

Ethan yawned. "And I'm too tired to even make a pass. But I'll give you a ride. Judging by the empty glasses, Maggie's had her fill of vitamin C."

Amber shook her head while she stood up. "Well, I, for one, am full of energy. Too bad I have to take my party home with me."

"Look, I can drop off Maggie and . . . "

"Never mind. You look like you could melt." She walked over and gave him a kiss on the cheek. Maggie blew out a gust of air and stood up. "Enough romance, boys and girls." She grabbed her purse with one hand, Ethan's hand with the other, and led him toward the door. "Fellow, give me a ride home. You two can play tomorrow."

Amber was by herself. No problem. She was her own party of one. When the juke box played some Creedence Clearwater Revival, Amber let the music fill her. She left Gilley's only under the influence of the music and the knowledge that life was good.

The overall bliss stayed with Amber the whole way home. By Lake Street, her radio began playing *Spirit in the Sky*. She tapped the first *Goin' on up*, her fingers beating out the rhythm on the steering wheel. By the second verse she was floating, and when Norman Greenbaum reached *Never been a sinner*, she was a true believer. She let the force of the song fill her, sucking the marrow of its message even when the radio station had gone on with other golden oldies. She kept on singing those words. She parked the car never havin' been a sinner. She danced her way up the front steps knowing she had a friend named Jesus. She opened her front door and wacked it shut with her hips, then kept right on dancing, gliding through the doorway and into the hall where she flung her purse onto the narrow black table and kicked her shoes toward the weathered, wicker hat rack in the corner.

The high eventually ebbed to blissful contentment, the kind of comfortable that eventually comes to bare feet after a long day of pointed shoes. She switched her dance to the deft escape of ballet movements long abandoned—her one hand firmly placed on the granite countertop for balance, the other extended and straight. *Toes up and point, heels down. Switch feet.* The cadence of childhood lessons played from her memory, and the symmetry of moving in perfect time to music only Amber heard seemed perfect. She stopped to take her bows. "Thank you for believing in me," she said, to one end of the room and then the other. "Thank you, thank you, thank . . ."

Charles Helm stood at Amber's door, beating a folded newspaper against his right hand, then slammed it to his side. "I cannot believe she would do this to my Lilly." His jaw trembled with righteous indignation. "She knows better. She knows." His hand trembled as he put the key into the lock, then he grimaced. "She doesn't even have the sense to lock her door." He slapped the paper again, once. "But then, what can I expect?"

Amber was so caught up in the rightness of the moment, she was oblivious to his presence as he watched her dance and bow to the unseen audience.

"I suppose you thought we wouldn't find out about your little escapade with the police? Honest to God, Amber, are you trying to put your mother into her grave?"

The voice threw her into a lurch. "Daddy." She stumbled, more like a child caught in the midst of abject naughtiness than a woman surprised by an intruder, straightened her skirt.

Amber's father stood in the kitchen doorway, the picture of distinguished businessman clear down to the well-placed graying of the hair at his temples as if even nature knew not to mess with Charles Helm. He was the image of Brooks Brothers perfection, suit without a wrinkle after a full day at the bank, not one speck of dust lodged on his shoes, the soul of collected presence. That is, except for his face. His lips were a tight line, and his dark eyes bored into his daughter's anxious face.

"Well, what do you have to say for yourself about this?" He held out a newspaper and watched her, the parent waiting for an answer from the naughty child. The trouble was, the child had no idea what she had done. His next words dripped cold wrath. "Emily Rathbourne called my private number at the office. It seems she's connected to an unnamed member of the school board who wanted to pass on his concern. She didn't want to disturb me while I was working, but how did I feel, she wanted to know, about my daughter . . ."

Charles took in extra air and his chin trembled as he continued as if struggling to mouth the last word. "And then I picked up today's *Trib* just to make sure." Panic grabbed at her while she forced herself to look calm, letting her father go on. "It isn't every day, after all, that one's daughter . . ." the family relationship came out more like a term of profanity ". . is hauled into the police station for aggravated assault."

Amber faced him, her mouth making little noiseless motions like a freshly landed fish drowning in the air. He had slipped in like smoke and now demanded accountability. Certainly there was a sound or two mucking about inside her, but her father's obvious wrath had managed to freeze her voice box while she wasn't looking. All she could manage was a stumbling, "I didn't do it."

"You didn't—let me see what this says." He opened the newspaper and read, ". . . accused of inflicting bodily injury by the girl's parent."

Amber pictured the words highlighted in red. She held up her head and responded in the voice of a small child, "He wasn't a parent."

"I see. Evidently assaulting nonparents is permissible then." The calm of his voice seared Amber more than the earlier anger.

She thought of the mesh of friends at Gilley's, the laughter and the congratulations and the ebullience of knowing that a child had stood her ground and grown, and they had been a part of that. She thought of all the stories she had taught her students, all the heroes discussed returning with the boon and filled with the sweetness of success. Then she thought of how, in many of these stories, the success was short lived. That sometimes the gold turned to ash and the hero faced tests even more formidable and chilling. What good did it do to conquer the world when your family thought you a villain?

I can't do this anymore. They want too much. Amber knew that she had to collect herself, but there in that house, in the dusk of an early fall evening, she felt sun struck. Jocelyn's first words rose from somewhere deep within Amber's memory, unbidden and bitter. "I dance around the abyss, and evil smiles." No wonder it smiles. It knows it will win.

"Sit down, Father. Let's talk about it." Before either one even moved, Amber knew what the words would be and how she would react. It had been all been said before. Her whole life.

Charles had not so much as acknowledged her invitation to sit. He stood firm, statued by the same sense of history. Perhaps he knew that. Perhaps not. What did it matter?

"If you choose to so callously ignore your mother's fragile state because of this, then I'll have to take steps to protect her." For such strong words, Charles Helm looked implacable, digging down for even more rebuke, his tone a lashing. "I cannot believe that I would have such a. . ." He paused, indicating a search for words, although Amber worried as much that he was trying not to slap her. But his body did not move so much as one flinch. And where his words had been delivered in such heat, now they turned surprisingly tender.

"Daughter, I remember when you were a baby. I watched you, lying there in your crib, and I felt such a surge of pride. Here was a piece of myself, a child that I would watch grow into grace and beauty."

His face darkened. Pain etched itself in his eyes and the set of his mouth.

"Your mother almost died giving you life." His voice cut the air, each word enunciated uttered with spite. He had been full of heat and tenderness. Now he turned cold.

"How can you forget that?

"How could you take a chance on killing her now?"

Amber's face remained the same, but her heart lurched, just as it had every time she had been reminded of the toxemia that had hospitalized her mother for three months. Never once had she forgotten the suffering her mother had endured. How could she?

No one would let her.

"Daddy . . ." Her voice lowered to a hush, almost a prayer. She had to start again. "Father, you know that I love you both for all you've done, and I know how much Mother risked.

"And you know that I would never, ever do something to endanger her. . ."

Charles cut her off. "Then how can you so embarrass us? How could you betray us!"

The stiffness of his body language relaxed. That was the familiar signal for Amber to show remorse and placate the parent as was her due. In times past, when Amber had been cast in her role as Disappointing Child, she had been alone and she had played her part well. Tonight was different. Tonight, there had been celebration and friendship and Amber was not alone. Amber met her father's gaze, one adult to another. Her silence spoke for her.

Charles narrowed his eyes. "What should I expect? I have a daughter who doesn't even know enough to lock her own door at night." His face was a stone.

I'm supposed to beg for forgiveness, throw myself on the mercy of the Helm Court. That's how it's always worked.

Not now.

"I'm sorry that you and Mother cannot have more belief in me. Or concern, for that matter."

Seated across from the man who had run her life—up to this point—she could feel the taking in of his breath, the clenching of teeth. One simply did not speak to Charles Helm that way, least of all his daughter.

He stood up and walked toward the door, never looking back, never even so much as hesitated in his steady, poised movement out the door . . . and for sure, Amber thought, out of her life. He had left the newspaper on the chair.

Amber reached over and opened it to the page her father had read to her. Nothing about teachers or assaults. She picked her way through the paper until she found the article, nothing terribly long, just an accounting of a public school teacher being questioned about an assault on a student's mother. She scanned it, turning red at its censure, and then tossed it aside. Old news.

He must have memorized the article.

He didn't even care that I'm innocent.

How much time passed before she was able to move, before she could react to the knowledge that the man who had taught her to ride a bicycle, who had taught her to dance for Miss Lathingham's Eighth Grade Cotillion, this man had called her an embarrassment? Seconds? Minutes? She would never know. She was in a vacuum, still dressed in her silk tee-top and linen skirt, a well-dressed woman back from a party. The walls of her first floor, normally comfortable and symmetrical, veered into strange shapes, weird trapezoids, morphing just about the time the left side of her head began to pulse at her temple, and the pressure of twenty-five years as the dutiful daughter blew.

She picked up a throw pillow off a chair and began beating the chair. "I betrayed you? *I betrayed you?*" She beat that hapless piece of furniture, her rage gripping her fingers, the thrust of her anger rhythmic in its intensity. "I pulled down my dress over those knobby knees you so despised. I pulled up my socks and took those stupid riding lessons even when I was sure I'd fall off that stupid horse and get bitten by its stupid teeth. I did everything to be your perfect daughter, to pay you back for my audacity at being born to Mother Teresa, I-almost-died-don't-you-owe-me, friggin' Lillian." No one heard her, of course, and nothing was moved by her outrage, except, of course, for the chair and the pillow. But they didn't protest beyond a dull thud.

Her body finally gave out. Tired from the aerobic demands of chair beating, she sank to the floor and cradled the pillow as if it were a child and she a remorseful abuser. Irony of ironies. She had almost lost her job intervening for a child. She most likely had lost her parents because of that intervention, and now, she, the rescuing angel had just reacted like the worst of the child beaters.

Minutes later, she sat on the edge of the bathtub, letting the water run through her fingers. She stood up and let her clothes drop to the floor, then kicked them to the side.

While she lay soaking in the tub, the tension of the confrontation slackened to a sense of remorse as the adrenaline dump wore at her. But the toll on her body ebbed and a new feeling took its place.

Satisfaction. Laying in that tub, her head resting on a folded towel, she not only felt satisfied, she felt pleased at that satisfaction. For the first time, she had actually stood up to her father instead of helping him put on the hair shirt she usually wore when he was angry.

Damn, she felt good.

The good continued, even grew in the late hours of that night. Warmth and a sense of indulgence as she soaked there in her tub, lolling in a comfort zone, certainly, that was good. The blanket of self-righteousness—she had stood up to her father for crying out loud—that was really good. When the laughter came bubbling up out of nowhere and rode her like the wind on a carnival ride in July—that was an unexpected good. When the moment had passed, she leaned her head back and sank more deeply into the water, brought her shoulders forward and made a sluicing sound, pulling in air through her teeth while she pursed her lips. It was late, and a stack of papers waited to be graded, but right now, in that tub, was a rush of relaxation that made her suck in her breath and feel indulged in pleasure. That wasn't just good; it was a good far beyond any pleasure she could remember. She was cleansed, body cleansed, soul cleansed, a cleansing soft and deep and full of a rightness as pure as a child at prayer. What could be more perfect than the beauty and warmth of her bath, this baptism of clemency. She had kept her ground. She owned herself and her life.

Still, that night, images of scuffed patent leather shoes and drooping anklets haunted her dreams.

Luckily, dreams fade in the morning. And two mornings serve even better. Forty hours went by, a day-and-a-half of excitement, anxiety, and the need to hide behind a mask, even from those close to her. On Sunday morning, Amber's eyes scanned the street as she leaned down to pick up the paper. Today was a new day, only one day before her life returned. Even the morning agreed. The sun was out, shards of light breaking through the gold and orange of trees just starting to turn. No mask needed today.

She didn't see the damage right away, not until she stood up. Even then, it didn't register as more than a fleeting sense of something not quite right, the kind of first reaction to an oncoming car about to sideswipe you. Then she saw it. Really saw it for its own kind of sideswipe. Big, ugly, black letters scrawled across the side. "BITCH" Some miscreant, some pond-scum-sucking-dilrod had spray painted the word along the entire side of her car. Krylon black. Huge letters. The car door looked like something from a bad horror movie.

My god. Who would do this to her?

Barefoot, clad only in underpants and t-shirt, Amber dropped the paper onto the front step and strode to her car.

Its sleek chassis had sent fingerlets of love clear down to her toes and she had taken in whiffs of new leather for months, loving every intake of breath. When she drove it, she was beautiful; she was free. Now the car was scarred, like a beautiful woman whose face has been slashed by a psychopath. Amber felt her breath take hold of her, squeeze at her lungs in sudden jerks and spasms, the sight permanently working its way deep into her memory bank, so rank and defiling was its message on a day meant for calm and good.

Her jaw clenched and her eyes narrowed.

She would not cry, would not react in any way that might pleasure the bastard responsible for this. The worst seventy-two hours of her life had not bested her. She had faced down her accusers, all of them. Those in the legal system, those others, the spineless twits who whispered behind her back and wondered with their sniggering questions, they were just bad memories.

All the best of her breeding took hold of her.

The universe that housed all those against her did not have enough force to warrant as much as a single tear drop from her, not even a blink, nothing to show any vulnerability. Seething inside, she kept her face a stone. The street was empty. She nursed her resolve for herself.

She turned and tromped up her front steps, dropped the paper onto the porch chair, and went inside. She gathered cleaning rags, abrasive cleaning pads, a bucket, and the strongest cleaner in the kitchen. Once outside, she made a line to the car and began scrubbing.

Anger fueled for the better part of an hour. If words could melt paint, the entire car would be nothing more than primer. A little of the black came off. Most of it remained, a sign for the entire neighborhood to know that not everyone loved Amber.

After an hour, she gave up, gathered up the equipment and marched back to her house. Balancing the bucket on her hip, she opened her door, let herself in, and set the gear in her sink. Then she sat on the floor and watched the wall.

Body shops wouldn't be open until Monday.

Good thing God made cabs.

Chapter 29

By 8:00 Monday morning, Amber owned control again. Her car would be ready in two days. The taxi that dropped her off two blocks from school had sped away. She was simply a young woman catching exercise by walking a few blocks. No need for gossip. No questions about an empty space in the parking lot. Better yet, no word from the parent front except a bit of grumbling from a mother left out of the loop. She'd hear from them again. Just not today.

Today was glorious. Today, Amber sat at her desk, ready for that first charge that came with kids and first hour.

"Wanna be my homecoming date next week? I'll buy you a mum." Ethan had popped into Amber's room, morning cola in hand. She stopped writing directions for her first class and laughed while he waggled his eyebrows in mock homage to dirty old men everywhere. "Then I'll give you plenty of candy and we can climb into my silver jalopy and find someplace to neck."

She smiled up at him, gawking like a star-struck groupie. "I'll have to ask my parents if I can stay out that late." She batted her eyes, then gave a dramatic sigh. "Oh wait, Daddy's not talking to me. Guess I'll just have to ask my mother." She mocked a stricken look, gaping her mouth and widening her eyes. "Wait a minute. She's not speaking to anyone."

Ethan laughed. "Yeah, they're not too happy. Eatin' rage ain't all that tasty to people used to prime rib and champagne."

Amber's tone tried ominous as she put on her best Lillian voice but her eyes sparkled and her sigh was empty. "And poor Mother, all in a snit over Daddy being 'holed up at the club or in one meeting or another for the last two days.'" She stopped and shook her head. "Mother is just fat with rage right now. I almost feel sorry for Daddy." She watched Ethan's scowl and slowed her words. "I said 'almost'. I nearly burned my hand on the phone, the lady was so hot." Amber flipped her hand at Ethan and then, to strengthen the gesture, let her fingers do a funky pirouette.

The reckoning would come. Lillian would discover the reason for her husband's behavior and the mighty parental team would have its full score of wrath, but that would all come later. Right now life was school, Ethan, and oh yes, working on that homecoming date.

"Well, you big brawny stud-muffin, I'll be wearing hot pink and purple. Probably get my tongue pierced, so the necking might be a little tricky, but we can always dirty dance under the moonlight."

"Pick you up after school, hot stuff. We'll get some practice time." He shot her a gotcha sign and left, his whistling obvious and comical as he walked along the empty hallway.

Amber felt the smile that lingered on her lips while she turned to the pile of mail waiting for her on her desk. Last week's deluge had at least trickled down to life-before-suspension. A good sign, definitely a good sign. Two brochures promoting teacher activities she already used, a Stumps catalogue for prom—God help us all, prom loomed on the horizon—and a folded sheet of paper, probably a memo from Duane, she thought as she opened it.

Aint U got it?
yer still a bitch!
Die bitch !!!!

Her first reaction was pure teacher laced with denial. The note was definitely not from Duane. Duane could spell.

The second started with fear. Die? Bitch? Then a fury. Some moron had called her a bitch! Wanted her to die?

She flicked the paper away as if it were covered with squirming insects. While it settled in the air a second before falling, Amber's temper flared. "Of all the stupid. . ." The words slammed from her and then shut down to a thought-filled seethe.

She cursed bad luck and swarmy fools who used cars as graffiti pallets and sneaked their way into teacher mail. She was the one who had won for crying out loud, the one who had taken on the world and her father—both equal matches—the one who was going to the dance with the man whose face had promised her much more than just a mum.

Then she stopped and turned back, picked up the note and crumbled it in her hand, and made a perfect three-point toss into the wastebasket. Take that, Cretin. You're not worth the time for a second shot. Winners did not succumb to terror tactics from idiots. They were trash, just like the note lying amid pencil shavings and dirty Kleenex. Just to prove her point, she sent her middle finger upward as a final note of derision. Of course, she checked first to make sure no one was watching. She shook her head and went back to preparing for the day. The kids would be here in fifteen minutes, and she would be ready.

The note was tossed and gone as it should be. All that remained was a bit of music in her head and a few concerns over subordinate clauses.

Chapter 30

"Can't sleep, huh? Ya' got your light on, I can see ya walking around."

Amber held the phone out in front of her. This was Thursday, the night many teachers referred to as "Friday Eve" in anticipation of the end of the week. Her fellow teachers may have shut down for the night—especially since the whole school would be doing football madness next week. But tonight, she had a slew of papers to grade, and she was not in the least open to any kind of silliness.

"Who is this?" Her voice sounded drowsy, raspy, angry like someone just wakened by an ill-timed salesman.

Bet you're thinking about sleeping. Maybe even sleeping like the dead."

Amber's jaw muscles tensed. *Sleeping like the dead.* A car drove by in front of her brownstone, its quiet passing eerie, almost alien. She glanced at her watch. It was after midnight, and yes, she was still up. Tired but not quite ready yet to put away her grading pen. Right now that was a moot point.

"Who is this?" She repeated herself while her survival mechanisms started to awaken, and she tried to identify the background noise, a subtle din of voices with an occasional yell, some laughter, a crack of something being hit—billiard balls? Before she could narrow these vague impressions to something more definite, the line went dead.

But if those noises were from a barroom, how would the caller know she was up? She hung up her phone, then hurried to the front door. The dead bolt and chain were secure. She had made sure of that, in part, after her father's parting shot the night before. She had even drawn the blinds tonight. Now she took a peek from the right side.

Outside, the street light was encased in low fog. Temperatures at night this time of year turned her street into a little London, so romantic she used to think. Now the fog brought thoughts of a different London, the one where Jack the Ripper waited for his white-throated victims. A late night phone call definitely awakened a girl's imagination. What could be out there in that fog weighed down on her, like the night, moist and heavy.

Knock it off, Amber. It's probably some drunk with the wrong number.

Then she saw him, just a shadow propped against the building across the street, a dark blur that was definitely male—funny how gender showed even in silhouette. Her logical mind told her that it was just somebody waiting, maybe having a cigarette. He certainly wasn't using a phone. One arm would be up if he were. The form indicated no danger. The tingle on the back of her neck and the wetness between her breasts and under her arms knew better.

Just as the refrigerator sent out a late night whir, the phone rang again. She jumped back a step and shuddered—once, twice. Her throat felt like it was choked with dry bread. She looked toward the front door, craving the sound of Maggie's voice telling her everything would be all right, then turned around and headed for the stairs to her bedroom. Silly child. Shadows and voices were benign. Nothing for an adult to fear.

How about a message scrawled across your car door? Or a threat sent by computer? In the daylight, the most obscene directives could be dismissed. Night was altogether different. She checked the lock—one more time, just in case—then crossed the room and started up the stairs. The first steps were fine. Nothing to fear. Midway up, the backs of her neck and hands tingled and she felt a wad of tightness in the middle of her chest. She scolded herself for her childishness. What was she—some middle school baby sitter afraid of a few sounds? Still, she moved slowly, her legs wooden, muttering, "It's only a prank. It's only a prank. It's only a prank." The words became a prayer, the air in front of her filling with them.

By the time she reached her bedroom, the prayer fell victim to panic. The eeriness of the downstairs silence made her want to run and leap beneath the covers like a little girl scared of the alligators under her bed frame. As if to summon calmness—or prove to herself that she wasn't an idiot, she took her time turning on the light switch on her wall, but then locked the door, even while chiding herself for the act. The outer Amber might want a mature approach, but the inner Amber still wanted to crawl under the covers.

It makes no sense that you're standing in this room, a grown woman who just locked her bedroom door because of a phone call and a shadow. Get a grip and get to bed. She turned out the light, headed toward her bed, climbed in, ready to cocoon herself, as she always did, in her bedding. The fan above her whirled, blanketing her with a steady swirl of air. That and air-conditioning allowed Amber to snuggle in bedding even while the September night stayed just cool enough to sleep with a light blanket. Maggie liked to tease that the tactile Amber was playing princess-and-the-pea, a sure sign that she was truly her mother's daughter. Amber acknowledged the tactile and ignored the rest. The pureness of the high thread-count cotton sheets and the airy comfort of a duvet-covered comforter surely sewed by angels was a luxury she craved for its pure nightly bliss. No matter how ornery the kids, or how many papers she had to grade, Amber could count on the pure self-indulgence of her bedding, even if it meant owing her mother for the luxury.

Tonight, though her body could not indulge itself. The sheets were the same sensual cotton that she loved, the dome of bedding the same cloud. But where her skin normally felt soothed, right now it felt prickly, her muscles stiff and aching and violated by the sweep of cloth against her. The night weighed on as she tried to sleep. A voice seemed to hover somewhere near the blades of the ceiling fan. *I can see you walking around. Bet you sleep like the dead.*

Chapter 31

All that night, shadows pelted her until she woke, restless and fretful over things she could not name. In the morning, Amber knew that she had dreamed. She just wasn't sure what those dreams had been. Lying there in her bed, fitful and tired, she only felt their ghosts. As the day went on, the workings of Friday took over. The remnants of the night softened, blurred, and then dissipated like morning fog.

The weekend came and went uneventfully. A movie date with Ethan—mediocre film, great company. A Sunday afternoon of flea marketing with Maggie—more laughter than bargains. All told, two days of leisurely regrouping and rest. No shadows. No nightmares. Now it was the school week. Rest time was over. George T. Clausson High School was caught in the throes of homecoming mania. Definitely, no rest here.

Comet orange and blue. It covered the walls, the lockers, the faces of teens normally energized but now at a full blown state of frenzy. Spirit Day. The Tuesday of homecoming week, the first of four days birthed from the gods themselves, so old was the tradition, the apex of a ritual guaranteed to shut down any semblance of learning for a solid week. Monday was anticipation and final plans. Tuesday slid the school into the four-day span for football players to enter the halls of Valhalla, courtesy of crushing the arch rival, Horace Van Meeter High School's Titans.

For the entire faculty, the festivities couldn't end soon enough.

Last Thursday's phone call had acted as a prelude to a series of high school pranks. Either the moon had been full for everyone, or that silliness on the phone was the kickoff for a mass of juvenile antics. This morning, the head office had received the news that Clausson's cheerleaders had driven plastic forks into Van Meeter's field. The athletic director had been checking for some kind of fungus thing on the fifty yard line when he heard their giggles. He even had confiscated a Fork U from the Comets sign about to be impaled right over their precious bulldog. Clausson's administration was not amused and the presence of a cheering section at the traditional kickoff pep assembly could be minus the cheerleaders this afternoon.

Then came Justin Davis. He was one of Clausson's resident victims. The poor freshman carried a Bible with him every day which set him up for harassment as much as his perpetually runny nose and asthmatic wheezing. When a football player pushed him against a locker and tried to paint a Comet on his cheek, that was the final of an endless series of straws. Justin reared back and smacked him with his Bible. The player wound up with a bloody lip, and Justin was cooling his wrath in the principal's office.

Privately, Amber smiled over Justin's attempt at self-defense, hapless though it might be, but the incident weirded out an already weird day.

Now at 1:00, the last class before the pep assembly, Amber was writing assignment directions on the board—as if the kids would focus for more than thirty seconds today—but she was spurred on by a commitment to at least make an effort to keep them corralled. Two senior fullbacks, bodies painted in school colors, walked the hall, one a blue smurf weighing in at 250 pounds, the other, six feet of solid pumpkin-hued muscle. Just as they passed by her door, they started a chant. Comet Glory! Like any normal adolescent assured that his immediate demanded gratification, each banged a rhythm on a locker to punctuate the warrior call.

Warrior calls always took precedence over academics during homecoming week.

Amber had forgotten that. She threw the chalk on the tray. Ten steps and she was out the door. "What the hell do you think you're doing!" No telling which was worse, the decibel level or the words themselves. Either way, the world around her stopped. Inside the room, students watched the doorway, waiting. No one could speak. Miss Helm never swore. She might yell when something was really bad—usually *the look* was enough—but swearing, that was for Coach Tinneli, maybe Mr. Bryson, but never for Miss Helm. In the hall, the blue and orange twins stood frozen, banging fist in hand, mouths open, gaping at each other.

Gritting her teeth, Amber collected whatever composure she could muster. Luckily, the shock of the moment gave her a few seconds to gain control. "Gentlemen, please try to make it to the assembly without destroying the school. Thank you." She turned and walked back into the room. The entire class was hushed. That is except for Roger Duclous in the back row who smiled and raised both hands, thumbs up. Amber's look let Roger know that the teacher was not amused.

"Grab your reading books and free-read until the bell rings." No one even dared breathe wrong. Every student in Amber Helm's fifth hour class went to the bookshelves to grab the novels of choice, row by row, just as she had taught them, while Amber went to her desk and picked up her reading book, managing the impression of a sane woman, given the circumstances. Sitting on one edge of the desk, she pretended to read.

Sipping the coffee that went everywhere with her and waiting for Amber to bring her attention back from whatever fascinated her outside the window, Maggie watched her friend. The faculty parking lot could not hold that much interest. Maggie had watched this Amber often enough, knew the signs of the silence that hid the shifting gears of Amber's mind when she was troubled. She waited, but not without a little fear herself.

Amber might lose it—after all, what was red hair for if not to warn *Temper Ahead*—but Amber never, ever, under any circumstances, lost it in front of the kids. Maggie decided to at least try intervention. "Look, it's not like you've had the easiest month . . . " Amber's shoulders tightened, then let loose a spasm even as she stayed fixated on whatever it was that was drawing her attention. "The point is, you let loose and goofed up. It's over. The pep assembly is in almost full throttle and we're late. The kids are busy yelling their brains out and have forgotten what happened, and even if a couple of them do remember, they'll chalk it up to the aftermath of all the craziness that's happened these past weeks." Amber shook her head. Maggie could hear the uneven breathing.

Enough was enough. "Amber, you're human. Get over it."

Amber turned around. "You're right." She nodded once in agreement. "We're late." She strode toward Maggie, grabbed her arm, and together they headed toward the gym. Comet Pride awaited.

Homecoming Days were hectic enough. No sense in letting a few seasonal pranks add to the stress.

Amber completely disagreed with her best friend on a few things, among them the status of mornings. Amber Helm's theory on mornings was that there was nothing inherently wrong with mornings. They just needed to start later.

Just not this morning. In the wee hours of a Wednesday morning, for Amber, it was a call for down-home celebration, part of the frenzy that had gripped her school. Wrapped in a flannel robe, her feet bare, Amber danced in her side yard, her hands clutching a brown wallet above her head, like a football player hot dogging after a touchdown, oblivious to the threat of the ref's whistle. Voice subdued in spite of the celebratory grinding, she rasped her victory song.

"Only losers are sore. Winners feel no pain." She held her head toward the sky.

"Hear that, Skippy?"

Skippy was Amber's catchall name for anyone who annoyed her. In this case, there were several Skippys, all bound for a comeuppance. The thought of a collection of swarmy men, each wearing a "Sucks to be Skippy" tee-shirt floated through her imagination. They had dared to heap threats upon her, one violation after another, but finally, enough was enough, and justice had finally announced herself.

Last night, at 11:30, someone named Al—she had heard it as in "Goddamnit, Al, you're supposed to scare the bitch, not wake up the neighborhood" had tried to climb the iron trellis on the side of her house and vandalize her window. Already spooked, she had lain awake in the dark listening for more night sounds. She got them all right.

First, the partner in stealth. Then a cat's wail and the clank of spilled garbage cans. Finally a neighbor's "What the hell's going on?" as he emerged from his back door, flashlight in hand, temper in overdrive.

Al and company had fled, leaving a sack of road kill guts ready for smearing. He had also left his wallet, evidently swept from his back pocket in the rush to flee the scene.

A name.

Amber scanned the driver's license again, soaking in the relief of seeing what had been faceless harassment. Al Franek. Born August 25, 1969. Height and weight of no consequence. But ah, the picture. A typical driver's license mug shot gone even more wrong. Al had a zoned look that brought up memories of Laverne and Shirley reruns and fuzzy dice. Watery blue eyes and thinning blonde hair, a face pitted with acne scars and a rather nasty scar along the right side of his face. Amber couldn't wait to see his expression once the police talked to him. She knew that her business with Al and company would have to wait until her prep hour. She knew that she had to contain herself until 10:20. Lord knew there had been enough excitement. But she knew—by all the saints that her friend Maggie held holy—she knew that she'd be on the phone to Officer Calavari once 10:21 hit. Let Al and his buddies sit there and stare at those gray walls.

Wednesday mornings were usually slow. Monday and Tuesday were off-nights for crime—even criminals took off the first part of the week. So when his caller gave her name, Detective Calavari could give his undivided attention even though he couldn't quite figure out what to think about talking to her. He cleared his throat and managed professionalism.

"Miss Helm. Of course I remember you." How could he help but remember. He had known in his gut that she was innocent. Dammit, he had known. It was that know-it-all lawyer. Dobron had pushed him just far enough to lose the edge of his common sense. Lawyer's fault. Not his.

Good thing the kid had broken and the whole mess was over.

So what did Amber Helm want now? He leaned back in his chair.

"What can I do for you?"

An explanation later, Calavari had made an appointment for Amber to come to the precinct. He'd make good on his promise to catch those punks. He owed her that.

When he hung up, he went looking for his partner. They usually didn't cover pranks, but this time they would.

Friday. Finally. School was out. The band had played. The kids had cheered. The football team had flexed its collective muscle while the coach promised, like he did every year, that School Spirit would pay off in glorious victory on Friday night. Amber and Ethan had just grabbed a bite to eat at Gilley's and now stopped at Material Acquisitions to check out windows that promised everything from jeweled Harley pillows to vintage clothing. A whiff of fall smoke hung in the air—someone was ignoring city leaf burning regulations—and the sky held that early evening haze that separated day and night right before the street lights blinked on.

"So why the million miles away?" Ethan's hand massaged her neck, his thumb rubbing in a little circle to check out tension.

Amber's answer came after several seconds of silence, more a question, hesitant and quiet. Her head stayed straight ahead while she spoke. "What makes you think I'm not here?"

"I don't know. Maybe because you haven't said a word for five minutes." His words were soft, a match for hers. Amber gnawed at her lip and stayed silent. He tried again. " Maybe the way you've kept your eyes focused on that really ugly pink feather thing. What is it? A bed for an ostrich?"

She turned to him and managed a half-smile and a raised eyebrow. "It is pretty ghastly. I guess I was just in awe." More humor. Definitely more humor.

"Don't fool me, young lady. I know better." Her head stayed still but the smile was gone. Ethan plodded on. "I know when there's a crisis in your life. You didn't want cheesecake for dessert. That's a major sign."

Amber laughed and blew out a whoosh of air as if dismissing something internal, then shook her head. "I'm sorry. There's something churning up in me, but I don't know what it is. I should be all about happy right now, but I can't seem to work up the energy. I guess I'm just tired, that's all. So many papers, so little time."

She put her arm around Ethan and hugged. Her head felt good against his shoulder.

Amber was tired all right, but she had left a lot untold, all the collective needles that had been pricking at her sense of safety. Sure, Detective Calavari had assured her that the police would put a stop to the pranks, but all she had was his verbal commitment and a name. Al.

A nasty message in black paint. A note and that phone call. The feeling in the back of her neck that someone was watching her. Frank and friends had spooked her just enough to keep her looking in spite of assurances.

It nettled at her and wouldn't let go. And from the look on Ethan's face, it was more than a nuisance. She hugged Ethan once more, just for good measure and her own sense of assurance.

How sad, she thought, the things that we hang on to when it's so much easier to let go. *Well, Frank, my man, look's like it's you and me at noon. There's only room in this here town for one of us, and I ain't movin'.* Let him pull his silliness. It couldn't hurt.

She lifted her head off of Ethan's shoulders and grabbed his hand, pulling him as she started walking away. "Let's carry on, pardner, saddle up and head 'em on out." Ethan looked at her strangely, but didn't say a thing. He just gave a curt little nod and followed.

Later, when the two of them lay naked, Ethan chuckled and said, "Here I was worried about you being tired," while he stroked her face, and bent to dust the side of her face with light kisses.

"Now I'm the one who's tired," came as he nuzzled her neck and bit at her earlobe, his hand still wrapped in her hair he had pushed upward. "Such a nice kind of tired."

Amber purred, making little noises of contentment while she wiggled her toes. Funny, she couldn't for the life of her ever remember her toes so caught up in the need for movement like this. But then, she thought, she'd never wanted so much to keep purring and stretching. If this kept up, she'd be licking cream like the most spoiled of pets.

"Things have changed in these three years."

His voice still had that depth and humor in it with these words, but Amber felt a catch in her chest. She pushed down her worry and took in sensation. This was no time for ghosts. Please. Sensation won, and she let herself ride it.

"Before, when we were just kids . . . " He muffled the *just kids* as he moved his lips downward, nibbling and kissing and tasting. ". . . when we were first so hot for each other . . ." This time he bit lightly and followed with a swish from the tip of his tongue. ". . . I wouldn't have spent as much time learning the finer parts of your body." Good girl, Amber—nothing to worry about after all. Ooh— hit that spot again, yeah, and keep doing that thing with your tongue.

Chapter 32

As the night wore on, both Ethan and Amber renewed past discoveries—found that what they had enjoyed about each other before remained, the hardness, the need to bury and be buried and revel in the dampness and the heat.

A fluke had brought them together. So much had happened in a few weeks. But they had weathered it all. Found each other again, harmony out of chaos.

For them, morning came at 6:30. Ethan woke first. He rolled on his side, reached across and touched Amber's lips, then pulled his hand down her breasts, his index finger stroking in light circles. Then he leaned in and whispered, "Ready for breakfast?"

Amber pulled her head tight against the pillow, stretching her neck. "You bet. How about you, over easy?"

No one had to tell a boy from Iowa twice.

When they finally made it downstairs, the food metaphors lingered along with the afterglow. Amber sat on a barstool while Ethan made coffee, grinning at him—not the toothy grin of a little kid bent on mischief, but a full out sensuous indulgence grin, as if she had awakened and plucked her dream, then slid it inside her to hold for the entire day. Her head was tilted up and her whole face stretched with her grin, eyes narrowed and knowing, lips together and freshly moistened by her tongue, a very happy, very well-satisfied tongue. A well-satisfied Amber. She leaned back for effect and put her feet up on the counter. It was seven in the morning, definitely time for coffee, just a few hours before they would have to face students all day. Coffee, definitely a good idea. Still, her mind was not on the task at hand.

"If you tasted any better, you'd be made of chocolate."

He smiled. "Yeah, and then I'd be addictive."

"Some addictions are worth it." His head was turned toward the coffee maker, but his body preened at the compliment even from the back.

"Coffee will be ready in a minute." He turned and looked at her. "Anything else I can get you Madam?" The words came out with a leer as he moved toward her. "A croissant? A Danish? Perhaps a well-deserved bonbon?" His hands reached out and covered her feet at the instep, and he began to massage, rubbing at the top with his thumb and using his fingers on the bottoms. "How about if I just come around and . . ." Leaving the suggestion open, he matched her smile and moved his hands upward, now working her ankles.

Amber leaned her head back and closed her eyes, let herself be wrapped in a rhythm of bliss that coursed through her like the rocking of a small boat on a gentle lake.

The phone rang. It was her father.

Her chair was the color of Merlot, a deep burgundy vinyl. The cushion made a funny whooshing sound whenever she stood up to check the clock or pace—now about every ten minutes instead of five, now that she had slowed down to a pace. The sound didn't go with the room, a merging of mauves and gray and the deep color of her chair. The hospital called it a "Family Center" in an effort to sound comforting, but the old fashioned term of waiting room was far more appropriate, just like the furniture and steel gray of the flooring. They reminded her of the precinct, not as tarnished and worn as that place had been, but for a room where family could float in agony waiting for news, it was appropriate. Evidently, the hospital had wasted its money on a decorator. No one can soothe fear with the stroke of decorating magic.

Ethan had offered—wanted to—go in the back with her. When she refused, he reached into his pocket and pulled out a half-used package of lifesavers and placed it in her hand with a hug. "Chew on the red ones," he said with a smile, ". . . they have the best mo-jo." Then he gave her a gentle shove toward the doors that separated them. He would take care of calling the school and explaining the crisis.

Charles sat across from her, bent forward, arms resting on his legs, his face pointed toward his daughter. A nurse walking by might think that Charles and Amber were in a conversation lull, that maybe the middle-aged man was trying to find words of comfort for the pale-faced woman rocking in her chair and rubbing her hands like a modern Lady Macbeth. Someone might even turn back and look, feel a pang of concern for that silent couple sitting there amid the din of emergency workers.

Amber knew better. No mo-jo here. Her father's eyes never moved, not so much as flickered. She kept at her hands. She had to use her thumb to test for feeling, make sure the numbness inside her didn't spread and turn her to stone. They had been here for twenty minutes, a lifetime really. How was Ethan doing in the lobby, she wondered. Did he get hold of the school in time? She had given him a quick hug, a detached piece of herself. That was before she had raced past the admissions station, following the tech that took her to this room of deadened colors. Her cheek stung where he had kissed her quickly; strange that she should feel that when the rest of her was shut down.

She tried to talk to her father. "How long before the doctor comes?"

Certainly a question about a schedule would prompt a response. Charles Helm was a man who worshipped at the holy grail of schedules.

He said nothing.

The walls started to close in on her. She knew better than to think that walls could move; she was an adult wasn't she? But the space in that cubbyhole they had appointed for family was narrowing, she could feel it, just like she could feel the silence of her father. Probably why so much of the rest of her was numb. All the stimuli around her soaked up all her response.

"It's your fault. You know that."

The sound swirled around in her head, meaningless noise, before it gathered the strength to register as a comment. When it did, she felt it in spasms. Shame. She was a woman who lapped up the responsibility of shame daily. If her students didn't love to learn —as if that were an option in the teenage brain—her fault. If a parent called Marti or a meeting ran late or Jo's schedule didn't work, somehow she was to blame. And if her mother died . . . she couldn't bring herself to finish the thought.

Amber closed her eyes, head bent, and breathed in, forcing the air out between her teeth. She swallowed once. "Daddy, I am so, so sorry. I never meant . . ." She couldn't even finish the thought. A silence hung there between them. They might as well have been strangers on a train, each focused on what lay once they arrived. Only these two had no sense of what the arrival would bring. When Charles finally spoke, his words came out in a cold rasp.

"You never mean to do anything, Amber. But somehow the worst is done." His whole body was motionless, eyes on the wall as if the sight of his daughter disgusted him. It probably did.

"You run through life as if you are the only one affected by your decisions. You never think about the rest of us, how we are affected by your foolishness. Your mother is fighting for her life because of you not *meaning* it." He stood up and walked away, as if she were no more than an annoyance invading his space.

Amber stayed in her chair as he walked away, felt the smallness seep throughout her body as shame sank her with its drowning power.

A nurse stood at the station desk, hunched over and rubbing her neck. When she turned to look at Amber, her identity tag was white and black against the blue of her uniform. Nancy Pellet, Head Endocrinology RN. Endocrinology. Long word, familiar word, word that had seeped through Amber's life whenever Lillian's diabetes went haywire. This was a woman who had some answers. This was the woman who was making her way toward Amber with pursed lips and a sense of self-imposed control.

"You're Mrs. Helm's daughter, aren't you? I'm sorry, I've forgotten your name." She sat down next to Amber, the request for an answer hanging there.

"Amber. Amber Helm." Her eyes hung on the nurse. She was waiting for some answers, but fear stuck in her throat like wadded cotton.

Nancy Pellet took the time to look at the chart. Amber's left leg bounced in the nervous twitch her body saved for special times of crisis.

The stranger with the name tag, this nurse of importance and answers, set the clipboard on her lap and centered her shoulders before she spoke. The she spoke firmly.

"Your mother's still brittle, but the crisis is over. She's regained consciousness, but the insulin shock has left her dazed and confused. We'll be keeping her overnight."

Nancy folded her hands on the clipboard and leaned forward. "Miss Helm . . . this may sound inappropriate. If so, forgive me." She tightened her lips and hit her knees with board three times, short and static, then shook her head. "The thing is . . . we've talked and talked to both your parents over the years about the dangers of your mother's disease, and absolute need for diligence in maintaining even blood sugar."

Amber closed her eyes. "I know. Believe me, I know about my mother's condition. I was seven the first time the ambulance left our driveway."

"Then you understand the dangerous game she's playing."

"Game?" Lillian was barely out of a coma, and this woman spoke of a game? Amber's voice scaled in anger. "What do you mean, 'game'?" She gathered herself into an air of sanctimony.

"My mother is a ill woman with a debilitating disease. Her condition is no game."

The nurse met her attitude, mettle for mettle. For a caregiver moments ago treading nervously, the news now was all business. It had to be. "Look, I fully realize the severity of Type 1 diabetes. What I have to say to you stems full well from that realization." Nurse Pellet pointed to the very chairs that minutes ago had been occupied by Amber and her father. "Let's sit down and have a heart-to-heart."

The two women sat there, heads together, Amber's arms on resting on her legs, her hands folded. Nancy was bent forward to respect their privacy, but her hands held the chart that defined Lillian's condition, her hands firm, signaling knowledge and professionalism.

"I've been with this hospital ten years. Do you know that your mother has been here at least once a year?"

Amber nodded mutely. She fully knew every mote of her mother's medical schedule, but the nod seemed to be appropriate.

"Every time, and this is crucial to understand, Miss Helm . . . Amber . . . her visit to the ER has been precipitated by wild swings of blood sugar."

Amber sat back in her chair, head up and eyes pointed straight at the nurse as she answered.

"Doesn't that argue the seriousness of her condition? I'm sure that stress as well as her body's attempt to fight this disease . . . precipitate these attacks." Amber emphasized the very word the nurse had used. She could play this game too.

"That's the point. Stress has nothing to do with it. Neither does the severity of her condition."

Amber kept looking at this woman, growing wary, even as she stayed willing to listen. No one in the hospital had ever talked to her about her mother. She had always relied on her parents for information. Or nothing. Without thinking, Amber reached into her pocket and held onto the roll of candy Ethan had given her. The movement gave the nurse time to continue.

"Thirty years ago, I could not say this, but we have made great strides in helping diabetics lead safe lives. This is the twenty-first century. And your mother's disease can be fully regulated by proper testing and a well-regulated diet."

Who was this woman to give her such news? The words fell from Amber's mouth.

"Then why does she need to come here? Why is my mother so ill?"

"I've seen many patients as ill as your mother. Some . . . most do very well, if they want to." Nurse Pellet's pause wrapped itself around Amber's throat and squeezed. But the words, when the words came, it was Amber's heart that stiffened.

"Amber, your mother plays with her disease. She plays with her insulin dosage, she plays with her diet." The nurse paused, letting the words gain meaning for a daughter who wanted only health for her mother. Then she brought up a possibility, one that could shake this daughter's world.

"Have you ever heard of Munchausen disease?"

Munchausen? That was child abuse. "That's when mothers make their children sick. What does that have to do with my mother?"

The nurse's eyes softened imperceptibly. This was a tough discussion for a woman whose whole being seemed stretched with concern. The eyes may have been softened, but Nancy's lips tightened. "That's Munchausen-by-proxy. Munchausen's is self-inflicted." The words hung there. "Sometimes . . . in fact, more often than we want to imagine, the attention a patient receives from an illness can become addictive."

"My mother plays with her life, even dares death so that we'll pay attention to her? The mother who sang birthday greetings to wake her daughter every July 14? The one who took her to lunch at the top of Marshall Field's every Christmas season, just two girls enjoying a Christmas tradition?

Was this woman nuts? The sheer impossibility of the words shook Amber to her core. No daughter could readily accept that kind of news. Even if the news was the truth. The birthday song was no more than a prelude to the tale of a mother putting her life on the line to birth the daughter. The lunch always had a price of subtle criticism at manners not quite up to snuff.

Amber's mind was a whirlpool of swirling thoughts, thoughts chaining her to the chair as she tried to sort through this roil. The bustle of the hospital had settled into a din, nothing important, nothing distinguishable. Nothing remotely enough to compete with the force of Nancy Pellet's message. Her mother playing with her life just for attention. All these years? Lillian could indulge in purposeful exaggeration if she needed to. But play with her life? A hairline crack took form, turned into the smallest of fissures.

Amber was a seven-year-old child again, not consciously, but the feelings of the little girl she once had been poured through her, the horror, the fear, the utter sense of desertion. The process drained her.

Think. Make a move. Do anything to warm up the chill that held her.

Ethan was waiting for her. Probably sitting there, arms between his legs, hands folded, that's how he usually sat when he waited.

Better not keep him waiting.

She didn't even feel herself rising from the seat and walking toward the lobby. The walking dead don't know where they're going, and that was she was at that moment, a white-faced zombie going about her business.

"It's all right, Baby, it's all right." When had she reached him? She felt his arms around her as sensation, but inside, she was still cold. His body was warm, but nothing could penetrate the weariness that held her inside. Ethan was asking about Lillian. Was she stable? Would they be able to see her in the morning? The words went in, she was sure. But they were garbled, words above the water while she treaded beneath trying to hear the faraway message. While his arms held her and his hand brushed at her hair, she tried, really she did, to feel his touch and know comfort.

"She's stable." She shuddered.

Ethan and Amber walked away from the lobby and out into the parking lot. The air hit her as soon as they went through the double doors, fresh and real. She looked back at the lobby, unable to separate herself from its hold. Standing there right inside the first set of doors was a man watching her, a beefy guy who looked like a has-been linebacker scarred by a few too many games, and far too many beers. There was something so familiar about him. Amber's body shook involuntarily, caught up in shivering, trying to place that form. It hovered in her memory like an object shrouded in fog, but before she could frame a conscious impression, he turned and walked to the desk.

Silly girl. Now you quail at strangers. She shook her head and chided herself. Then a pall of depression weighed on her. *Mother is stable all right. One for the good guys. Too bad my life can't be.* The wish was a quiet whisper, far too soft to hold even the hope of change.

Ethan put his arm around her shoulder. "Are you sure you want to teach today? They'd certainly understand if you took a mental health day."

"No. I'd go crazy at home. Work will keep my mind occupied."

He gave her a quick squeeze. "C'mon, then. Let's get to school."

Amber's body obeyed. Her mind stayed focused on the hospital. Her mother had passed the crisis. Lillian would be home by this time tomorrow, tired but ready to face life.

Life.

That nurse must be crazy, Amber thought to herself.

You're defining crazy? She swatted the thought away like she might a pesky fly buzzing in annoyance.

Chapter 33

Amber and Ethan stood on her porch. They should have been planning the last details of a getaway weekend. They should have had their heads together, their smiles slick with the thought of the trip. Instead, two days after the visit to the hospital, they stood apart, arms folded, mouths no more than twin slashes. Three years ago, on a hot day in July, they had stood on a porch much like this one, a time when they had moved from writing team to friends, when Amber had cried, a few noiseless tears unleashing a wailing that had left her depleted. Today, Amber wanted to cry again. She had felt her hurt start in the back of her throat, knew her arms had reached around herself and locked themselves in a body language that in no way spoke of love.

She'd always hated when she cried. She felt the tears well, sting at her eyes and throat, but she willed herself to stay calm—or at least look that way. Once, on that porch so long ago, Ethan had held her and let her cry out her burden. Her anguish wet his favorite shirt, a tattered remnant of loyalty to some high school team, her mascara smudging the team logo. On that August afternoon, Ethan had sat there, listening to a girl he thought not much more than a spoiled princess as she shared a hurt she couldn't even voice intelligently, so new was the knowledge that had risen to the surface.

That Ethan belonged to the past. "Don't you get it," this one said, his face and voice pocked with the storm of his anger. "Listen to you." He raised his head, turned his voice a nasty falsetto. His chin was tight. "Ethan, I want this weekend, just like we planned, but I can't desert my family." He met Amber's eyes and he spoke in a firm hiss. "Desert your family? For God's sake, Amber, it's a weekend. Two days." Breathing out, he covered his face with his hands, then let them slowly slip down. His eyes had turned black. "'Ethan, you're my best friend, but I have to go.' Shit. It's the letter you dumped me with all over again."

The letter. 'I love you Ethan, or I love what we could have become, but I have to go. My family.' Evidence of Amber's cowardice.

"That isn't true."

"The hell it isn't." Where Ethan's words had risen, loud and firm, all accusation, now they turned caustic once again, his volume lowered but his words still marking her. "'How can I leave my mother when she's so ill?' The volume grew, and his eyes snapped. "Easy. You take off with me to Galena just like we planned." His face was empty of any compassion and his voice turned surgically cold. "You can't leave your mother? What? Is she going to suddenly die if we slip away for one weekend? Who gave you that kind of power? He shook his head, and his faced turned to a mask of contempt. "Or maybe it comes down to you're just a scared little girl feeling guilty because she's afraid of Mommy. What the hell kind of hold does she have on you?"

Amber started forward, swinging her hand upward, flat-palmed. Midway into the second step she stopped, turned her head and looked at her hand. It shook with want, white, fingers splayed, a mean hand ready to deliver retribution. She wanted to gasp but was too angry to even manage a show of surprise. The sound of his mean laughter brought her eyes back forward. Ethan was standing there, dressed in this trumped-up epiphany, reading her reaction and looking at her as if he were the end-all expert on her psyche.

She wanted to hit him all the more, pummel him until he was mush, then stand over him and spit. But she stood fixed. Her hand relaxed and the fingers stilled.

When she finally lowered her arm, she straightened and looked at him, her head and shoulders thrust forward. This time her voice was low and raspy. "How dare you think you know me." She whipped around. She did not want to see him, the all-knowing Mr. Michaels, walked away from him, then leaned her body against the railing, her arms at her side, her hands shaking as if to dry them of some unseen wetness.

She turned to look at him. There was enough space between them now for safety. She could breathe again.

Ethan edged out whatever was going to come out of her mouth with his own speech. She was playing the same record again, the one played when her back was against the wall. "How dare I think I know you? How *dare* I think I *know* you?" The meanness was gone, but Ethan was definitely still laughing. In fact, he seemed to be having a good old belly-chortler, arms crossed, eyes closed, whole head shaking as if this were the funniest goddamn thing in the world. Amber knew full well that nothing was funny. Not to her. She knew it the way kids know giggling, automatic, a welling of air and throat and soul, the way a victim knows death seconds before the gun fires.

The moment of reckoning. It was out there, in front of them, swirling in the air, little bits of truth like dust motes in a beam of sunlight taking up the atmosphere, a mysterious universe unto itself and yet part of them, a vacuum and a wall. The sounds of traffic, its swish of tires on pavement and radio music and impatient honks of Chicago traffic passing by had been a part of their night, but the traffic noise had died with the last notes of Ethan's laughter. All was quiet except for the breathing on each side of that wall.

Ethan looked at her. His eyes were not only open now, they were fixed on her face, searching, his gaze moving from her mouth to her eyes as if imprinting each detail for a memory. Don't touch her. The urge to feel her was making him feel impotent, as if her mere presence owned him, provoked a primal urge to protect and possess. What if he kissed her? What if he kissed her senseless, let her fear flow into him and die.

One sign, Amber. Give me one reason to stay.

Dammit Amber, do it now.

But she stood there. The promise of what could be lay dead there on that porch.

Then he reached out and touched her face, running one finger along her cheek and down her mouth.

"I know you."

Amber felt chilled and hot at the same time. That, and a strange sensuality from the soft touch of his finger. She could accept the pounding of her heart, the warmth that spread across her shoulders and neck. The chill she ignored.

The tightness in her belly. The welling of the tears she had tried so hard to stem. That, she could not accept.

His last words came in a strange monotone. "Amber, there is one thing that I know, one thing for sure. Loving you isn't enough. It ought to be, but it isn't. It kills me to know that. It would be so easy, just to go out there and kick someone's ass and take my woman home to my cave. But the loving of someone doesn't save her, doesn't make her whole, make her ready for the love you want to give her. I didn't know it, not the least part of it when all this started that summer, when you cried and I held you and thought I could take on the universe, just me and my woman. Then you left." His voice lowered. Amber could hear the trembling, the catch between the words. "This huge rage took over, breathed for me and lived in my gut, fed on my misery and my sense of abandonment. When I saw you again, everything stopped for that split second and I skated back to anger again."

He stood up. Amber knew his body was wrapped in memories that no longer mattered, that his eyes not dare to even look at her. "You asked me once, how could I not have followed you?" He paused. "I was a fool then, just a kid who didn't know what to do except hurt. It's different now. Now we're adults." Another pause. "Or we at least think we are." He took a step back. "I'm going to walk out of here. Walk out without a moment of pause. This time, you have to come to me." His words caught in his throat. "I'll wait for you, but I won't wait forever."

Amber swallowed her own words, first the ones of protest, then the ones of promise. She just stood there taking in the truth. Her chest and throat trembled. She ached for what might have been, grieving already what couldn't be.

He touched her face again, this time with a gentle smile. No words.

She asked him, "What are you doing?"

"I'm storing your image for when I ache and want to come back. I have to be strong enough to stay away." His lips pressed together and he nodded. "When you're ready."

Amber could only stand there like some starstruck kid in love with the boy she could never have. When he spoke next, his words tore at her.

"You've given yourself to those kids. You put your career . . . hell, your life on the line for Jocelyn. And now you're just that scared little kid looking out the window at an ambulance that's just a ghost. You value everyone and everything you care for, but you can't value yourself."

Ethan turned and walked out. The door only gave a slight whooshing sound, far too slight for the jolt the sound sent through Amber's body. Amber held her breath, straining to hear more. The silence sliced at her until she heard the start of a car engine. She could hear the end of her in that sound, the damning blackness of a noise that she couldn't even name even though she felt its power running through her, shutting her down.

It's over. The thought hit her, laughed at her, fed her with its bitterness. She drew in a breath. Ethan's cologne—was it a remnant of him still here or had she conjured the scent as a futile connection? She moved to the window to watch for emptiness. Ethan's car was still parked across the street. He hadn't pulled out yet. A shudder hit her throat, a strange sensation for hope.

Ethan's eyes locked onto hers, then he turned his attention away from her, jerked the car into gear and drove away.

A gust of wind caught a crumpled paper cup someone had discarded, blew it at the curb. The cup bounced and tumbled twice, then lay there, worn and tired, just gnarled wreckage of what it once had been.

Across the street, a man sat on a park bench jotting down something in his notebook. Amber did not notice.

Chapter 34

Five weeks had gone by since Ethan's arrival. Five weeks of panic and safety, of love and rage, of redemption and desertion. Five weeks with the man she hated to love. Dickens knew his stuff all right. Best of times. Worst of times.

Tension had isolated them after Ethan had peeled out of her life. He had turned the corner in his gray car, turned the corner on them. His presence in the school for his last few days as artist-in-residence had filled her with a want that almost sickened her. Before the confrontation, before the bliss of the man had squeezed through her, so long ago, she had run into his office to blather out an apology. In the days since that final fight, she had hid in her school room too wrapped in fear to see him. Amber had thought those last days the worst of times. Right now, though, right now was the worst. Ethan was leaving George T. Clausson High School to return to Iowa.

Like any other morning, Amber was at her desk by seven-thirty. This morning, though, her thoughts were not on lesson plans or anticipatory sets for motivation. She had found the candy Ethan had given her, the lifesavers to give her courage. She had stashed them in her purse and forgotten them. She took one out of the package and put it in her mouth. Laying back in the office chair, head back and eyes closed, she felt the cherry tartness as she kept the candy between her tongue and the roof of her mouth.

Ethan was leaving.

You are so stupid, woman. The man loves you.

If he loves me, why is he leaving?

She swallowed the candy. The flavor swept down her throat and disappeared. She tried to protect herself from her thoughts. The kids would be here in thirty minutes. Did she have enough copies of her work sheet? Sam Carmichael would lose his by fourth period. She should keep an extra. If the kid would just clean his locker, she wouldn't have to keep extras. She and Ethan had watched Sam stuffing empty pop bottles and reams of school work back into the locker, usually while the two-minute warning bell was ringing. Sam Carmichael's locker was two doors down from Ethan's office.

He should have listened. He should have waited. She kept her eyes closed and rocked in her chair, lost in thoughts too tumbled to be called thinking. No more candy today.

Somehow, the day proceeded even though the irony of explaining motivation and conflict to sophomores made Amber's hands press the chalk a little too hard as she outlined discussion questions on the board. The squeak made several kids cringe. One student even laughed, "Hey, Miss Helm, no need to be mad at the guy. It's just a story"

Oh, Travis, if you only knew.

3:30. Zero hour. Amber stood in her empty room weighing possibilities. She could just stay here. They certainly had said their good-byes. She could go to the coffee and ignore him.

He surely would be ignoring her, and with all the chaos of a faculty putting closure to this project, no one would notice. Well, Maggie and Marti would know. But they also knew the story.

And Ethan knew. The tears Amber had battled all afternoon forced themselves on her, like a tornado of sad rising from her gut. She grabbed for the tissue box, made ready to grab a wad, instead ran her thumb down the side and threw the box to the other side of the desk. Both of her hands clenched into fists with a will of their own. Her nails cut into her palms. She could have screamed. She could have cried again. Either response would have been appropriate for the moment. Instead, she drew in a breath, deeply. She would say goodbye and Ethan would know her heart. She was a adult for crying out loud. And adults realize that good-byes don't last forever. She squared her shoulders and went out into the hall toward the cafeteria, Maggie's usual plea, *Help me, Mary, Joseph, and all the saints* riding in her head.

Amber's steps echoed in the halls, her heels clicking on the tiled floor. Funny how kids turned these halls into a massive din, each step creating its own sharp clatter. Here she was, a hairsbreadth away from facing Ethan, and the only thing she let herself focus on was the sound of her shoes against the floor. But then, all she could do right then was walk.

The doors to the cafeteria were open and waiting. Inside, teachers chatted and ate, a usual after-school ritual, trading stories and gobbling free food. Dé jà vu. She had walked into the same setting only six weeks ago, innocent, unprepared for the tumult that would come. The same people today cackled, the same ones clapped their peers on the back, the same ones listened to those with the best stories. The only one in her vicinity who had changed now held on to her room keys, fingering the cool metal. A little support. Time to face Ethan and keep their bridges from burning.

Maggie rushed toward her, concern on her face. But before Amber's friend could say a word, Amber held up her hand in the same hushing movement she used on her students.

"Maggie, don't say anything. I'm going to talk to Ethan for a few minutes and then leave. I owe him that much."

Maggie face was an empty pallet. She looked like a tall mortician ready to provide sterile comfort to the unknowing bereaved.

That's not Maggie. She should be knocking away my hand and limping off. Amber took a small breath and twisted one side of her mouth into a cynical grin. Before she could say, "What's up?" Maggie simply said, "Honey, he's gone.

Gone. Ethan was gone. He had left her.

She might as well have been Alice dining on mushrooms. Before her, the doors to the cafeteria stretched and loomed. The air itself closed in on her. She felt cold. She felt a sweat creeping up her back. The laughter of teachers inside, no more than thirty feet away, turned tinny.

He loved her. He had moved inside her, sheltered her from the outside. He was a part of her.

He was gone.

Maggie stood there, her face an empty pallet except for her eyes. Maggie's eyes waited to help a friend.

Amber's throat gave a spasm as she turned and stood there in the hall. She had thought she had time to mend them. She was a fool.

The honesty drained her, the knowing that Ethan had demanded all of her, not just part, that he was right, that this was permanent. Outside, students ran toward the weekend. Fifty feet away, teachers had started their own celebration. Here, at this moment, in this forlorn hall, a chill settled on her arms.

A universe away, Ethan had called her a brat. One week ago, he had called her a coward.

All she knew was that now, in this vacated hallway, she ached for another chance that would never come. She would spend the next forever aching, longing for something to fill the hole 212 that had started eating at her heart the moment he was gone.

Maggie held out her arms and let Amber fall into an embrace. She smelled of the last remnants of spice. Held by the lanky Maggie, Amber lay against her best friend to sob dry regrets.

"Go ahead and cry, girlfriend."

There was nothing else to do.

Chapter 35

The rain should have made her feel good. It always had before. Safely tucked inside, she listened to it hit the windows. The sound of rain, something about its beat in syncopation with her body rhythm, that and the safety of being inside, away from the hard splat on the windows. She did her best thinking when the rain hit. The rain of early fall was a special indulgence , a gust out of nowhere, its coolness and cleansing welcome after the last heat of the year.

Too bad the rain was wasted.

Amber had expected that she would be a basket case, that after the meltdown after school, she would sink into outright hysterics. Lying on her sofa in the early evening, one part of her listened to the rain, tried focus, her breath flowing in a steady rhythm, her mind detached, floating or stuck—she couldn't tell—in places she didn't have the will to name. The only sign of emotion was the tightness of her lips pressing against each other.

She blinked her eyes and shook herself. She would come to grips with the loss of a man who once again had dropped out of her life. But his words crept to her consciousness, then stayed there, playing over and over, like a computer program on an endless loop.

Scared little girl. Guilt. Value. The ghost of a child watching an ambulance drive away.

Her mother had called earlier, wanted to know whether or not she would be attending the fall cocktail party at the club Saturday night—after all, their friends just never saw enough of her, and Charles' clients always loved her flair and wit the few times they were able to see her. And of course, Lillian was better after that scare, but you never knew what could trigger another. Translation? Amber had better show up.

Then Maggie called. Any other time, they'd hit the Pour Fools' Bar on a Friday night to listen to live Blues. That was the last thing Amber needed and both of them knew it.

"Let's skip the Blues tonight and have a two-woman pity party at Mr. Peasley's. We'll cry and eat bagels, drink coffee until we puke." Maggie had such a way of getting to the grist of things. They would meet at 8:00.

Right now, though, Amber indulged herself, drifting to some far away place, listening to a din of words muddling themselves as each segment fought for control. *Scared. Guilt. Value. Ghost.* Ethan's last words surfaced from the muck of her mind, demanding, moving into focus. She might have beat them back; the old Amber of three years ago certainly would have. But she let him have his way. She was not strong enough to fight them. Or perhaps she had let them win.

You are not a scared little girl. You cannot be a scared little girl. Your value comes from who you are and what you do. She let herself sink into what he had said, tightened her arms around herself and huddled into their grace. She was still calm, even passive, her state more one of realization than fatigue.

The rain had stopped. Cars went by, the sound of their tires hitting puddles a whooshing noise, just enough of a niggling sound to keep Amber from concentrating. She sat up, mussing her hair with her hands in the same distracted motion she had always used when befuddled. Maybe her hands could shake up her hair enough to put her mind on track.

The thumping bass of some driver's radio joined the splashing of the rain water sound. Amber turned and looked at the window. Two kids, oblivious to traffic, jumped in puddles next to the curb, kicking an occasional can tossed toward the gutter. Where were their parents? Kids didn't belong on a busy city street, unprotected. Especially this close to dark.

She set to plumping the pillows on her sofa. Plumping pillows was a noble pastime. Plump enough of them and maybe her life would lay less flat. The gray taffeta one made her mad. She could form the others, but that gray square would not bend to her will. She threw it one-handed at the sofa's arm, stood up, and marched over to grab her sweater from the chair next to the front door and headed outside. As she stood on her front porch step, the smell of early autumn after a rain hit her, a cooling, fresh smell that invited her to walk. The air held a crispness, a welcome relief after the late summer heavy heat. Mrs. Antolini from two doors down was walking her dog, talking to it like a child.

She could go back inside and wallow or she could walk. Walking had to be better than sitting on a sofa waiting for pillows to cooperate. So, she walked.

Amber picked up her pace as she rounded the corner onto Delaney Avenue. A breeze hit the back of her neck and cooled itself into her hair. The air held a remnant of wetness but nothing like the oppressive humidity of the first month of school. Strange. That simple reflection brought a pressure to her throat, one she hadn't prepared for. She picked up her pace. The rhythm of her steps soothed her, that and the clean smell of the air. *I should be grateful instead of such a sorry mess.* The thought worked its way through her body. She was grateful. Ethan had been a surprise in her life. She found herself laughing at that thought. He had been an unexpected force, a storm that had whipped in, dumped much needed caring and aid in her life. A storm. And like all storms, he had blown away, all the way back to Iowa. She stopped and crossed her arms. The sky was a mixture of gray and pink and the dark blue of early night. When she had stood on her porch, the neighborhood had bustled with people just like her out for breath of fresh air. Now, two blocks from her home, the same neighborhood was quiet. Instant ghost town. Even the cars were gone.

The sound was so strange. She could only hear a few footsteps behind her, just a few in rhythm with her and then silence. She turned around and pretended to look back toward her street as if she were waiting for someone. A man looked into the window of a small boutique. He had a big form, slouching posture. He was smoking a cigarette. That's all she could tell for sure in the fading light, but something deep in the most basic part of her brain chafed at her. Something about the scent of the smoke and the build of his body. Something about the way he seemed to be checking out a boutique that was closed while he turned his head part way toward her.

Her knees locked, and she breathed in quickly. *You walk this way to school every day. You've been on this very place late at night, all by yourself, walking back from Duffy's.* The self-talk didn't work, so Amber started walking again, listening for the footsteps. She went about a block and stopped again. The footsteps stopped.

Why this on a Saturday night when all the businesses had been closed since five and no one was there to run to?

Alarm and dismay worked their way through her, then dread and the first tinges of fright. But right along with the fear was anger, a snort of ire followed by indignation. Maybe it was her father's dismissal, maybe the injustice of losing the man she loved. Maybe even the memory of bitch scratched on her car Why should she be scared? Where had scared ever got her? Whatever the reason, fear didn't stand a chance.

Amber turned around and walked slowly toward the source of the footsteps. The man dropped his cigarette onto the sidewalk and stepped on it, casually looking past her. Even seeing half of his face gave her a sense of the whole—beefy like the rest of him, a face marked with acne scars. His nose was a bulb, pockmarked with huge pores. She could have hung her purse on it. Black eyebrows jutted in a straight line toward the center of his face. The man was definitely a bruiser.

She stopped two feet from him and faced him, arms folded in defensive posture. "Do I know you?

He looked down, his face blank. "I don't think so."

Her head tilted, more a reaction of surprise than a need for a new perspective. There, on a familiar street in Chicago, her mind sought the connection that eluded her. It was there, she knew it. She stood her ground.

"I know that I've seen you before, I just don't know where."

He looked at her like someone might look at a Pekinese, mildly amused by the snipping of an insignificant animal yipping at his feet.

"Look, you're a pretty girl and all, but I don't know you. Ain't never met you. You gotta mistake me for someone else." He said the words, but his eyes were blank. The man was lying.

Amber mumbled an apology as she turned and walked toward the coffee shop, but his form, something about the scent of his cigarette and the way he hung his head low niggled at her.

A weird anxiety crept along her neck. She crossed the street and walked to the corner, then turned left. By the time she was midway on Forrest, the anxiety level notched up a couple of levels. She stopped, reached down to fix an imaginary untied shoe lace. When she turned her head to check out the street, he was at the corner. He ducked behind Lacey's Tap like a kid playing spy. Amber stayed where she was, knees bent, playing charades with the lace, then stood up and starting walking again. She increased her pace until she at Wan Hin's Specialty Market, then stopped. The building was shaped like a "U", the store's front window inset and crammed with fliers announcing gourmet deals for the sushi crowd. A green awning connected the ends of two brick walls. Amber moved toward the window as if her life depended on the latest eel treat and stood against the inside of the brick wall, her heart pounding so much she worried that she wouldn't be able to hear footsteps—if there were any.

There were.

The vestiges of the last few weeks had alarmed her. Now they took over. The fear. The embarrassment. The outright wrongness of all that had happened. The sight of that word smeared across her car door. She swung around to face her opponent, whomever that might be. For one second, an image of her hurling herself at some total stranger nearly held her feet. That second passed quickly. She was too heated to stop.

Sure enough. Mr. Beefy.

"That's it! You moron!" In an outright fury, Amber grabbed at the monster bag she called her purse and whacked him. He backed up, arms raised against this harridan who was pummeling him.

"You can tell Frank or Fred or whoever sent you that Jocelyn's gone. It's over!"

When the last of her spleen was spent, her victim lowered his arms and looked at her, his lower face warped by twisted lips, his eyes dismissive. "You *are* crazy. She told me you were crazy, and she's right." He squared his shoulders and walked backwards, his hands held firm in front of him just in case.

Amber's face clouded over. *She.* She? Amber moved toward him, her voice demanded answers.

"What do you mean 'she'? Who's after me?" Her arm started back, purse clutched.

The man pulled at his jacket as if checking for creases and ran his right hand through his hair. "I'm not paid to give answers, just to make sure you're not off on some tangent." He shook his hand and brushed his jacket. "And most of all, I'm out of here." He pushed past a startled Amber and walked off.

Heart still racing, her jaw trembling, Amber stood there, clenching her fists and shaking. She aimed for something to do, here on a deserted sidewalk in Chicago. Couldn't the store fronts talk to her, let her know she was all right? Nothing came to her, anxious though she was. Instead of taking action, she walked backed to the wall, leaned against it to keep from falling over, and felt the rush fading. The aftermath left her tired, lightheaded.

The evening plans were the last thing on her mind while she gathered herself. Then she looked at her watch. Oh-my-God. Maggie.

Mr. Peasley's was empty except for one couple. The couple, a middle-aged man and a younger woman—a daughter perhaps— sat still, silently finishing the last of their coffees. The younger of the couple looked at her coffee cup, her right middle finger edging the rim of the cup. The man stared past her out toward the street. Neither showed any much sign of life, especially to each other.

Maggie sat on an aluminum bar stool, swerving in agitation and looking at the clock on the wall above the door. The clock was a huge timepiece, yellow stars and a white moon against a dark blue background, hand painted by a friend of the owner. The red minute hand drooped, knocked askew by an angry customer with more strength than sense, and a solid right arm. Usually Maggie had some wisecrack about art having no respect.

Right now, she could have cared less about the clock. She swerved on that stool, fuming, occasionally banging her heel against the metal frame. The quiet of a coffee shop amid rows of bars on a Saturday night usually meant the peace to hash over whatever needed to be discussed until the topic reached a sensible conclusion or enough absurdity to provoke them to laughter. The pungent familiarity of freshly ground coffee centered the girls on those Saturday nights when they'd rather talk than do the bar scene.

the normal pattern was Maggie rushing in late to see Amber grin and point her finger to Old Droopy above the door. Tonight, Maggie had been there ten minutes. That made Amber fifteen minutes late. Where was she?

The clanking of tin utensils in the back made Maggie jump. She had just caught her breath when Amber walked in. Before Maggie could get even one sacred name out of her favorite litany, Amber closed the door and rested against its frame, shutting her eyes and breathing deeply. Maggie watched her best friend walk to their favorite booth—just as the couple slid their chairs and stood up to leave—sit down, then put her head between her hands and rub the top of her forehead with her fingers. All the metallic clanking in the back room, all the traffic outside, all the sound of steps Maggie counted waiting for Amber to show, they all slid into insignificance. She crossed to the booth, sat down across from Amber, and stretched her hand toward her friend, barely touching amber's fingers. Her voice was a both a demand and a plea. Yet the usual sarcasm was replaced by the softness of concern. "Where have you been? You look godawful."

Amber looked at herself in the mirror above the counter. She saw a disheveled woman, white faced, hair askew, whipped into frenzy by the Chicago wind. She felt for the security of the purse clutched at her chest.

"I'm sorry I'm late," she said, her voice a monotone. "This guy was following me and I had to hit him with my purse."

Maggie half-rose from her side of the booth. "What?"

Ignoring the ire of her friend, Amber added, "I think somebody paid him to follow me" Dipping her head, she let go of the purse and rubbed her forehead with her fingers as if that could erase the last half hour.

Silence lasted long enough for Amber to catch one breath. Maggie had been panting, a friend either in the beginning of strong labor pains or too astonished to find the words, any words, to convey her thoughts. When the panic ebbed she found them—in spades.

"Are you nuts? Are you out of your everloving, friggin' mind?" The sacred names rose from her, one each louder than the previous one. "Jesus, Mary, and Joseph, help us all." By now Maggie was hyperventilating. "A man follows you, and you hit him with your purse?"

Amber's head sank down toward the booth's laminated table and rested on her folded hands. "What was I supposed to do, walk clear to the lake until he got tired?" She sounded like one of her sophomores trying to worm out of detention.

Maggie's voice met the challenge, a firmness in her tone that she usually reserved for school. "Let's see. People scrawl on your car. Maybe they want to carve on your body as well?"

This time, Amber sat up and leaned against the back of the booth. "No. It wasn't Frank. The guy looked like he could have been one of Frank's bully cronies, but he said the weirdest thing." Amber screwed her lips together, knotting a furrow between her brows.

"He said, 'She'—'she' thought I was crazy, 'she' knew I needed watching."

Amber folded her hands again, looked at her friend, and calmly asked, "Who is 'she'?"

Chapter 36

The sounds came from both of Amber's worlds. From an outer world of clatters and swishes, the normal sounds of Chicago morning banging its way into city business. From deep within her, whispers only intent on building a dream, oblivious to the pull of a city awakening. Bits of the dream murmured, *Don't leave. Stay with us. You belong to us. We promise you answers. Stay with us where you belong.* The tug between the two worlds chafed at her. The city called and the dream began to bleed away.

As with most moments of first consciousness, remnants of the dream stayed, last bits fighting to keep itself alive. Outside Amber's window, the city traffic bustled by, an occasional honking splitting the din. Inside, lying in her bed, Amber kept her eyes closed against the assault of the morning, letting shapes and touches of the dream stay with her. She had been witness in the world of that dream, not the focal character of some anxiety in the normal dream world, rather an indiscernible presence firmly positioned above a circle of rock that looked like the ruins of an ancient amphitheater.

At the very center sat a small girl sitting on a stool in the middle of the dirt ground, a circle surrounded by stone walls pocked with caverns, specks of darkness against the brown and gray of the stone. The child's head lay down on her lap, her thin child arms wrapped over her head for protection as if she feared a pelting of boulders from the walls. Red hair swept up in ponytails had swung on the ground as the little girl shook. Amber still felt that child's terror. She knew that, even while the images swirled in half-life while they fought to stay. A hissing came from the caverns, some high-pitched and echoing, others low like the far away rumble of thunder.

She, they whispered, taunted. She. The little girl moaned as the sounds covered her. Amber knew that she had to save the child. *Hang in there, little girl. I see you. Hang in there until I can sweep down and save you. I'll cover you with my arms. The voices won't hurt you.*

Amber had been poised on the edge, looking at the child. Guilt and fear nagged at her. That child. That poor little girl.

Later, Amber would turn over that moment of insight, how it had swirled around for hours, for days, for years, just waiting for the right time to make its presence known. Something in the genes, maybe in the deepest recesses of the mind, what locks away what will pain us, demands unconditional certainty of betrayal. The flow of knowledge stops, the anger abates—for just a while—waiting for the heart to process the grief.

For now, she let it be, allowed it to tumble its way into some kind of sense. The truth rose slowly, so deep within her, moving up through her bones, her muscles, coursing through her veins—she felt it like an effluvia of emotion, liquid and warm. Amber tried to quell it, dismiss it as a remnant no more valid than the proverbial body flying naked or student missing a college exam. She tried to find her way out of that confrontation, but the truth won out and spoke.

It's you, Amber. It's you. Don't you recognize the red hair sweeping the ground? Don't you know that hunched form?

Wasn't denial the first reaction to a trauma of this magnitude? Not so. She was struck by the intensity of her reaction, the way that her response ruled her, drowned any thought of denial. Anger followed truth, uncoiling, slowly at first, the pull on the coils of that tightly wound knot rusted with disuse. Amber felt it like the first taste of sexuality, deep and fearful yet touched with promise. And why not? She had spent too much of her life disconnecting from her feelings. She was an emotional virgin. Oh yes, that knot resisted, moaned and creaked like an arthritic old man rising on a cold morning.

The next sign was a sense of tightness in her arms, then a tingling.

She had betrayed Amber. She.

Her mother.

Amber's sense of self began to buckle. Only then did denial try its hand. Why not. She'd had so much practice lately.

Lillian was her mother, the one who did up her ponytails with blue ribbon, the one whose eyes misted over when Amber and her horse nailed a jump, who said *Oh my precious darling, aren't you the best ever.*

For the longest moment, Amber held out hope, held onto the family scenes she thought had mattered. She could be wrong. Could be. What weight did a dream hold?

No longer the soother of broken children outside her personal realm, she spoke to herself gently, for the first time. All the weight in the world, my child. All the weight that has haunted you and laid you low since you a child.

She thought she had been angry before. But this anger was a burning, consuming holocaust. She stood, paced the floor, pulling at her hair and pounding the back of her head with her fists. All these years, nothing but betrayal. That night, after the encounter with Frank, she had told Ethan that her parents loved her. She'd always believed it, put that belief at her very core.

What a fool.

About that precious darling thing, Mother, I would love to take your compliment, hold it in my hand—then trounce on it for the self-centered garbage it is. And even if you meant it at the time— what—two seconds, maybe, I could only trust the knowledge that faithlessness consumed all our tomorrows.

That pronouncement liberated her. Freedom meant a calming, a newness of insight so seemingly simple and so absolutely mind blowing.

Lillian did not love her. To Lillian, Amber was no more than an object. Just a pitiful object that let guilt and need ride her like some sick trainer trying to break a horse.

The she that haunted Amber's dreams was no specter. It was a solid woman, one who manipulated the perfect sigh, the perfect tone for the moment, the one who watched her family play their roles—Charles the Enforcer, Amber the object. It was almost funny, in a perverse and creepy way.

Amber's pacing had slowed during this revelation. She sat in her favorite chair, where she had so often wrapped herself in the throw her mother had given her for a Christmas present. This time she sat wrapped in her new knowledge, the throw discarded, lying there on the floor next to the chair, ignored, forgotten.

Suddenly, she was hungry. Consumed by hunger. She moved to the kitchen, opened her cupboards, and sat on the floor with her hoard. Cookies. Chips. A box of saltine crackers. She ate them all. Devoured them. She couldn't stuff the food fast enough. The energy of her emotion devoured the calories. She couldn't eat fast enough.

Then she was tired. She pulled a cushion from a nearby bar stool for her head, one of Kikki's choices, a yellow toile to match the wallpaper. Amber wanted to spit on it, but she couldn't muster the energy. She lay there, head on toile and slept for two hours.

When she woke, she still felt spent, full of regret and wistfulness at time lost. While she moved through the chores of the day, the image of her inner child stayed with Amber and grew, the image of a child whose only measure of worth lay in saving her mother... Scared little girl running from guilt—whispers of guilt, threats of guilt. The more she ran, the more the guilt controlled her.

The critic gave a farewell taunt. *You're pitiful, Amber Helm. Mama's ego fattens on your guilt, and you just wait for her to serve up more.* Then it dissolved like a vampire hit by streams of light.

The grown Amber reached her arms around the child Amber, hugged her with a feral protectiveness. As these first few moments of truth wheeled through her, she let the child within her grow comfortable with hope. The child who had watched the ambulance drive away so long ago. The child who had wrapped herself into a knot of pleasing. The child who would hollow herself, walk away from becoming at the sight of a mother's frown or the scent of criticism laced with Chanel.

The words asserted themselves within an empty room.

"Little girl, you've waited long enough.

"No more."

Chapter 37

Oak Hollow Country Club was a well established club, one of those places where gentlemen smoked their cigars and ladies made plans to aid people they wouldn't be caught dead talking to. Hundred-year-old oaks lined the fairways like sentinels, and spring through fall, dogwood bushes and swaths of wildflowers—meticulously groomed to look natural—filled in the picture perfect landscape. In summer, the golf greens were as clipped as the speech of the help. In the winter, deer came from the woods surrounding the area, never venturing too close, just making their presence known to please the clientele, especially the ones expecting repentence.

Inside, where Amber and Lillian were about to talk, rich walnut paneling and dark leather arm chairs sat in silence and darkness, so very suitable for what Amber had in mind. She waited in the chair farthest from the door, letting one word slip through her like fog caressing a coastline. It wrapped itself around her deepest parts. It gave her courage, cemented her purpose.

She. She.

Memories tumbled forward, each one a domino toppling through her mind. Family portrait night. A ten-year-old girl in a navy dress—girls with carroty hair should never wear pink—that would look cheap. She had kept her pose while her mother took a twenty-minute break to rest herself. Her diabetic condition and all. In the photograph, the dress was lovely, of course. The child's face was a mask.

Mother-Daughter Tea. The grimace and slight turn of the head, poised and dismissive. Amber had used the wrong fork. Again. Outside this room of waiting, ball room musicians warmed up the cocktail hour with swing music. It was the night of the annual Fall Celebration. The ballroom itself glittered with topiaries filled with sugared fruit and fall leaves, their trunks wrapped in ribbon. Six-foot glass urns filled the room with candle light, softening the sheen of the decorated topiaries. Wrought iron benches had been strategically placed for quiet conversation, and tables lit by smaller versions of the urns waited for those more inclined to mingle. Lillian and her committee had outdone themselves once again.

Amber's mother opened the door to the conference room and stepped inside, then quietly closed it behind her. "Tell me, darling, whatever is it that is so important we have to meet here?" She stepped forward and sat down, facing her daughter, and smiled. "I, myself, want to be in that beautiful ballroom soaking up the ambiance." Lillian's voice, so cultured and self-possessed, hovered over Amber like a mist. "Amber, are you paying attention?" The words were curt, laced with hurt.

While Amber watched Lillian sit there, she allowed herself the shudder, just a small reflex out of habit. Totally still, Lillian smiled at her daughter, her one hand at her throat, fingers splayed, the other resting on a side table.

An "I'm sorry" started out of Amber's mouth before she squelched it. Amber hardly knew where to begin, but her mind was definitely not on apologies. "Mother, I hope we can . . ."

The door opened before Amber could finish. Charles Helm stood in the threshold, the light from the hallway creating an aura around him. "Whatever you girls have to gab about, you can do in the ballroom." To an outsider, his tone may have seemed light. Amber knew better. She had felt its cast before. It meant *You are insignificant. Do as you're told and behave yourself.*

Lillian's straightened the skirt of her dress and stood up. She brushed one hand against the other as if disposing of imaginary crumbs. "Absolutely. Duty does call." She walked toward Charles, grabbed his arm and left the room, a trail of "Come along, Amber" floating in indifference to the needs of the daughter who still sat in her chair. The couple kept their eyes forward.

Amber forced control. She felt her skin tighten. The blood in her veins thickened, toughened her need. "Do not—do not let them win," she muttered. The ownership of her life, her soul. All that she had missed in her childhood. She swallowed, a movement geared to stem the emotion that piled behind her eyes, tightened her jaw. Several deep breaths and she was ready.

With a command of all that she had ever dreamed of being, she stood up and walked into the ballroom.

Her mother and father were standing by one of the huge urns, talking to the Carruthers'. Charles and Edgar were comparing golf grips, and the women were caught up with the room's decor. Edith Carruthers was gesturing at the highlights while Lillian took in the compliments with her usual panache. Amber didn't need to hear the words. She had watched this scene over and over most of her life.

Putting on her country club face and straightening her posture, she stepped toward the foursome.

"My, Edith, you look lovely tonight. New hairdo?" Before the woman could answer, Amber said, "Excuse us a minute. I have to steal my mother for just a minute. I'll have her right back." Butter could have pooled around them. Amber had been schooled well.

Charles Helm watched Amber's face, his gray eyes steeling. "Edgar, why don't you and I get a drink? And Edith, I thought I saw Meredith Ostering looking for you." He patted Amber's hand. I'm sure that whatever you and your mother have to chat about will be finished by the time I get back." His voice was even. Amber recognized it for what it was.

When the two women were alone, Amber grabbed her mother's hand at the fingers. She knew that her hand gripped them too tightly, but her own did not obey the command to loosen themselves. Lillian winced. "Whatever has gotten into you, child?" Amber let go of the hand, lifted her chin.

A waiter stopped near the two women. "I know that you, Mrs. Helm, have to skip these treats, but Miss Helm, may I entice you with a chocolate-coated strawberry?" He chuckled a little, almost a tssk. "They're sinfully delicious."

Amber looked at the tray. They might as well have been snakes. With the control drilled into her for better than two decades, she smiled.

"No, thank you, Edward, chocolate is the last thing on my mind right now. But thank you for asking."

"Very well, I'll leave you lovely ladies to your talking." He started to turn, then looked at Lillian. "By the way, Mrs. Helm, you

have truly made this a room of beauty. But then, you always do."
With a nod, he slid away to another couple.

Lillian rubbed her hand. "Isn't he sweet."

Amber's reply came out a hiss. Her throat ached, her heart too.
"You hired that man?"

With the same chilled look Amber had seen so many times
before, Lillian answered. "Man? What man?"

"A man has been following me, Mother. A professional."

Lillian's smile never so much as flinched. She matched
Amber's sibilance. "Are you out of your mind? Do you realize
where we are?" She lifted her hand to her hair. "Get control of
yourself before I have to get your father."

"Daddy's busy right now. And I've never been more in control.
You're on your own."

On that, Lillian's head tilted up and her mouth tightened.
Amber knew that look.

"A man, Mother, a big burly man who said that 'She' had hired
him. Tell me the truth; don't you dare lie. Did you hire that man to
follow me?"

Lillian nodded, an imposing nod, hardly a movement really,
more an affirmation of her right to control. If the temperature of
her words could have been measured, the air would have frozen.
"I did."

In Amber's mind, the two words grew, twisted into malignant
forms, slid into the forms of the topiaries to disappear into the
flowers themselves, the gray of their evil mixing with the
warmth of the greens and golds where it would grow like
rot, then return to choke her. "I see." Amber rubbed her
tongue against her top teeth. In some dim way, she
understood.

"Could you possibly find it in your schedule this evening to
explain why you found it necessary to have me followed?" Sarcasm
and anger flickered from her words like lightening. It was no longer
a question. It was disbelief.

"Of course, I hired him. Someone has to make sure you're not
making a complete fool of yourself. After that tawdry affair right
under the eyes of your Uncle James, I knew I was right to keep an
eye on you."

Amber's voice was taut and hollow, like an abandoned schoolroom waiting for the sound of a bell that would never ring, a futile place stripped of children and hope.

"You knew about that? That was three years ago."

"Well, it wasn't three years ago that you took up with that boy again." Lillian pulled her lips together as if she had eaten something tart. "And it certainly wasn't three years ago that you almost went to jail for involving yourself with some ghoulish creature." Lillian face relaxed, and she looked at Amber with a softness that made the daughter wince. "You must know that we do what we do for your sake. After all, darling, we do love you."

Amber's eyes narrowed. "Oh, you love me all right. You love me so much you use love like a club."

Lillian looked at her as if she were a toddler. "Hush, Amber, you're making a scene."

"A scene? A scene." The words started in amazement and ended in a declaration. "A scene, my dear mother, is when a little girl disobeys, when she screams because she can't have friends over, or she can't get dirty, or she can't get even speak her goddamn mind." The words were too soft to be heard by anyone outside their circle. Amber heard them pounding, as if they could resurrect the dead.

Lillian response was a whispered sibilance. "Don't you dare take that tone with me, and don't you dare use profanity with your mother."

Amber ignored her. She could not get the words out fast enough, harsh enough. "A scene is when a child cries in her room, all alone, because she's sure that her mother is dying and it is her fault, and that never, never again can she be herself lest her mother become distressed."

Lillian glared at Amber, or glared as much as she would allow herself in this public place. Her voice lifted slightly, a scream for her.

"None of this is my fault!" She stepped back and smoothed her hair. Amber, we are finished with this conversation." The seconds that passed in silence between them might as well have been an eternity.

Several heads had turned. In that silent gap. Amber felt their stares. A tingle of excitement stirred in her, gave her the courage to see Lillian for who—and what—she was. Little spots of energy pulled themselves into being while she took in the sense of violation. The spots coiled and churned and began warming in places that had seemed dead and cold for so long. She wanted to snap at the power of the affirmation.

Her mother, standing there, looking like the queen herself, suddenly grew smaller, less imposing in her royalty. Lillian was no queen. She was simply a woman. Not even a mother.

"Don't feed me that crap." It was an accusation, not an order. It was also loud enough to draw a bigger audience. The stares turned to whispers as ground zero spread. While men talked business at the bar, and couples two-stepped, those close enough reacted, eyes glinting, some leaning close to hear better, others smiling at what they knew eventually had to happen. Blood was being spilt, and the sharks couldn't wait to close in.

"Someone will have to get your father, young lady. I simply cannot abide this." Lillian closed her eyes and swayed.

With a tone fitting for a playground dare, Amber snorted, "Take too much insulin today? Or is this just for my benefit?"

She turned to the closest table. "Know what she's afraid of? I might actually grow enough of a backbone to tell her to go to hell."

"Amber!" Charles was back. He supported his wife with one arm. "You will stop this nonsense immediately." He used his free arm to gesture toward the crowd. "And you will apologize to everyone for this insanity." His voice turned to a low, feral growl. "You must be out of your mind. What are you trying to do? Finally put your mother in her grave?"

Amber laughed. "Kill her? Nothing can kill her. She's indestructible." Amber paused and let the next words spill with derision. "That is, except for her own silly games."

Lillian's face was mottled. "After all we've done for you, you ungrateful little bitch."

Amber's voice started as a purr. "Oh, I'm grateful all right. Grateful for the house, grateful for the car, grateful for it all." Her voice fell flat. " But bitch?" She smiled, a tight smile, her lips no more than a slit. Only then could she speak. "No, Mother, that's your department."

Charles and Lillian Helm held on to each other, a united front of silent shock. Amber watched them. It was all she could do. Her parents could have fallen to their knees, weeping and gnashing teeth and asking for the grace of God's forgiveness, and all she would have done was watch. That in itself was a bit of grace.

Amber turned and walked out of the ballroom, knowing where she would go and convinced that she had the right to go there. Before she left, though, she reached into the pocket of her jacket, took out her car keys, and dropped them on a tray. Someone would find them. For now, she could take a cab. She could walk clear back to her apartment if she had to.

Then, she would buy her own car. She needed a car, one that was her own.

Maybe a red one. While she waited for the cab, a door opened and the riffs of "Satin Doll" rolled out to the parking lot. A breeze shook the tree tops in accompaniment. Amber never looked back. Instead, she danced. She was all alone, no more than a shadow of movement. She danced, arms outstretched as if she were waiting for a lover, feet sliding across the asphalt. She danced, sure in the knowledge that it was only three miles to her house and 318 miles to Iowa City.

Why not? She had already taken the longest journey, the step to the 86th degree.